Jolly Roger

Thomas J Leveque

Bishop Publishing—Lancaster, California
Paperback ISBN: 979-8-9882786-0-3
Hardcover ISBN: 979-8-9882786-2-7
eBook ISBN: 979-8-9882786-1-0
Library of Congress Control Number: 2023908628
Title: *Jolly Roger*
Author: Thomas J. Leveque
Digital distribution | 2023
Paperback | 2023

This is a work of fiction. The characters, names, incidents, places, and dialogue are products of the author's imagination, and are not to be construed as real.

Dedication

For My Children
Julie, Holly, and Grayson

Acknowledgement

First I would like to thank my Father whose life and stories helped shape this novel. My Mother for her unwavering belief in my talent and abilities. My sister, Margot and brother, John, for sharing family experiences, stories and memories and for their guidance throughout my life. My children, Julie, Holly, and Grayson for standing by me and believing in me when there was no reason to do so and for my wife Lisa who puts up with me on a daily basis.

I would also like to thank Joan Bauer who read countless versions of this book and was always there to offer her advice and support.

I would like to thank Lake Charles Louisiana and all my Aunts, Uncles and Cousins who live there, both past and present. You are always in my heart, memories, and imagination.

Finally, I would like to thank Emily Hughes and the team at New Book Authors for making my dream a reality.

Prologue
Katrina

Oil Rig, Gulf of Mexico
Off Louisiana Coast
Tuesday, August 23, 2005

*I*t *began with a soft breeze against my cheek. I was uneasy, standing on the rig looking southeast. It was about 1:00 am Friday...Katrina had been down- graded to a tropical storm, but the barometer was still dropping. By 3:00 pm it was a hurricane again and its track had changed. It was heading our way. By 5:00 the next morning it was a Category 3. Still coming.*

The water was getting choppy, and the wind was picking up. You could see the clouds gathering on the horizon, a frenzied, churning dark gray mass coming our way. I woke up Sunday morning to the report that it had been up graded to a 4 then by 7:00 am to a 5. The wind was up around 100-110 mph, and you couldn't tell the difference between the rain and the return from the gulf. The water was up around the base and the rig deck was alive with the thrashing water. It got closer to noon, but the sky was almost black.

It was then that it all went to hell. The wind howled and the top of the rig near the winch snapped and slammed into the deck about six or seven yards away. I didn't think it got anyone, but it was around then that guys started going missing. A huge wave slammed against the side of the rig and threw me to the deck. I was trying to crab my way to the hatch, but the waves kept slamming us. I heard men scream, but I couldn't open my eyes enough to see.

A wave, bigger than the last, caught me and I cart-wheeled across the deck. The water had me pinned against the railing. And then I saw it, a two-masted schooner heading straight for the rig. I heard voices cascading over each other through the storm. It took me a minute to recognize they weren't speaking English, but by that time the ship was right up on us. Just as it was about to smash into us headlong, I locked eyes with a tall slender man with dark hair and a piercing blue gaze standing at the helm. Then, a bolt of lightning seemed to strike just where I was standing, followed almost immediately by the loudest clap of thunder I'd ever heard. I realized I'd shut my eyes. When I opened them, the man and the ship were gone.

****

Lake Charles, Louisiana
Chretien Home
Present Day

This transcription, painstakingly written on a yellow pad by Roger Chretien, had been thrown across the room. In fact, the entire upper floor had been ransacked and generally turned upside down. If that wasn't odd enough, in the corner of the small study was a body. A body lay wrapped in the Jolly Roger, with two crossed cutlasses on the chest just below a cocked pistol. Roger Chretien, Professor of American History at McNeese University in Lake Charles had been given a pirate funeral.

Part One
Hurricane Category 1
Very Dangerous

Chapter I

"…It was a skull and crossbones."

Johnny

The air roars about three and a half inches from Johnny Chretien's left temple as he sits looking out the window of an Embraer ERJ 140 as it flies over the flat, lush green marshy ground of Southwest Louisiana. He cranes his neck but can't see the Lake Charles Regional Airport. He hopes it's up ahead. There are stories of the time the pilot landed at the wrong airport. Well, he won't worry. He just hopes Jenny is there when he arrives.

He closes his eyes…he hasn't been back since Pop died…almost twenty-five years now. Roger came to California for a visit once. You couldn't really call them close. They seemed to have drifted apart after Pop died. He tried to call Roger once a month but, at least, they talked at Christmas and on birthdays. Well, Roger called on his birthday. He was really good about that. Johnny couldn't remember if he'd called Roger on his or not. He must have. He was almost sure that Roger had turned sixty this year or was it next year…maybe last. Johnny leans back in his seat. God they were getting old. When had that happened?

He rubs his knee for about the millionth time. This may be the future of commercial aviation, but at just over six feet, there is no place for his long legs. It's stupid. There are only forty-four seats and there is no room for legs…or baggage…or apparently scotch. Although, as he looks out the window, he is beginning to wish he'd asked for row twelve and the emergency exit since the plane is flying too low and too fast. At this rate, the plane will overshoot the runway and he'll wind up in the parking lot of McNeese University. Which considering his brother's job is kind of ironic if you stopped to think about it…Johnny decides not to think about it

Jimmy

James Chretien slumps in his seat at Café Du Monde on Decatur Street in the French Quarter. He rubs his tired eyes and lets out a huge sigh. He's sorry Roger had died and all that...it is rather peculiar after all. Drowning is such a horrible way to die, and Roger had always been a good swimmer, he won a medal for it in high school...or was it track.

All James knows is he doesn't want to be here. He hates to fly...he hates to take the train...he hates to drive. Why he had decided to drive from New Orleans to Lake Charles is beyond him. He hates Louisiana. He hates the people. He hates everything about it...well...he rubs his face and thinks about coffee on the back porch swing and his mom's gumbo and then there's Pop's crawfish bisque.

The waitress brings his coffee and plate of hot, crisp beignets. This brings a smile to Jimmy's face for the first time in days. This is the moment he's been waiting for. He inhales deeply getting the full effect of beignets, powdered sugar, and the aroma of dark rich coffee.

He realizes this is the reason he came to New Orleans. It's the smell. Some people complain about it, but for Jimmy it's magic. An amalgam of the briny, fishy smell from the Gulf. The industrial, chemical smell from the Mississippi. The dense, complex organic smell coming from the bayous and the mold and decay from the French Quarter. These smells when combined with the aroma of dark roast coffee and hot beignets creates a smell that is uniquely New Orleans.

One more thing...he furtively looks around and reaches into his inside coat pocket. He brings out a silver flask and hesitates just a moment before he opens it and pours a healthy dollop of dark, almost black, thick liquid onto his plate. Jimmy dips a beignet into the dark syrup and pops it into his mouth. Beignets and Steen's...it doesn't get better than this. OK, so he doesn't hate the food so much or really the people. Right now, he hates Roger for dying...and maybe Johnny for... well the jury is still out on Johnny, but probably him too.

He takes a sip of coffee and pops another Steen laden beignet into his mouth. He closes his eyes in pure contentment, but a frown begins to creep in. No, he knows he doesn't hate anyplace or anybody. He is angry. Angry at himself. Angry, that he had to wait for Roger to die before he came home. And, if he is truly honest with himself, he is afraid. Afraid of what is waiting for him in Lake Charles.

Jenny

Jennifer Chretien pulls her rented, slate gray Ford Fusion into a space at the Lake Charles Regional Airport and checks herself out in the mirror. At twenty-two with her auburn hair hanging loose and free, her father's amber eyes, well really the Chretien eyes, but thank God not the Chretien nose, she's happy with the result. Jenny looks at her watch. Her father should be touching down right about now, and she doesn't want to be late.

Jenny realizes she's beginning to fall in love with Louisiana and doesn't understand why Daddy had never brought her here. He always had a kind of love/hate relationship with Louisiana. He and Uncle James always argued about who made the best gumbo or jambalaya, but she always felt there was much more unspoken. Now she is here and for the first time in…well forever, she feels like she can breathe, can relax, can be…herself. She feels like she's been running a marathon for her whole life. Getting the highest grades so she could get into all Honors classes. Taking all AP classes and getting into UCLA. Receiving not one but three degrees. As if Business, Philosophy and somehow, French Literature would better prepare her for law school.

Now in the Fall she would be off to Loyola Law and get ready for a profession she really doesn't care about. But for now, she doesn't have to worry. In a weirdly ironic way, Uncle Roger's death couldn't have come at a better time. She can't explain it, but she feels oddly at home. It's kind of creepy staying at the home of a dead guy…even an uncle. Uncle Roger seemed like he'd been pretty cool…for an old guy. She wishes she had known him, but she isn't sure her father had known him either…not really.

Jennifer is sure her father doesn't know about Margot, Roger's lady friend, and she is glad she had arrived before her father. He is difficult sometimes and there are things he needs to understand before he starts huffing. Like he and Uncle James are not going to be in charge. Margot has definite ideas about what is going to happen, and she needs to be heard.

5

Jennifer shakes her head. She knows Daddy is not going like it. He always wants to be in charge…no, that isn't right, he always wants to think he is in charge. For all his blustering, Daddy is never really in charge. He's cute, funny, and sometimes charming, which was more than you can say for Uncle James, but he isn't in charge. Her mother had been in charge when they were married. His secretary is in charge at work and she's in charge whenever she stays with her father. Who is in charge when he is by himself, Jennifer has no idea.

Margot

Marguerite, *Margot*, Sallier sits in front of her vanity and primps. She pauses to really look at her face and is satisfied with what she sees. At 57 she likes the way she matured. She isn't 30 anymore and she doesn't try to look it, but she's still cute. Margot isn't used to using her feminine wiles to deliberately manipulate men, but she is going to knock the socks off Roger's fuddy-duddy brothers and prove she belongs here. Hell, her great, great, great, grandfather, Charlie Sallier, founded this stupid town. Besides, there are things they need to know.

She reaches over to a small, intricately inlaid cedar box and opens it. The pungent scent of cedar drifts up. Lying in the cedar box is a deep blue velvet pouch and inside, a brooch. It belonged to Charlie's wife, her great, great, great-grandmother, Catherine and is about two inches wide, made of gold and has a finely carved figure of deep purple amethyst. It is beautiful…or it would have been if the figure had been the expected cameo silhouette. A shiver ran the length of Margot's spine. Her fingers closed, clutching the brooch. It wasn't the profile of a lovely lady … it was a skull and crossbones. And there is something more, something else that scars this unusual piece. There is an indentation just off center and a crack…a crack dividing the skull almost perfectly in half.

Roger had been excited. It had been the first clue, the first indication that there was some truth to the legend of *Laffite's Treasure*. Margot shudders again. That had been the beginning, but that's also when things got weird. She is sure someone was watching them and then two weeks later, Roger was dead. She isn't exactly sure what is going on, but she knows there is more trouble to come. She shuts her eyes and makes a solemn vow. Roger's death will be avenged. She'll see to that.

6

Antoine

Detective Sergeant Antoine Francois Durel, an African American, powerfully built ex-marine, is not a happy man and as anyone in the Lake Charles Police Department can tell you, that does not bode well for anybody. He does not like mess, and he considers a body wrapped in a pirate flag to be a mess. Someone is going to have to clean it up.

He picks up his coffee cup. Actually, it isn't an ordinary coffee cup. It is an antique Limoges porcelain demitasse cup. He always takes a minute before taking the first sip. It is the last remaining cup from a set that belonged to his great grandmother. He thinks of the history this cup has seen. He looks deep into the cup and seems mesmerized by the deep dark brown liquid as it caresses the sweetheart roses painted inside. He takes a sip and makes a face. "Damn...a perfectly perfect cup of coffee ruined by a pirate funeral."

He picks up the manila folder dropped off by the M.E. and thumbs through the seventeen-page report. Seventeen pages to ruin his coffee, his day and make a mess. Not only does he have a dead college professor wrapped in a pirate flag. He has a dead college professor wrapped in a pirate flag who drowned, apparently in his own study.

Perhaps Chretien was taking a bath...Antoine searches the report...with his clothes on, and with his last gasping, dying breath, got out of the tub, staggered into the other room, wrapped himself in the flag and died on the floor... No, he has to face the fact. It is a mess. Detective Sergeant Antoine François Durel is not happy.

Sallier Landing
1816

The mist, rising off the lake's jungle green surface as the sun peaks through the cypress trees, obscures Laffite's ship, the Pride, a two-masted schooner as it glides silently up the Calcasieu river toward the landing across from the Sallier cabin. Men, women and children from the nearby Atakapa village, descendants of the ancient Ishak tribe, calling themselves the 'Sunrise People,' throng the shore.

Laffite himself jumps from the rail of the quarterdeck to the sandy beach and walks toward a handsome man with a regal bearing emerging from the gathering on the shore. Crying Eagle embraces Laffite, who, with a show of appreciation, offers the chief a small chest of brightly colored trinkets. The chief holds the chest up for all his people to admire.

A commotion on the ship behind Laffite catches the captain's attention. He hurries to the ship in time to help his 16-year-old daughter, Denise, as she scrambles over the ship's rail, to the shore below. A murmur of admiration from the crowd on shore as Jean stands back to admire his daughter. She is the image of her mother, and he realizes she is the same age as Christina was when they married.

Catherine Sallier comes out on the cabin's front porch and waves to Jean and his daughter. Denise hurries to Catherine as Laffite makes his way through the crowd, laughing loudly and thumping the backs of well-wishers. He stops at the bottom of the porch steps and looks up at Catherine. "Comment ça va, Katerina."

Catherine smiles, "Mais tout va bien, Jean."

He nods and climbs the steps, hugging her briefly. He smiles and urges Denise forward. She shyly reaches into an apron pocket and brings out a deep blue velvet pouch. Hesitantly, she offers the pouch to Catherine, who looks to Jean. He gives a small nod and Catherine looks into the pouch and sees it contains a beautiful amethyst and gold brooch. Catherine takes it from the pouch and admires the piece of jewelry and attached gold chain.

Her brow furrows as she looks more closely at the figure on the front of the brooch. She cocks her eye at Laffite...a skull and crossbones? He shrugs and she runs into the cabin to look in the

8

mirror, putting the pouch on a table and sitting in front of a large mirror. Denise and her father follow her in.

Catherine fumbles with the clasp and Jean gently takes it from her hand and fastens it around her neck. Admiring herself in the mirror, Catherine flings her hair over her shoulder. She rushes to Denise and kisses her sweetly on the cheek. She turns to Laffite. She hesitates but hugs him and lightly kisses his cheek.

No one in the cabin notices the commotion outside. A small gasp escapes Catherine as she looks up to see her husband standing in the door. Charlie looks from his wife to his friend, locked in an embrace. A suspicion confirmed, he raises a pistol. Laffite instinctively moves between Charlie and Catherine. He spreads his hands and steps towards Charlie, imploring, "Charlot."

In one move Charlie sidesteps Laffite, fires the pistol at Catherine and runs from the cabin. The sound of hoof beats echo through the bayou.

Laffite rushes to the side of Catherine now lying motionless on the floor. He looks to Denise who stands rooted to her spot. Jean gently turns Catherine over and gazes at her lifeless face. Suddenly, she gasps for air and opens her eyes, looking frantically from Jean to the door from where Charlie fled.

Denise and Catherine lock eyes. Denise looks down at the brooch hanging around Catherine's neck. Her eyes follow the young women's gaze and Catherine slowly lifts the brooch. It's damaged. There's a large indentation in the side and the skull is cracked in half. She looks from Jean to Denise. The brooch saved her life.

And Charlie Sallier? He was never seen or heard from again.

Chapter II
"…him being dead and all."

Jenny

The ride from the airport is pretty much as she expects. Daddy is a mix of petulant boy angry that his boyhood town has changed and mature attorney who is there to take charge of a burdensome situation. It's amazing to Jenny how her father can be disillusioned, juvenile, wide eyed, world-weary, and a jerk all at the same time. Well, that is Daddy, and she loves him.

She opens the door and lets her father, wheeling his suitcase, go in first. He stops abruptly just over the threshold, eyes darting from side to side. "It's different." He smiles and shrugs. "I guess I shouldn't be surprised. It has been over twenty years."

John is clearly surprised…and disappointed. His face brightens as he leaves his bag and heads straight for the kitchen, through the back door and out to the screened porch. Jenny hears the unmistakable squeak of the porch swing. He calls airily, "How about some coffee?"

Jenny shakes her head. This is typical Daddy. Why couldn't he say something while they were on the way to Uncle Roger's? Now she will just have to go back out. Not that Starbucks doesn't sound good. "You want the usual…a grande, non-fat, latte with four raw sugars?"

"No honey, Uncle Roger must have coffee here. Check the cupboard. It's probably Community Coffee…paquet rouge."

Jenny doesn't know what that means, but she goes into the kitchen and opens the refrigerator. "We don't have to worry about food for around a billion years."

"What?"

"Casseroles. People have been dropping off casseroles since I got here. Margot assures me is a Louisiana thing."

"Well, she's right about that anyway."

Jenny starts looking through the cupboards. She finds what she's looking for in the third cupboard. Her degree in French literature finally paying off…a red pack of coffee clearly labeled Community. She looks on every countertop but can't find the coffee maker. "Found the coffee, but I don't know where the coffee maker is."

Her dad's voice calls out from the swing, "It's probably in the oven."

This puzzles Jenny, but she opens the oven and stares in. Her brow furrows as she brings out a white enamel pot like thing that is in two parts, a larger bottom receptacle with a smaller cylinder resting on top. This in turn is sitting in a slightly larger, burned-out, beat-up aluminum pot. "I suppose this is it, but I don't know how it works. There's no place to plug it in."

The porch swing stops swinging, and Jenny clearly hears her father huff. She hates the huff. Her father opens the screened door and peaks in. His eyes sparkle when he sees the pot. He grins at Jenny, "Watch and learn."

He takes the nestled pots to the sink. He removes the white coffee pot and fills the outer pot about half full of water, puts it on the stove and turns on the burner. Jenny looks perplexed. He checks the cupboard beside the stove and brings out a smaller pot, fills it with water and puts it on the stove to boil. He locates a tablespoon and measures four heaping tablespoons of coffee into the top cylinder. "Now we wait for the water to boil."

He walks out of the kitchen and calls over his shoulder, "I'm going to unpack. When the water boils, pour it in the top…slowly. Don't let it spill all over the store."

Jenny watches her dad wheel his bag up the stairs, bumping on each step. She turns back to the stove. She can do this. She stares at the pot for a while and nods. They are right. It doesn't boil when you watch it.

Johnny

Johnny wheels his suitcase down the upstairs hallway. He peers into a room. Roger's room…he doesn't want to stay there. He checks out the next room. This was the room he shared with Jimmy when they were kids, but he sees Jenny's things. He hesitates and looks in the room across the hall. This had been his parents' room when he was

11

young and then just Pop's after Mom died. He can't bring himself to stay in there. James can have that honor.

He chooses the small room down at the end of the hall. Roger had converted it from a guest room into a study of sorts. He bounces on the couch. It is one of those convertible sofas. He can make do with this.

It takes him about 30 seconds to put his clothes away. He doesn't have many. He doesn't need many since he doesn't plan on staying very long after all. He zips up his case and puts it on the floor. The very place Roger's body was found, as luck would have it. Of course, Johnny doesn't realize it at the time.

He looks around the room and sighs. A long time since he was in this house. A picture, perched on the desk catches his eye. He walks over and picks it up. Here they all are. Mom and Pop and the three boys. He vaguely remembers this picture. He looks around twelve or so. It was some family gathering. John looks at his mother. He remembers that dress. It seems like his mother had always worn that dress … and Pop, standing there in his hat. And there he is, standing with Rog and Jimmy. God, they looked goofy.

He looks up and sees himself staring back, reflected in a mirror. Now he just looked old and tired and something else. He feels the *cold breath of death on his neck* as some writer or other has said. Johnny thinks maybe Thomas Mann, but he isn't sure.

He shakes off the dark feeling and sees an old black and white photo just under the desk blotter. Chretien Point, the family plantation…a stately, old home sitting on the banks of Bayou Bourbeau. He had been there once when he was little, just before the family sold it. He remembers it as a place of wonder and mystery. He hasn't thought about it in about a billion years. He wonders why Roger has it on his desk.

As he lays the picture down, he glances at the back. Written in Roger's doctorial scrawl was: *Hypolite, Fèlicitè and Lafitte, 1819.* John would have taken more time to consider this but wafting up from the kitchen is the inviting aroma of coffee.

Jimmy

James has been driving his rented *Smart fortwo* around this stupid town for over an hour. "It's not that big a place, for crying out loud," He thinks…and speaking of size…he tries again to find a seat

12

position that allows blood to flow all the way to his feet. He sighs. "*Fortwo* is an overstatement."

He looks around and realizes he has no idea where he is. Everything looks different. Someone has turned all the streets to one-way and he's almost positive that he has passed this corner before.

There is a part of him, the analytical, shrewd, clever and Harvard MBA graduate part, which knows he should just call Johnny, who is probably at this very moment having coffee on the back porch swing, and ask for help, but he would rather die first. He must concentrate. It is only five or six blocks from the lake. If he is on Shell Beach Drive, it's between Lake Street and Alvin. If he gets to Sallier Street, he has gone too far.

He should just have paid for the navigation system, but he knew where he was going. In desperation, he gazes heavenward. "Pop" He implores. "I know you're up there gazing down at your eldest son and laughing but please help me find the house."

The *Smart forshit* sputters, misses and with a loud sigh, rolls to a stop. James looks up and finds himself, as if by magic, in front of his boyhood home. He smiles, "Thanks, Pop."

Jimmy pops the hatchback and gets out his bag and wheels it, jauntily, up the front walk. All desperate thoughts gone. He is Jimmy Chretien coming home from his freshman year at LSU. He throws open the front door and takes a deep breath. "Is that coffee I smell?"

He looks around the front room and his face falls. "It's different."

Antoine

He closes his eyes and throws the medical examiner's report on his desk. "This can't be right,"

He mutters as he picks up the phone and punches four numbers. The line clicks, but before anyone can speak, Antoine jumps in. "Doc, what're you doing to me? Why are you making a mess?" He waits for a response. "What do you mean, what do I mean? The professor …Chretien." He listens but can't contain himself. "Yeah, I know he drowned, but it's the water I'm talking about. What the hell do you mean brackish?"

Antoine closed his eyes. He tries to listen patiently. "Doc…doc." He says as politely as he can. "Can you shut up for just a minute?"

Doc shuts up.

"I'm sorry doc. Can you just tell me where the water came from?" He manages to listen to a complete sentence. "Contraband Bayou...that actually makes sense. It goes right by the university." Antoine freezes. "Not near the university?... Further out...near Prien Lake...No doc, you don't have to tell me how you know. I believe you...But doc, you made a mess."

Antoine stares off into space. Why was Chretien out near Prien Lake? What was he doing that got himself drowned? And how the hell did he get back to his house? I mean, him being dead and all.

Margot

Margot pulls her Barcelona Red Toyota Prius behind what appears to be an oversized kids Power Wheels, abandoned in front of Roger's house. She checks her make-up once more before she gets out, glancing over her shoulder as the *Smart fortwo* sighs and farts.

On her way up the front walk she wonders how much she should share with Roger's brothers. He was always so vague about them. They weren't close, but Roger was always strangely protective about them. Like he was preserving them in a box until the time was right. Kind of like her brooch...cherished and valued, but not for every day. She takes a breath before she rings the bell.

Margot flashes what she hopes is a charming smile that dissolves into a relieved exhale when Jenny opens the door.

Jenny whispers, "They're on the back porch."

Margot nods nervously and takes a deep breath... it smells of Roger. Everything will be okay now. She feels at home in this room. After all, she helped him pick out the new furniture.

Margot turns as James and John come in from the kitchen. Maybe, this will go well. Covering her nervousness, she looks around. "This is my favorite room. I was with Roger and helped him pick out this new furniture."

The brothers trade looks. "That figures," bounces between them silently.

Margot sees the exchange and blurts out. "I'm Margot by the way."

She looks to Jenny, who shrugs. "It seems my father and uncle have forgotten their manners."

She gives them a look, arching an eyebrow at her father. He coughs and steps forward. "I'm John…I know you were close to my brother. I'm sorry for your loss."

James spreads his hands in an attempt to appear inclusive. He's at his pompous best. "I realize this has been hard on you, but John and I are here now, and we can take care of all the…the arrangements. Take on the burden, as it were."

Johnny agrees, "Yes, certainly. We will, of course, keep you in the loop."

The two brothers look at each other with smug satisfaction. Jenny shakes her head and looks at them like they've lost their minds. She turns to Margot and is about to speak.

Margot cuts her off. "You arrogant bastards. You weren't part of his life before he died, and you think you can come in here now and take over his death. He got along fine…more than fine, without you before and he doesn't …we don't need you now." She turns to Jenny, trying not to cry. "If they want to be part of this, you know how to reach me."

Margot glares at them daring them to speak, turns on her heels and slams out the front door. Jenny watches her leave and turns back to her father and uncle. "Smooth, very smooth."

Chretien Point
1818

The wind howls as the rain lashes the stately plantation known as Chretien Point. The acres of cotton and sugar cane wave in the wind and majestic oak trees surrounding the house bend as the gale force squall rages. Bullfrogs croak and alligators thrash when the banks of Bayou Bourbeau overflow as a torrent of water surges past the plantation.

Inside, the rooms are bathed in the warm glow of kerosene lamps. In a room off the main hall Hippolyte Chretien and his wife Fèlicitè sit around the poker table sipping brandy with their gentlemen guests as their wives sip coffee in the drawing room.

Fèlicitè, cheroot clamped between her teeth, raises the stakes another hundred dollars. Hippolyte wisely folds as he proudly watches his wife call and rake in the pot. He shrugs as the other men grumble. Fèlicitè just smiles and blows smoke rings.

Hippolyte signals for another brandy as the hallway door quietly opens. Fèlicitè watches as a house slave bends to whisper in Hippolyte's ear. His eyes dart to hers as he listens to the message. A subtle nod of his head tells her all she needs to know. He downs his brandy, stands and with a curt "Good evening, gentlemen." He follows the house slave out.

Without a word, Fèlicitè rises and moves to the sideboard against the wall. Using her body to block the view from the table, she slides a drawer open and removes a derringer, secreting it in the folds of her gown. With a well-mannered bow, she excuses herself and follows her husband.

She pauses at the front door, opens it a crack and peers out. Her husband, cloak over his head, hurries through the storm with a man she doesn't recognize. Fèlicitè grabs a cloak from the coat rack and holds it over her head as she follows her husband into the torrent. Moving from tree to tree she follows silently, pistol cocked at the ready. Peering around a tree, she sees her husband joined by another man. Fèlicitè would know him anywhere...Jean Lafitte.

She lowers the pistol and watches as Lafitte produces a flat tin box. Hippolyte nods and gestures for the others to follow. As they hurry off seemingly oblivious to the raging storm, moving deeper into the dark bayou, Fèlicitè leans against the tree and ponders the meaning of what she just witnessed.

Chapter III
"Is this what he was killed for?"

Daz and Diz

A bluesy jazz riff from an alto sax overflows a third-floor balcony of Lagniappe House, an elegant plantation style mansion with a vast lawn sloping to Shell Beach Drive and the lake beyond, now a home for retired musicians. Dazincourt, Daz, Broussard, a seventy-year-old African American with eyes closed, fingers flying and ponytail bouncing in time to the music is one with his instrument.

A clarinet counterpoint suddenly joins in creating a sound that is both wistful and melancholy. The sax suddenly stops, and Daz opens one eye and glares at the figure in the doorway. Dennis, Diz, Dampiere, exact twin of Daz except he's white and bald, grins from around the mouthpiece. Daz faces forward looking over the balcony thinking deep thoughts. "You know, Diz, Mozart and I have a lot in common."

"Daz, do tell."

"Well, for starters we both hate the damn clarinet." He looks back beyond the balcony, while Diz thinks about this.

"You know it's a pity you don't have something else in common with him."

"Like what?"

"Like dying young."

Daz grins back. "That's good. That's very good."

Diz bows and looks over the balcony. "Margot here yet?"

Daz looks out at curved drive and shakes his head. "Don't think so. Haven't seen her."

"Maybe she's with Roger's brothers."

"Don't think that's going to go well."

"Why not?"

"I think they're kinda jerks."

Diz resumes his swinging. "Can't be all bad, daughter's sweet as pie...I was thinkin' we should get some tunes together, just in case."

"Just in case what?"

"Just in case Margot asks us to play."

Daz can't believe what he's hearing. "She damn well better ask us to play. Who else she gonna ask?"

"So, what do you think, 'Nearer My God to Thee'?"

"Okay...we gotta do 'Saints,' but how bout we mix it up with a little 'Down by the Riverside'."

"Gonna be the best damn jazz funeral this Parish has seen in forever."

"Right you are, my brother."

Margot

Margot finds herself driving along Shell Beach Drive aimlessly. She'd promised herself that her visit with Roger's brothers would go better, but they are such jerks...such men. She knows they're hurting too. They have, after all, just lost their brother, but they are such...men. She knows she should turn the car around and go back and apologize. That would be the gracious way to do things. The Louisiana way...the Lake Charles way, but she isn't feeling gracious. She is still damn mad.

Feeling a little better, Margot swings her Prius into the curved drive at Lagniappe House and pulls into the spot marked, **Director.** As always, when she gets out of her car, she gazes up at the old house, waving to Diz and Daz. She was still in nursing school when her grandfather died leaving her this place. She vowed then and there to turn this home into a haven for musicians, because her grandfather, although he couldn't sing or play a note, loved music and the people who made it.

She closes her eyes and listens to Diz and Daz working on a jazz riff to Saints, probably for Roger's funeral...she makes a mental note to ask them to do it. Someone else is softly playing Beethoven's Moonlight Sonata on the concert grand in the parlor until it is drowned out by someone crushing Proud Mary on an electric twelve string. Life as usual at Lagniappe House.

Instead of going in through the main door, she turns left and heads for a smaller door to the side. This is her private entrance. It opens to her sanctuary, refuge, retreat. It's only a small part of the sprawling mansion. It is, however, her small part. As she reaches out with her key, the door is flung open with such force that it knocks her to the ground. Margot is vaguely aware of a large shape running by her. She reaches out, but the shape is gone. As she struggles to her feet, she looks in through the front door and freezes. The room is torn apart. Drawers thrown to the floor, papers strewn everywhere, furniture up ended.

Margot's first thought. "Who could have done this?" Her second. "This is what Roger's house looked like."

Antoine

Antoine, wearing fishing waders, is knee deep in Contraband Bayou as it winds toward Prien Lake. One part of him is looking for the scene of a crime if there is one. One part is wishing he brought his fishing pole since that pool up ahead looks like a promising spot for redfish and part of him is listening for gators.

He notices a spot just on shore that looks odd to him. As he slogs over, he spots a young alligator, about a foot and a half long, eyes closed, sunning himself on a log. He can't help but wonder if Mama is nearby. His next thought stops him. "Is this case worth being a gator's lunch?"

He looks cautiously for Mama. He scans every possible hiding spot but doesn't see her. His attention is once more drawn to that odd spot-on shore. As he gets nearer, he sees trampled marsh grass along the shoreline. Something happened here. A gator fight...or is this where Roger Chretien died? The sun catches a glint from something on the ground. He bends down to pick it up but freezes when he hears a soft gurgle behind him.

He drops the shiny object into his breast pocket before turning slowly to scan the bayou behind him. A pair of cold, dark eyes stare at him from just above the water line...ten feet of an overprotective Mama. Junior slips off his log and glides to his Mama's side. As Antoine weighs his options, his hand slowly moves to the small of his back where his Smith and Wesson lies nestled.

Never taking his eyes off Mama, his fingers finally curl around his weapon. He brings his gun to the front and assumes the position. He looks at Mama. Mama looks back...a contest of wills. It seems like an eternity until the big gator blinks and slowly sinks below the surface. Antoine warily backs up, his eyes darting from side to side looking for the ripples that will tell him if Mama is gone or merely playing with him.

How long he has been holding his breath, he doesn't know. Never turning his back on the bayou, Antoine holsters his weapon, then remembers the shiny object he dropped in his pocket. He reaches in and pulls it out. A round coin, crusted in muck. As he rubs the black crud from the coin, gleaming gold glows in the afternoon sun. He looks closer at the Coat of Arms in the center, something written in French around the edge and a date...1806. "Is this what Roger Chretien was looking for?" Or more to the point. "Is this what he was killed for?"

Jimmy

James stands, suitcase in hand, peering into the guest room. He scowls at John's suitcase. "This is typical."

James shakes his head and looks back down the hall. Now he must decide...Rodger's room or Pop's. He couldn't face Rodger's room, but Pop's room is, well, Pop's room. Squaring his shoulders, he heads back down the hall. He is, after all, the eldest...the head of the family. He should take Pop's room. It will be a comfort to the rest.

He slowly opens the door and sticks his head in...the faint scent of Old Spice. He remembers standing on a stool in the bathroom watching Pop shave...then the splash of the aftershave. Almost reverently he quietly enters the room, laying his suitcase on the bed, and opening the closet door. Pop's clothes...this is almost too much.

James sits on the bed and gazes around the room. He hasn't been in this room since Pop died and now Rodger is gone. It is down to Johnny and him. When had he become the old one? He catches a glimpse of himself in the mirror. He looks like the old one. When had that skin under his chin gone all saggy? When did he get old? This isn't fair, he is still middle-aged. He glared at the mirror, then sighs. "Middle aged if I live to 130."

He makes a face at himself. He needs something that will remind him that he is still a vital, virile man with his best years still ahead. Jambalaya...he will make jambalaya. No old fart can make jambalaya like he does. It is settled. He'll make a list for Jenny. She won't mind running to the store...not for Uncle James' famous Jambalaya.

Johnny

On the back-porch, Johnny sits on the swing, staring off into space, holding an empty coffee cup. He stops abruptly and looks around and calls out. "Where is everyone?"

No one answers and John frowns. He has no idea when Jenny and James left. Margot...he remembers when she left. He winces at the thought. He could have handled that better. He stops to think. He and James could have handled that better. Well, really James. Where does he get that "taking on the burden" and "keep you in the loop" stuff?

He can be a real asshole sometimes. John closes his eyes. He knows he can be a real asshole, too. Then a realization hits him. Rodger...Rodger is dead...he drowned. "How did he drown? Where was he...who found him?"

There are times when he is astounded at his own stupidity. There is a person who knows the answer. A person who was is this house not an hour ago. A person that he dismissed...shooed away. He begins swinging again. He needs to fix this. He's the only one who can. Then it hits him. The answer is obvious. Gumbo...he'll make a pot of gumbo. No one can be mad when they have a bowl of gumbo. He'll ask Jenny to call Margot. No one can say no to Jenny. She can call right after she goes to the store to pick up few things. She won't mind...not for her dad's famous Gumbo.

Jenny

Jenny pulls into the Market Basket parking lot. She left the house more than a little annoyed. She's not sure what annoys her the most. The fact that both her uncle and father would assume she'd like nothing more than dropping everything and go to the market, or that she isn't more annoyed. Uncle James makes a mean Jambalaya and her dad's Gumbo was always one of her favorites.

As she gets closer to front door, the tantalizing aroma from the smoker near the front of the store hits her full force. Maybe this time she'll get the courage to try the Jalapeno Boudin. Her mouth begins to water with anticipation. She can't believe how much life in Louisiana is centered around food. It's a way of life, a reason for being, a contact sport. When you finished one meal you began planning the next. If she isn't careful, she'll gain a hundred pounds and have to be wheeled out of the state.

Jenny snags a shopping cart and takes out a long list. First things first, shrimp, crab, oysters, then some andouille. She wants to check out the crawfish. She's never had crawfish and she'd like to try it. And they need more 'Slap Ya Mama.' She'd become addicted to it. She turns down the coffee aisle. "Chicory or not to chicory, that is the question." She shrugs. "Depends on my mood."

Her phone begins to buzz, and she fishes it out of her jacket pocket. She brightens when she sees Margot is calling. She's next on her list. "Hi, Margot, I was just going to call you." Something is not right. "Margot…are you there? What's wrong? She listens, frowning. "Are you okay?" Her frown becomes alarm. "I'm at the store. I'll finish up and be right there…Don't be silly. I'm coming." She turns the cart around and heads for checkout.

Contraband Bayou
1820

A sleek pirogue skims the dark water of Contraband Bayou. As two men row silently, Jean Laffite sits in the stern, eyes shut listening to the night sounds of the bayou. Bull frogs, alligators, crickets, and owls...an eerily soothing chorus. Without opening his eyes Lafitte points to a copse of cypress trees in the middle of the bayou. He holds up his hand and his two men raise their oars, the boat gliding silently with the current.

Then, as if by magic, there is a gurgling rush of water, and a small island appears under the Cypress Trees as the tide rolls out. The small boat drifts ashore as Laffite nods toward two large chests next to him. Each chest bears the Coat of Arms of Napoleon Bonaparte. The two men wrestle the chests from the boat as Lafitte throws two shovels ashore. Silently the two men begin digging a hole big enough to hold the chests.

As the hole gets larger, one of the men stops, leaning on his shovel. He obviously thinks the hole is deep enough, but the other man keeps digging. After a quick look to Lafitte, the man joins his companion and keeps digging. When he is satisfied, Lafitte motions toward the chests. The men heave them into the hole. Then, they pick up their shovels and Lafitte nods imperceptibly.

As one man begins filling in the hole, the other moves behind him and with a mighty whack sends him toppling into the hole. Without sound or expression, he continues filling the hole until the chest and man can be seen no more.

He picks up both shovels and climbs into the boat pushing it from shore. He and Lafitte take up the oars and begin rowing back up the bayou. Lafitte pauses and turns to see the water churning and covering the small island until nothing, but the small grove of cypress trees is seen.

Chapter IV
"Nobody messes with her family."

Antoine

Antoine pulls his mud splattered, Dodge Durango SXT into his marked parking place behind the Lake Charles Central Police Station. Holding the phone in the crook of his neck, he changes out of his wading boots into his cognac Florsheim wingtips, throwing the boots into the back. As somebody comes on the line, he grabs the phone. "Hey, it's Durel."

He pauses impatiently as they spew inanity. "Yeah, I'm great. Listen, could you send a team out to Contraband Bayou." More inanity. "Yeah, where it flows into Prien Lake. Also check the northeastern tip of Coon Island." Walking to the department entrance, he moves the phone to his other hand as he fishes in his pants pocket for his badge and slips it on his belt.

"I'm looking for a place where something could have been dragged ashore." He listens, closing his eyes and rubbing his brow. "About the size of a body and if you find anything make a plaster cast…and tell them not to break it this time."

As he walks into the station, a young female rookie behind a plexiglass partition, catches his attention, waving a letter. He looks at her. She says nothing, just waves the letter. He resigns himself and walks toward her. "Yes, officer."

She pushes the letter under the partition. "Mailroom thought you should see this…right away."

Antoine picks it up and starts to walk away. Suddenly he freezes and turns back to the rookie, trying to keep his voice steady. "When did this come in?"

"The clerk said a couple of days."

Antoine takes a beat. He senses a mess in the making. "A couple of days?" The rookie scratches her chin. Antoine looks away for just a second. "And they thought I might like to see it?"

"They thought it might be important."

"Did they...officer?"

"Thibodeau, sir"

"Officer Thibodeau...Thank you."

As he walks away, Officer Thibodeau calls out. "One more thing."

Antoine stops and turns...did she really just Columbo him? "Yes, officer?"

"There was a break-in at Lagniappe House."

"That's Marguerite Sallier's place. Was she there...was she hurt.?"

"She was roughed up a bit...reports on your desk."

He mutters all the way passed the double doors, the interrogation rooms, and the break room. He's muttering as he passes the wall with the wanted posters, the jet ski for sale and roommate wanted notices. He mutters all the way to his desk, where he sits and lays the letter, face up on the desk and picks up the report on the break-in. For a moment he stares at the letter and the report. He grabs a letter opener and pauses. "Okay then, first things first let's see what Roger Chretien has to say."

He slices the envelope open.

Jenny

Sitting outside Lagniappe House, Jenny pauses after starting the Fusion. Margot says she's okay, but she's obviously not. She's scared and it must have to do with Uncle Roger's death. She must make her father and Uncle James see that there is more at stake than Uncle Roger's funeral. There is something dangerously wrong and the sooner they both realize that the better. The question is how.

Margot is coming over for round two and they have to get out of their own way. Her brow furrows, Jenny backs out of the parking space, heads for the exit, and turns left onto Shell Beach Drive. As she ponders her next move, her phone rings. Alexis announces: "Daddy." Jenny presses the connect button on the steering wheel. "Hi Dad."

"Where are you? I got to get cooking."

Jenny plunges ahead. "On my way now. Listen Dad, something's happened...It's about Margot."

"What's wrong...she's coming isn't she?"

25

She hesitates just a second before going on. "She'll be there, but Dad someone broke into her house…he was there when she came home."

Silence on the other end.

"Dad?"

"I'm here…was she hurt? I mean is she all right?"

"She's okay. She was knocked down and is banged up a bit, but she's alright."

There's pause until Johnny responds in a quiet voice. "Do you think…I mean this must have something to do with Roger?"

"It must…but now you need to listen to Margot…both of you."

There's a brief hesitation. "We will…I'll talk to James. You know how pig-headed he can be,"

Right, Uncle James is the only pig-headed member of this family. It must somehow be linked to the Y chromosome. Jenny wonders briefly if anybody has done that study. "Please, Dad, do that. I'll be home in a few minutes."

Jenny clicks off. She's worried. If she's right they could all be in danger, and she will not let anything happen to her father. Nobody messes with her family.

Daz and Diz

Heads together, Daz and Diz stand outside Margot's front door. A concerned look on his face, Diz weighs their options. "Jenny's gone…the police are gone. Do you think she feels up to seeing us?"

Daz crinkles his forehead. "Don't know…if you were her, would you want to see us?"

"Well, I'm not sure. I'd always have time to see me…but you can be very draining."

"I'm draining? You suck the life right out of…life."

"The red, red robin ain't bob, bob, bobbin along when you show up either."

Before Daz can respond a muffled voice from the behind the closed door speaks.

"Come on in, guys. I'm okay."

The door swings open and Margot ushers them in. As they enter Daz and Diz look around at the overturned furniture and drawers and papers strewn around. Margot places a dining room chair in its proper spot. Daz and Diz exchange looks. Daz tries to look deeply into Margot, beyond the pretense. "What happened here, Margot…what's going on? And I

26

don't want to hear you got it under control because you don't. Someone was looking for something."

Margot tries to bluff her way through, but after a look at Diz and Daz, her exterior calm crumbles. She collapses into the chair. Daz and Diz look at each other helplessly. Diz touches Margot's shoulder. "Can I get you something? A glass of water…?"

Margot shakes her head. "No, thank you." She shuts her eyes and begins to shake all over. "I don't know what to do. I'm scared." She looks around the room. "This is the way Roger's study looked when I found him…after he drowned."

Daz and Diz draw chairs up beside Margot. Daz looks around the room. "You never said anything about that night."

Margot covers her face. "It was horrible. I found Roger in his study…lying there. With stuff thrown around room."

Diz shakes his head. "I thought he drowned?"

"He did." Margot sees the confusion on their face and shakes her head. "I know…it doesn't make any sense, but someone was looking for something at Roger's."

Daz absently fingers an imaginary sax as he looks around the room. "I don't think they found it there."

Diz looks from Margot to Daz. "The question is, did they find it here?"

"I don't know. Roger was on to something." She thinks, smiling at some thought., "You know Roger. You know how obsessed he was with Lafitte's treasure. He found something. He didn't want to tell me what it was…not until, he was sure."

Daz frowns. "So, you think this is all connected? You think Roger was killed over some buried treasure?"

"I didn't at the time…or I didn't want to think so. But now it seems too much of a coincidence. Don't you think?"

Daz and Diz exchange looks. They don't know what to think. Diz tries to be helpful. "Well, someone was looking for something, that's for sure."

Daz gives him a look. Diz shrugs. "I mean, if they killed Roger, they must want it pretty bad."

Margot looks from to the other. "I'm scared. I've been scared since Roger died." She closes her eyes as a tear slowly trickles down her cheek. "I've felt so alone."

Diz and Daz stare at each other. Diz gives permission for Daz to speak for the two of them. "You're not alone anymore."

Daz and Diz look at each other in agreement. No body messes with family…and Margot is family.

Johnny

Still sitting on the back porch swing, Johnny slowly moves back and forward, thinking deep thoughts as Pop used to say. "When had he stop caring about Roger? When had he convinced himself, that he was somehow better than Roger?"

Johnny stops mid swing and takes a sip of coffee. Now Roger is dead. His brother is dead. "We used to play right on this porch."

Now, he would never have a chance to make it right. Johnny shakes his head. Plus, he'd ignored the one person who knew Roger best; the one person who cared about Roger. Abruptly, Johnny stands, a determined look on his face. "I've got to find James…got to figure this out."

Jimmy

James is in the kitchen opening cupboard after cupboard. "There has to be a proper pot for Jambalaya." He opens the oven and finds a cache of pots and pans. "Okay, here we go. Now were cookin' with gas, as Pop used to say."

He starts pulling out pot after pot, but none satisfy him. He pulls out a red enamel pot, but his eyes are on one in the back of the oven. Juggling the enamel pot, James reaches into the back and pulls out an ancient five-quart pot that's been seasoned with four or five generations of gumbo and slams it on the stove. "As usual I'm doing John's job."

Still mumbling, John comes in from the back porch and rinses his cup in the sink, turning to have a serious conversation, but James beats him to it. "Found your pot." James states, gesturing to the pot on stove. "Of course, I can't find the Jambalaya pot. How can I make Jambalaya without a proper pot?"

John looks at James holding the enamel pot like his brother has lost his mind. Sometimes James gets lost in the weeds. John points at the pot James has in his hand. "You're holding it."

James looks at the pot like some alien creature, finally really looking at it. "Of course, it's in my hand…where else would it be?" He slams the pot on the stove. "And where is that daughter of yours? How can I make a proper jambalaya without proper ingredients?"

He glares at John, who rolls his eyes. "Will you get a grip, please? She's on her way. Anyway, Jambalaya doesn't take any time at all.

Gumbo now, that takes time to get it just right." Changing gears, John holds up his hand. "Wait, it's not important. We've got to talk about Margot."

James wants to argue, but finally concedes the point. "You're right. I mean it's not like Jambalaya isn't important, but we should focus on Margot."

John pours coffee for himself and James, handing him a cup. He leans against the counter. The proper way to discuss important business in the kitchen. After taking a sip, John looks at James. "I got a call from Jenny. Someone broke into Margot's place."

James is shocked. "What? Is she okay?"

"She was roughed up some and her place was trashed."

"That is unacceptable. She is family."

The irony is lost on both of them. James takes a sip and puts the cup down. At his pompous best he turns to John. "There's something odd going on here. We've got to get to the bottom of this."

"We will."

They turn as the front door bangs open and Jenny calls out from the living room. "Will the chefs please come and help with the groceries?"

Margot

The foursome is gathered around the dining room table. John and James at either end with Margot and Jenny across from each other. Remnants of Gumbo, Jambalaya, salad, French bread and two bottles of wine adorn the table as they finish up their meal.

Actually, Jenny and Margot are finished, and they watch the guys polish off their feast. John sops up the last of the gumbo with French bread laden with butter, while James relishes his last forkful of Jambalaya. Both of them close their eyes enjoying the complex flavors as they roll over the tongue. Margot and Jenny share a smile, before Margot's gaze settles on the brothers. "I've got to say, I wasn't expecting this. It was incredible."

James and John beam at each other. James turns to Margot and raises his wine glass in a toast. "Well, you can take the brothers out of Looziana, but you can't take the Looziana out of the brothers."

John raises his glass to Margot as well. "Amen to that."

An unspoken agreement passes between the brothers. James clears his throat in embarrassment. "My brother and I need to apologize to you."

29

Ever the diplomat, Margot tries to wave it off, but James will have none of that. "No, this is important. We blew it the first time we met."

Jenny and Margot share an unspoken moment. "Who are these guys and what did they do with James and John."

James puts his wine glass down and gets serious.

"I realize…" He shares a look with John. "We realize that there is something else going on here and we have no idea what it is. We need your help, Margot. It's becoming clear that this isn't just an ordinary accidental drowning." He looks to Margot. "Will you help us understand?"

"I'll try, but there is so much I don't understand." James and John share a look and Margot is clearly frustrated. "I realize that this makes no sense, but it all began as sort of a game." The brothers are even more confused. Margot tries to explain. "We shared the stories our families passed down."

John nods in understanding. "Pop had all these stories…we were never sure if they were true or Pop being…well Pop."

"That's exactly what Roger said, but when we began to compare stories, Roger really got excited…" Margot takes out the brooch and lays it on the table. "And when Roger saw this, it all began to click. He became almost obsessed with it. He would be gone for hours slogging around Contraband Bayou and then he started saying he thought he was being followed. There was no proof of that and I thought that he was being paranoid, but a few days later…he was dead."

John and James examine the brooch. James fingers the crack on the face. He looks up in astonishment. "This is the brooch? The one Lafitte gave to Charlie's wife. My God, I thought that was just a story." With reverence John puts the brooch down. He looks to Margot, excitement dancing in his eyes. "And then what?"

Sadness passes over Margot's face. "Nothing. I think Roger found out more, but he was dead before he could tell me."

James looks to John who gives him an imperceptible nod. "What can we do to help?"

Margot looks defeated. "That's just it. I have no idea."

Sallier Landing
1822

The sun is just rising in the East as the birds wake in a beautiful harmonious blend of song. Catherine, waving off a bee, comes out onto the front porch to see the sunrise and closes her eyes, as the warmth of the sun, bathes her face. Her eyes fly open as she hears a soft sound coming from the river. A two masted schooner, The General Santander, emerges from the mist. A familiar figure stands on the quarter deck. Jean Lafitte waves. "Bon jour, Katerina."

He is helped ashore by a few of his men and limps his way to Catherine. "Jean, you are hurt. What happened? And where is your beloved boat?"

Jean waves his hand and spits on the ground. "It's the bastard Spaniards. They are responsible for both. I accept the leg, but I mourn the loss of my ship."

Catherine helps Lafitte up the steps. "Come inside, Jean, and rest."

Lafitte shakes his head. "I have something important to tell you, Katerina."

Catherine guides Lafitte into the cabin and helps him into a chair. "You should be comfortable here."

Lafitte sits and Catherine looks out the window. "Is Denise still on the boat? I'd love to see her."

"No, Katerina. I had to leave her with my brother, where she will be taken care of. She is not safe with me."

"Why, Jean, what is happening?"

Lafitte rubs his face. "The Spanish...I stay one step ahead, but they are closing in."

Catherine kneels next to Lafitte, and he puts his hand on her head. "Jean, is there anything I can do?"

"It is this very thing we need to speak about. I need your help." He gestures to the chair beside him. "I have some very valuable cargo that I am hiding. Do you understand?"

"Certainly, Jean."

"Very good, very good, Katerina. I must keep it out of the wrong hands. In case anything happens to me, I need to make sure it remains safe."

Catherine locks eyes with Jean. "Of course. I understand, Jean."

31

Lafitte studies her face intently for a moment, then takes out a small cedar box. "Katerina, in this box I have hidden everything about this cargo. If something happens to me, someone will come for this." He gets very serious. "Katherina, it is very important that you keep this safe. Can you do this? Can I trust you?"

"I will guard this with my life, Jean."

"Very good. Now help me up Katerina. I must get back to my ship. It's time to show the Spanish for the fools they are."

Catherine helps Jean to the door and watches as one of his men help Lafitte to his ship. Catherine's eyes start to mist as she waves to Jean as he stands on the quarterdeck. "Au revoir, mon ami."

She looks at the small box and then up as the schooner is again swallowed by the mist. Catherine knows she will never see Jean Lafitte again. She opens the box but finds it empty. Catherine smiles. It is in there somewhere. She removes the brooch Denise had given her those many years before, places it in the pouch and lays it lovingly in the box. It fits perfectly.

Chapter V
"Old habits die hard."

Jenny

Jenny is enjoying her last few minutes of peace snuggled under the covers as the sun streams through her bedroom curtains. Everything has been a whirlwind since her dad and Uncle James came into town. She snuggles deeper into the comforter and then she hears her dad calling from below. "Come on, Peanut, coffees ready."

Ordinarily Jenny hates it when her dad calls her 'peanut' but today she doesn't mind. She throws on a robe and heads downstairs. She pauses in the kitchen to pour the coffee and then heads to back porch. Uncle James and her dad are on the swing, so she takes the rocker. Her dad takes a sip and then ever the attorney. "So, what's on the docket today?"

Jenny takes a sip, thinking that they talked about this last night. Oh, well. "We are meeting Margot at the funeral home at 10:00 to finalize the arrangements. Then back to Margot's for an early lunch."

The brothers nod in agreement. After a sip, James has a thought. "We have to start digging into Roger's death."

John frowns. "You're right. Maybe we can talk to Margot about what she knows, after lunch?"

Jenny shakes her head. "Don't get ahead yourselves, guys. This is going to be a rough morning on Margot. Don't push her."

The brothers look at each other and sigh. John smiles. "I know…we won't. Old habits die hard."

James agrees. "Just give us a poke if we over-step."

Jenny has been waiting to give him a poke for years, but instead just smiles. "Well, I doubt it'll come to that. Just behave." Jenny finishes her coffee and gets up. "I'm going to take a shower and get dressed." She looks pointedly at her dad. "I suggest you gentlemen do the same. You all don't want to keep Margot waiting."

John shares a smile with James. "You've almost got it, but it's not 'you all.' It's one word…'y'all.' It just takes practice."

Jenny rolls her eyes. "I promise, I'll practice later…when I have time."

They get the hint and finish their coffee. John smiles at his daughter. "We'll be down in a bit." He gives his daughter a peck on the cheek and he and James go into the kitchen. Jenny watches them leave. A shiver runs up her spine. Something is not right…not right at all.

Antoine

Antoine sits at his desk staring intently at the roses in the bottom of his demitasse. He takes a sip and resumes his staring contest with the roses. Finally, Antoine pushes the cup and saucer aside. He takes out the Chretien letter and opens it. He reaches into his top desk drawer and removes the coin he found on the banks of Contraband Bayou and the report on the break in at Lagniappe House and places them beside the letter.

He looks around his office and finds a plaster cast sitting on top of a filing cabinet. He places it gently on his desk next to the letter, report, and coin. He stares at it for a moment, then turns it to the right 45 degrees and stares at it some more. Then he tries 180 degrees. He has no idea what he's looking at. "Duplantier!" He bellows. "Are you out there Duplantier?" He hears nothing. "Officer Duplantier, I have a sneaking suspicion you are out there somewhere…Please, Officer Duplantier, I'm not going to hurt you."

After a moment, Officer Duplantier pokes his head in doorway. "Yes, sir, Sergeant Durel, sir?"

"Officer Duplantier, you went out to Contraband Bayou?"

"Yes sir. I was told to look for any place where it looked like a body could have been dragged ashore."

"Yes son, I know…and you found one."

"I sure did."

Antoine smiles at the young officer. "And you did a fine job."

Duplantier beams. "Thank you, sir."

Antoine stares at the plaster cast. "The only thing is…I don't know what this is."

Duplantier tries to be helpful. "Well sir, that's a plaster cast. I was told to make a plaster cast of anything that looked suspicious."

"I know what it is son…and you thought this was suspicious?"

Duplantier gets very serious. "Well, yes sir I did."

Antoine just stares at the cast. "Thank you, officer. The only thing is I don't know what I'm looking at."

34

Officer Duplantier finally understands. "Yes sir, but you've got it wrong." He reaches across the desk and turns it about 15 degrees.

Antoine tries to look at it from different angles. "Son, do you have any idea what I'm looking at?"

Duplantier looks at it for a minute before shrugging his shoulders and shaking his head. "Not really sir. Could be a footprint, maybe a gator. Like I said it looked suspicious…very suspicious."

Antoine shakes his head. "I'm sure it was, son." He stares at the young officer for a moment…a long moment. "Thank you, officer, you did a fine job."

Duplantier turns to go and at the door gives a small wave. Antoine waves back. He looks at the three objects on his desk and picks up the letter, reading it for the hundredth time and frowns. "Okay, so Chretien thought someone was following him. That he may be in danger…and if anything happened to him Margot Sallier may be in danger." He checks out the postmark. "He mailed this the same day he was murdered. Why didn't he call? Why write a letter?"

He closes his eyes and rubs his forehead. "And the mess keeps getting bigger and bigger.

Margot

At a quarter till 10:00, Margot pulls into the parking lot of Louragan et Fils Maison Funeraire and parks, sitting alone in her Prius. The funeral is tomorrow, and she doesn't know if she can do it. Jenny has been great, but the brothers… she still isn't sure about the brothers.

Luckily, she doesn't have long to wait. Jenny pulls up in her Fusion and parks next to her. Before Margot can gather her things, Johnny springs from the car and runs to open the door for her. He offers his hand to help her out. "May I be of assistance?"

"Thank you, kind sir." Margot takes Johnny's hand and gracefully gets out of her car. "I really appreciate y'all being here."

Johnny looks over at Jenny and points to Margot. "You see, Honey. That's how you say it."

Jenny rolls her eyes. "Thanks, Dad."

Johnny bows. "Glad to be of service…We'll start on Nawlins next."

Jenny just shakes her head. Margot looks over at Jenny and James, gives them a little wave. "Thank you for coming. Jenny and I were here earlier and picked out a casket and made the arrangements. I hope it's okay."

James can't let Johnny outshine him. "It's entirely up to you. Whatever you think is best. We are here for support."

Margot looks quizzically at Jenny. Jenny just shrugs. She looks back at the brothers, "Listen, y'all, I appreciate what you're doing, but I need to know what you think. Don't tell me what you think I want to hear. Tell me what you think. He's your brother. I want you to be honest with me. Can you do that?"

She looks pointedly at the brothers, who look to each other and nod. Johnny guides her to the front doors. "Yes, Margot. Yes, we can."

James opens the front door, and they step into a darkened foyer. It's cool and the smell of roses, mums, lilies, and gladioli fill the room. Margot pauses and takes it all in. "This is the right place for Roger."

Jimmy

James steps through the doorway and comes to an abrupt stop. He remembers this place...the smell, the look...everyone was so goddam polite. This is where they went when Pop died. This is not right for Roger...not right at all.

Robert, a young African American man, appears out of nowhere. It's beginning to remind James of the Haunted Mansion. He can't be more than twenty...twenty-five at the oldest. He probably wasn't even born when Pop died. Robert steps forward and offers his hand to Margot. "Good morning, Miss Sallier."

He turns to the others; his eyes linger on Jenny. "Good morning, I am Robert Louragan. I'm the "Fils" in Louragan et Fils. My father apologizes for being late, he will be with us momentarily." He looks to include everyone and notices James scowling at him. "And you must be Dr. Chretien's brothers."

Margot steps forward. "Yes, this is James Chretien and John Chretien."

Robert holds out his hand and both James and John shake it. James somewhat reluctantly.

Margot turns to include Jenny. "Of course, you remember Jenny."

Robert gives Jenny a small but heartfelt smile. Jenny's face warms as she returns the smile. Robert holds her look. "Yes, I do. How are you, Miss Chretien?"

James watches as Jenny shyly takes Robert's hand. Their touch lingers. James looks at Johnny, poking him to see if he's picking up on any of this. John squints at Robert and clears his voice. "I'm sure she's fine."

Robert gets the message and gently let's go of Jenny's hand. Johnny shakes his head and gives Robert the 'I'll be watching you look.'

Robert clears his throat. "If you will follow me, Dr. Chretien is resting in our Chamber of Heavenly Repose."

James stops in his tracks, his eyes narrowing. "Resting?... Chamber of Heavenly Repose? Roger is not resting. He's..." James realizes this is not the Haunted Mansion...it's a Monty Python sketch.

Robert leads the way down a short corridor. He pauses outside a wide, rich mahogany door. The door silently slides open, and Robert ushers them into the room.

Standing at the foot of Roger's casket is a distinguished, African American man with slate grey hair, impeccably dressed, without a wrinkle on his face. He spreads his hands in greeting. "Welcome, to Louragan et Fils. I am Phillip Louragan. I am very sorry for your loss. It is a tragedy that brings you here. We share your suffering, as well. Dr. Chretien was a friend."

James stares at Phillip Louragan. He can't believe it. This man hasn't changed in twenty years. James steps forward. "Mr. Louragan, I am James Chretien, and this is my brother, John."

John steps forward and Phillip shakes their hands. "Of course, I remember you...such a sad day when we buried you father...You must call me Phillip; we are family."

James and John share a look. Phillip turns to Margot and Jenny. "Miss Sallier and Miss Chretien, welcome. I hope you will find everything to your liking."

Margot looks around the room. Pictures of Roger and flowers abound...soft music plays in the background. Margot closes her eyes, listening intently. 'On Eagle's Wings,' that was one of Roger's favorites. Her eyes start to mist. "Thank you, Phillip, It's all lovely."

James notices him change gears slightly. Phillip moves to the head of the casket. "Would you like to view Dr. Chretien?"

James is about to shake his head when he notices everyone else nodding. He hates this part. Effortlessly and silently, Phillip lifts the top half of the casket. Margot steps up and with tears streaming down her face, places her hands on Roger's hands. Jenny steps beside her, putting her arm around Margot's waist. Johnny joins them gazing intently at Roger.

He turns to include James, but James finds he can't move his legs. He can't take a step. He can do nothing but stare at Roger from behind everyone else. He's vaguely aware that the others are speaking. He hears snippets. "He looks so natural...He does look like he's resting...It's all so lovely."

It's only then that James realizes that tears are streaming down his face. He becomes aware that Phillip is speaking. "Dr. Chretien will remain here until 6:00 pm for visitation when he will be escorted to the Cathedral to lie in repose overnight until the funeral tomorrow morning at 11:00."

Johnny extends his hand. "Thank you, Phillip. We are deeply grateful."

Phillip gives a slight bow. "Of course...if you need anything please ask us."

He takes a step back and gestures to Robert. "Robert, could you see these lovely people out."

"Of course, Father."

He gestures to the family. "If you would follow me, please."

He leads them out of the room, then steps aside to allow them to pass, falling in step beside Jenny. They share a moment. A moment that is not lost on John.

While walking, James turns to include Robert. "Thank you, Mr. Louragan,"

"Please call me Robert. After all, as my father said, we are family."

As the others walk out the front door, James hesitates and looks around the room. A small smile forms. "Roger is in very good hands." James walks out into the bright Lake Charles morning.

Daz and Diz

Daz and Diz are on their third-floor balcony playing "Nearer my God to Thee "in a slow, mournful way befitting a Jazz Funeral, but Diz stops, shaking his head. "I think it's too slow."

38

Daz glares around his sax. "Diz, this is a funeral. How else is it supposed to sound?

"I don't know. A little more hopeful maybe. This sounds like Roger is damned forever in the fiery pit of hell."

"Well, that's your fault."

Diz can't believe it. "How can it possibly be my fault."

Daz explains. "We all know that the clarinet is not the happiest instrument. It sounds like a pig pleading for its life."

Diz is about to respond when Daz points to the driveway. Margot is pulling in followed by Jenny and the guys. An unspoken thought passes between the two. Daz gives a silent four count, and they break into a rousing rendition of Saints. Margot gets out of her Prius and waves to the guys. Jenny waves as she stands next to Margot. She gestures to John and James. "This is my dad and uncle."

They wave to the musicians. Johnny cups is hand around his mouth and shouts, up. "That sounds great guys."

They listen as Daz and Diz finish up, clapping as they follow Margot. Daz and Diz bow as they pass below them and into Margot's quarters. Daz can't help wondering about them. He finally turns to Diz, who shrugs. "I guess things are okay after all,"

"I guess they are, my friend."

"And do you know what? I think you're right about 'Nearer my God.' What if we pick up the tempo?" He gives Diz a look. "And see if you can get a more pleasant sound out of that…kazoo. That would help a lot."

Diz is about to come back with a zinger but shakes his head and smiles. "I'll do my best, Daz. I certainly will."

Johnny

Johnny looks around the table as they all finish their stuffed crab. He thought he was a good cook, but this is whole different level. "Margot, this is exceptional. I thought I'd had stuffed crab before, but apparently, I haven't."

Margot smiles. "It a family recipe handed down from Catherine, my great, great, great grandmother. It's been perfected over the years, but it all began with her."

Johnny raises his glass of sweet tea. "To great, great, great grandmother, Catherine, and her stuffed crab. She'd be an asset to any family tree."

Jimmy swallows. "Here, here."

Jenny gets up to clear the dishes. Johnny rises to help, but Jenny gives him a look. He sits back down, turns to Margot, and clears his throat. "I'm not sure what to say here, but I'm glad Roger got to spend time with you, and we are here to help figure out exactly what happened."

Margot bows her head. "I am most grateful John. Thank y'all for being here. I don't feel alone anymore."

Jenny brings the coffee service, sets it on the table and begins pouring. "Who's ready for dessert? Margot has pecan pie with or without ice cream."

Jimmy lights up like a candle. "Well, I don't usually partake, but today I'll make an exception…with ice cream, please."

Johnny shakes his head and laughs. "I'll have the same."

Margot starts to say no and then reconsiders. "Just the pie if you please, Jenny."

As Jenny leaves for the kitchen, Margot calls out. "And maybe just a skosh of ice cream." Jenny smiles and heads for the kitchen. "Be back in a jiff."

There is silence while everyone fixes their coffee and takes the first sip. Jenny returns with the dessert and takes her seat. Johnny takes a bite of pie and ice cream. His eyes close as he enjoys the sweet crunch of the pecans and creamy goodness of the ice cream, but then he gets serious. "It occurs to me that tomorrow might be good to watch people. To see if anyone looks or acts suspicious."

James nods in agreement. "John's right."

Jenny rolls her eyes. "Dad, this is not an episode of Law and Order. We are there to honor Uncle Roger, not to finger a suspect."

John coughs, embarrassed. "Of course, you're right. I only meant that if we see something suspicious, we should make note."

James agrees. "You know what they say, 'the killer always returns to the scene of the crime.'"

Chretien Point
1822

On this night Fèlicitè is restless. Hypolite is off somewhere doing who knows what. He is gone for days at a time and Fèlicitè wishes he would stay home occasionally. It is late and she steps onto the wrap around veranda off the drawing room. She likes to come out here before going to bed. The soft breeze, the sound of rustling leaves from the oak trees, the bullfrogs, crickets all singing their night song. This calms her. Suddenly, in the darkness, a presence. She reaches for her derringer. "Who's there." No sound. "I have a gun and I know how to use it."

A soft chuckle came from the darkness, although closer than she thought. "I know you do."

Fèlicitè recognizes that voice. "Jean, is that you? Hypolite is not here."

Jean Lafitte comes into the soft light of a kerosene lamp. "I know, I'm not here to see Hypolite. I am here to see you."

Fèlicitè is shocked by Lafitte's appearance. He is injured and obviously exhausted. "Jean, what's wrong...can I get you anything? Comes inside and rest."

Lafitte shakes his head. "I cannot, chere. I am barely one step ahead. You understand?"

Fèlicitè nods. "Of course, Jean."

Jean looks behind him. "I must hurry...Fèlicitè, I need a favor."

Fèlicitè spreads her hands in agreement. "Whatever you need. You know that Jean."

Jeans smiles. "Bon."

From the folds of his cloak, Jean brings out a small cedar box and hands it to Fèlicitè. "Take this, Fèlicitè and keep it safe. No one must know you have it...not even Hypolite. Can you do this?"

Fèlicitè holds the box close to her breast and speaks softly. "I will Jean. I will keep it safe. You may trust me on this."

This was what Lafitte needs to hear. "I do trust you, Fèlicitè...with everything I hold dear."

Jean looks over his shoulder and motions to someone deep in the trees. "If I can, I will return for it. If I can't, someone you know, and I trust, will come for it." Again, he motions impatiently. "Until then keep it hidden...even from Hypolite."

With those words Jean Lafitte disappears into the night.

Chapter VI
"I am The Resurrection and the Life."

Jimmy

James sits in the back seat of the Fusion. While John and Jenny are busy talking about who knows what in the front seat, James is alone with his thoughts. Mom and Pop at Christmas... Crab boils on Prien Lake...Crawfish bisque, shrimp etouffee, gumbo and jambalaya...LSU...coffee on the back porch and Johnny.

Most often his thoughts return to Roger. Roger, the scholar...the doctor, the history professor, the treasure hunter...that was the family joke, but more often now... Roger running, Roger afraid...Roger drowning. Roger being murdered. He tries to shake that final image but can't. It lingers like a foul taste.

James tries to focus on the here and now. He's the patriarch of the family. It's up to him to set an example...to show what it means to be a Chretien. In a short while, they will lay Roger to rest, and life will go on...but it can't. Not until they find out what happened to Roger. James doesn't notice when they pull into the parking lot of the Immaculate Conception Cathedral. He doesn't notice Johnny and Jenny get out of the car. He doesn't notice until Jenny speaks gently. "Uncle James...Uncle James, we're here."

James looks up surprised to see they are at church already. He reaches for the door and gets out looking at the tall spires of the Cathedral. This church represents God to him, it always has. Right now, he's angry at God and how He let this happen to Roger. He looks at his niece and brother. "Sorry, I was in my own world."

Johnny looks from James to Jenny. "That's okay, you're allowed. We all are, really."

Jenny looks at the Cathedral and sees Margot. "Let's go. There's Margot at the top of the steps."

James holds them back, draping his arms around them. Looking at both of them intently. "I want you to know how important you are to me. I want to be there for whatever you need."

Johnny and Jenny share a look behind his back. Johnny breaks away and hugs James back. "And I'll be there for you. Whatever you need…we both are."

James shudders. "I just got the most vivid image of Roger…of Roger dead."

Jenny pales. "That must have been horrible, Uncle James."

"It was."

Johnny guides his brother toward the church. "We need to make sure Roger is at rest." He looks James in the eye. "And then we will find whoever is responsible for Roger's death."

Jimmy's eyes clear of the dark places in his soul and he looks at Johnny. "Yes…yes we will."

Margot

As 11:00 approaches, Margot becomes more nervous. People keep coming up to her. Roger's friends, her friends, colleagues from the university, parishioners from the cathedral, acquaintances…and of course the merely curious. She doesn't know what her face should be doing. Should she smile, look serious or cry? Should she be the one consoled or is she the one to offer consolation? She finds herself telling a perfect stranger she is sorry for their loss. It's all too confusing.

At last, she sees Jenny, John, and James walking toward her. As they approach, Margot reaches for Jenny's hands. Holding on for dear life. "Thank you so much. It's such a relief to see you."

Jenny looks to her father and uncle and back to Margot. "You're not alone, anymore."

Margot smiles briefly. "But all these people…they expect something from me.

Margot is on the verge of crying and John steps to her side and speaks, softly. "You're the one who needs to be taken care of, not them."

James steps up. "Margot, you don't owe these people anything."

Margot shakes her head. "But they're friends." She looks around, considering. "Well, most of them."

43

John, arching an eyebrow, takes her elbow. "Why don't we go in and take our seats? All of these people, friends or not, will be here after all of this is over."

Johnny

Johnny sits in the front row, eyes darting back and forth. He's between Jenny, on his left and James on his right, with Margot on the aisle. That's about all he can see with his peripheral vision. He wishes he could turn around and look at the people behind him, but that would be…awkward. He knows something is going on behind him…he can feel it. Is it the killer or a witness? Perhaps, someone from his past. Is it the bully from sixth grade…or maybe old lady, Robinet, who used to sit on her front porch and yell at him in French every time he walked by? He takes a deep breath, pats Jenny's hand, and leans to James speaking softly. "Do you feel that everyone is staring and pointing at us?"

Jimmy leans into Johnny. "I do. Is that weird?"

"Not if they are."

Jenny nudges her father. "Will the two of you behave."

Johnny is about to speak when Margot turns toward them and gives them the look. They straighten up and face forward. Johnny feels like a six-year-old at Christmas Midnight Mass, sitting between Ma Mère and Grande Père. Johnny comes out of his reverie when Bishop Lisbony begins the traditional funeral Mass, spreading his hands to include everyone in the church.

"I am the resurrection and the life, says the Lord. He that believeth in me, though he were dead, yet shall he live and whosoever live and believe in me shall never die."

Johnny slips back into a reverie, only half listening to the bishop, responding by rote. He half hears the choir singing the 'Dies Irae' and his favorite hymn 'Be Not Afraid.' He listens to the lyrics…*Be not afraid. I go before you always. Come follow me and I will give thee rest.*

It isn't until Bishop Lisbony moves from the altar to the casket that Johnny comes out of his trance. He focuses as the bishop begins the final prayer. "To you, O Lord, we commend the soul of Roger Chretien, your servant; in the sight of this world, he is now dead; in your sight may he live forever. Forgive whatever sins he committed through human weakness and in your goodness grant him everlasting peace. We ask this through Christ our Lord."

Johnny answers. "Amen."

It is only then that full impact of Roger's death hits him. Roger was taken away from them. Why? What possible reason was so important that he must die because of it? He must find out who is responsible…for Roger's sake…for his sake…for all their sakes.

Jenny

Jenny stands next to her father as Roger's casket is wheeled down the center aisle.. She sees Robert and gives him a small smile. He looks at her but he's in professional mode and nothing can break his stoic expression. Jenny remembers the guard at Buckingham Palace and smiles to herself. She follows Margot out of the pew and down the center aisle following the casket. She is blinded momentarily, when she reaches the back of the church, by bright sunlight streaming in.

It takes a moment for her eyes to adjust and when she does, she's amazed at the number of people there. She's touched until she overhears some conversations.

"I hear he was murdered. I wonder what he did."

"Still waters run deep."

"I guess I never really knew him."

It goes on and on until Jenny is about to lose it. Not everyone is here because they love Uncle Roger or want to pay their respects. Many are here to gawk or get the lowdown…the latest gossip. She knows Margot has overheard the talk and moves to her side for support. Margot gives her a small smile of gratitude and shakes her head. "I shouldn't be surprised, but I am."

Jenny gives her hand a squeeze and it is then that she feels that something is not right. They are being watched. Somebody is watching them intently. She moves silently to her father's side, gives him a nudge, and leans in close so no one will hear.

"Dad, do you feel that something is wrong?"

Johnny doesn't look at her but is scanning the people around the cathedral.

"I do. We're being watched, but I don't know by whom. Can you tell?

"No, but I'm sure we are."

Johnny motions James. Reluctantly James walks over. "What?"

John nods to include Jenny. "We think someone is watching us."

James can't believe this. "Of course, we're being watched."

James motions with his head. "There's someone about 30 yards to the left, about 20 yards to the right and 40 yards straight ahead."

Jenny and John scan the area but come up empty. John looks back at James. "Are you sure? I don't see anyone there?"

James turns to glare at John. "Of course, I'm sure."

He gives a slight head tilt. "That guy standing right in front of us wearing the grey, double-breasted blazer."

Jenny and John scan the area in front of them. They see nothing. "Uncle James, there is no one in a grey double-breasted blazer in front of us...or anywhere as far as I can see."

Shocked, James looks all over. "They're gone...all three of them are gone."

Jenny and her dad share a look. John shrugs. "If they ever really were."

"Obviously, they were there. I saw them."

Jenny tries to calm them down. "We need to figure out where they went. They couldn't have just vanished."

John rolls his eyes. "And yet, apparently that's just what they did."

Jenny pokes her dad. "You are not helping, father."

Johnny let's go of it. "Okay, what do you suggest?"

"Let's spread out and see if we can come up with anything."

Jenny looks at her dad, who looks at James. They all nod and walk off, thinking they're being nonchalant about it, looking for someone suspicious.

Robert

After making sure Roger is placed gently in the hearse, Robert steps to the side to survey the crowd, trying to gage when they should leave for the cemetery. Today, however, is a little different. He's looking for Jenny. Finally, he spots her talking to her father and uncle. Suddenly, they break apart and walk off in different directions. They are walking with intent and Jenny is scanning the crowd. She is looking for something...or someone. "What the hell...?"

Now Robert begins to look. He isn't sure what he's looking for, but he's looking. Then he notices them. One, two, three men…maybe four. He isn't sure about the fourth one…but maybe four men all standing on the periphery…not quite part of the crowd. The first thing he notices is their suits. His dad taught him well. They are all slightly rumpled. They didn't get dressed for this occasion and yet here they are. He wishes he weren't rooted to this position. He sees Jenny, about ten yards away. She spots them, as well and is moving, discreetly toward them. Who are they? Family friends? … he doesn't think so. He speaks softly to himself. "What are you doing, Jenny?"

Robert is trying to decide what he should do…he feels compelled to protect Jenny, and yet he has a job to do. His predicament is solved when he gets the subtle signal from his father to begin moving people to their cars. Of course, the first person he heads for is Jenny. "Jenny."

She doesn't hear him. He tries a louder stage whisper. "JENNY."

She stops abruptly and looks his way. She gives Robert a small smile. Robert smiles back and makes his way to her side. "Jenny, what's up…what are you doing?"

"We think we're being watched."

"I think you are too."

This stops Jenny in her tracks. She looks at him seriously. "Really?... I thought I might be imagining it."

Robert shakes his head. "No, you are not. You're definitely being watched."

He takes Jenny by her elbow and begins guiding her. "We have to get you safely away."

Jenny looks at the crowd. "How, do we do that?"

Robert zeroes in on the limo behind the hearse. "You're going there."

Jenny gives him a quizzical look. "But I came with my dad."

Robert is undeterred. "I'll take care of that."

Jenny is still not sure. "What about Margot?"

Robert presses forward. "I'm sure, Miss Sallier will appreciate the company."

Jenny is beginning to see the logic in this as she and Robert reach the limo. Robert opens the rear door and Jenny peers in. Margot looks up, startled, but when she sees Jenny, she is deeply relieved.

She motions Jenny inside. "Thank God, you're here. I need you right now."

Jenny looks at Robert and smiles. Robert smiles back, helps her into the limo and closes the door securely. He catches her dad's eye and motions that Jenny is in the limo. John nods and waves to James. Robert begins to discreetly move people toward their cars. He looks around to find the four...or three men...but they have vanished.

Antoine

Antoine is standing on the periphery of the crowd. He has three men strategically deployed observing the crowd. He's trying to locate the man he spotted in the cathedral. It's more of a gut thing, but Antoine is sure he was watching Margot Sallier...and maybe the Chretiens as well. He sees Sallier still on the steps greeting people and the Chretiens...where are they? He finally spots them down among the crowd...heads together...talking about something.

Now where is that guy? He's beginning to think it was all in his imagination when he spots him off to the side. He is watching Sallier. Antoine looks around for his men and sees Duplantier. He's not even facing the right direction and that suit...the only thing missing is the word COP written on the back in Day-Glo orange. He shakes his head and adjusts earpiece and tries to speak inconspicuously into his cuff. "I have eyes on our suspect...at about ten o'clock."

He sees Duplantier check his watch and huffs.

"Duplantier."

He sees Duplantier look up, startled. "Duplantier relax, it's Durel. I'm not speaking about time. I'm talking direction...I'm sure they went over that in the academy?"

He sees Duplantier nod and try to figure 10 o'clock out. Antoine is becoming discouraged. "You have to turn around first...face the cathedral."

Now how to say this without sounding sarcastic. "Excellent, Duplantier...now the cathedral is 12 o'clock. Can you find 10 o'clock. "Yes sir."

Antoine exhales, relieved...Duplantier, however, is not finished. "What do I do now, Sarge."

Antoine can't believe this is happening. "You watch him, Duplantier...just watch him for now."

"10-4."

Antoine looks heavenward. Now, where's Sallier? He spots her still at the top of the steps. Good. Now the Chretiens…where are they? Still in the same place. Wait…they're splitting apart. Where are they going? He speaks into his cuff. "Watch the Chretiens. They're on the move."

Okay, the old mortuary guy is giving a sign to the young mortuary guy…the Louragans. Excellent…let's get this show on the road…wait where is the young guy going? He watches Robert take Jenny by the arm. Where are they going? He looks for Margot…now she's gone.

He spots the Chretien brothers milling about. Okay, they're safe. Now, where are Jenny and the young guy. He's putting her in the limo. Good…that's good. Sallier is in there too…even better. Now where is the suspect? He doesn't see him. He speaks into his cuff. "Anyone have eyes on the suspect?"

He gets two negatives and then Duplantier. "Sarge, I saw him follow Miss Sallier to the limo and then watch while she and the young girl got into the limo."

"Okay, Duplantier, very good information. You should always report movement like that, but that's my fault. I didn't mention that part. Where is he now?"

"He got in a car a ways back. "

Antoine nods. "Excellent, Duplantier…now could you go and take a picture of the car and license plate."

"Yes, Sarge, right away."

Then Antoine remembers the plaster cast. "Duplantier, why don't you write the information down too…in case something happens to the pictures."

He sees Duplantier nod, but just to make sure. "You do have a pencil and paper, right."

"I don't have a pencil, sir…I have a pen. Should I run get a pencil?"

"No, a pen is just fine. I just really need the information. Can you get it for me?"

"Yes sir, I can."

Antoine watches everyone head for their cars. He follows and climbs into his Durango. "Now, off to the cemetery."

He looks off into oblivion and shuts his eyes. "I hope Duplantier gets there. I really do."

Diz and Daz

Diz and Daz are tuning up near the grave site. Besides the sax and clarinet, they have Bobby on the muted coronet, Tommy on the trombone and Delta on the snare. Besides providing the best damn music in the Parish, they are on a mission. Someone is hurting people they care about, and they are going to find out who. Everyone is a suspect.

With a tilt of the head, Daz motions to the street and the line of cars snaking their way into the cemetery. "Okay guys we're on in a few."

The guys make last minute adjustments on their instruments waiting for the downbeat. Daz and Diz watch the cars pulling up, looking for anything suspicious. Diz points his sax toward cars pulling up rear and mouths, "Police."

Daz raises one eyebrow; he wasn't counting on a police presence. This makes their job a little easier. Then, he notices one, lone black SUV pull slowly into the cemetery and stop near the entrance. He frowns and sees Diz has noticed it too. "Who's that?"

Diz shrugs. "We need to keep an eye on him."

Daz gives a small gesture as the hearse pulls up and stops. "Okay guys, showtime."

He gives a slow, somber four count and they begin to play 'Nearer my God to Thee.' Daz watches the pallbearers slowly make their way to the grave and place the casket gently on the catafalque and step away. Bishop Lisbony and two altar servers process to the grave. Daz times the end of the song to the Bishop's arrival at the head of the casket. With a nod, Daz signals the cut off. He watches as Bishop Lisbony begins the graveside service. "Our brother, Roger has gone to his rest in the peace of Christ. May the Lord welcome him to the table of God's children in heaven…"

Diz and Daz scan the mourners at graveside. Diz motions to the cemetery entrance. The SUV is gone. They look for it, but it's nowhere to be found. Daz tries to get the attention of the police, but they are also busy scanning the crowd. Diz spots Sergeant Durel and tries to get his attention but he's looking off to the left. "What can he possibly be looking at?"

Daz nudges him. Bishop Lisbony is wrapping up. "Receive him, we pray, into the mansions of the saints. As we make ready our brother's resting place, look also with favor on those who mourn and comfort them in their loss. Grant this through Christ our Lord."

The mourners all reply, solemnly. "Amen."

As Bishop Lisbony and the servers process out. Daz and Diz look at each other and the others, give a quick four count and begin a stirring version of "When the Saints Go Marching In." The mourners start to mill about. Forming a line to pay their respect to Margot, James, John, and Jenny. Antoine motions for his team to spread out and watch. Daz, Diz, and the guys are jamming to Saints, Daz ponytail bouncing to the beat.

No one notices the glint of the sun coming from a small knoll to the left. A small girl starts to hand a bunch of lilies to Margot but drops them. Margot bends to pick them up. The band is playing: "Oh Lord I Want To Be In That Number." John leans in front of Margot to pick up the lilies as the band continues. "When the Saints Go Marching In."

No one hears the pop as John catches a bullet in the shoulder. It takes a moment for anyone to realize what is happening. When they do; they panic. Antoine shouts. "Get down. Everyone gets down."

People drop and Antoine motions to the knoll. Police run up the small incline and find…nothing. Next to Roger's casket his brother lies, crumpled. His red blood staining the green grass…blossoming on his starched white shirt. Diz and Daz have stopped playing and look helplessly at the scene before them. Duplantier rushes Margot to the limo, while Jenny, Robert at her side, and James kneel beside John trying to staunch the flow of blood. Johnny tries to keep his eyes open.

He's so tired. He tries to speak, but words won't form. He wants to ask…he turns from Jenny to James. Just before he loses consciousness, he wonders… "Why did the music stop. I was really enjoying it."

Dzilam de Bravo
February 5, 1823

Dzilam de Bravo is a small fishing village lying in the northwest corner of the Yucatan Peninsula. It's as quaint and picturesque today as it was then. Fisherman still ply their trade bringing their fresh grouper and yellow fin, with calamari, shrimp, and lobster for the tourists to enjoy in their legendary restaurants.

On that dark night in February, however, with a tropical storm raging, it is anything but picturesque. A battered schooner, the General Santander, runs aground on a white sandy beach. The ship has been almost destroyed by the hated Spaniards, barely surviving long enough to allow Jean Lafitte to make his final appearance in the village he had come to love. Under the guidance of his brother Pierre, Lafitte is lowered to the beach. On the ground his youngest daughter, Lucia, drapes her cloak over his shivering body, as he is taken to the nearest posada.

Lafitte is placed on the floor in front of a raging fire and Lucia tries to get him to take some pozole, but Jean, drifting in and out consciousness, is too weak. There on the floor of a small inn, in an obscure village in the Yucatan, Jean Lafitte, the gentleman pirate, takes his last breath.

The next morning dawns warm and clear. Flamingos, as if in tribute to Jean Lafitte, fill the sky, turning it a bright pink. The entire village turns out to pay respects to the man who had been their benefactor and their friend. He is laid to rest on the church grounds and a small cross, marks the resting place of Jean Lafitte.

Pierre and the crew manage to escape just hours before the Spanish arrive, but Lucia doesn't leave. She remains in the village, close to her beloved father. She lives out her life there, marrying a fisherman and having children. To this day if you visit the little village of Dzilam de Bravo you will see people with blue eyes and red hair. Descendants all of the legendary, blue-eyed pirate, Jean Lafitte.

Part Two
Hurricane Category 3
Devastating Damage

Panama City, Florida
October 1965

*I*t's 4:00 AM and Emil Disparte, a 33-year-old, commercial fisherman, drives his, ten-year-old, Ford F-100 across the crushed shell parking lot and pulls into a spot near the dock. He needs to get there early because ever since Hurricane Betsy hit the gulf in September, fishing has gone to hell. Well, anyway, the fish have gone somewhere, and no one can find them.

This is the longest dry spell Emil has ever known. He hasn't made expenses in over a month. He has a family to support, with a baby coming any day. He needs to do something. He's desperate.

He grabs his backpack and ice chest from the back of the truck and hauls them down the dock to his old, battered fishing boat, The Palermo, a 1931, 38 foot, Mathews Honey Badger. He tosses his gear and ice chest into the back of the boat, unties the stem and the stern lines, and pushes it off from the dock. Emil jumps in and makes his way to the cockpit and starts the engine. It purrs like a kitten.

Emil is proud of his boat. It is well worn but survived Betsy with not so much as leaky seam. He steers his boat out of the harbor and heads south southwest. The talk is, that's where the fish are…about fifteen miles out.

Emil pours a cup of coffee from his thermos and leans back in the captain's chair. It'll take about an hour to get there, but it'll be worth it, if he finds fish. He can't go home empty handed again. He reaches down inside his backpack and pulls out a new paperback. He loves mysteries and this looks promising. It's an Agatha Christie with Miss Marple. Emil prefers Hercule Poirot, but the cover looks good and besides…he has nothing else. Emil looks up and adjusts his heading a couple of degrees and settles back into his book.

About an hour later, Emil looks up, makes an arrow to mark his place, drops his book into his backpack, and cuts the engine. As he sits, drifting with the current, Emil considers what's before him. A vast expanse of open water. "This looks promising."

He shrugs. Actually, it looks exactly the same as any other place he's fished in the last month, but he has faith. He prayed to the Virgin last night and explained the situation. She should understand…she's a mother. He's just trying to provide for his family.

54

He pulls his nets out and throws them over the side. One on the port the other on the starboard. Before he has a chance to pour another cup of coffee, the nets begin to stream away from the boat, filling rapidly. Using the winch, he hauls up both nets. He's hit a school of redfish. As fast as he dumps the fish into the hold and casts the nets back in the water, that's how fast the nets fill up. Time after time until the hold is full. The Virgin has been generous.

It's not yet noon and he's heading back to the harbor with a hold full of fish. As he reaches for his backpack, Emil notices a shiny reflection from the deck. He walks closer to see and bends over to pick up a small, crud covered object of some kind. He's about to look at it more closely, but a wave hits broadside throwing the boat off course.

He drops the small object into his pocket and scrambles up to the cockpit and puts the boat back on course. He can't afford any delay. He must get these fish to market. The object forgotten; he settles into his seat with Miss Marple for the voyage home.

When he arrives at the dock, Emil finds he's the first fisherman back today and after unloading his catch, he's made more money on this day then during the past month. After hosing down the deck and hold, he heads for home...tired, but grateful.

At home, the first thing he notices is the commotion...people running in and out of the house, the second, the doctor's car. He scrambles out of the car and runs head on into doctor at the door. Before he can utter a sound, the doctor puts a reassuring hand on his shoulder. "You have a son, Emil, a strong, healthy son."

Emil rushes to the bedroom only to find his wife and son sleeping soundly. He shakes his head. "These two are probably the only ones more tired than I am."

He sinks into the chair beside the bed and closes his eyes. Just as he is about to drift off to sleep, his eyes spring open and he sits up straight. He reaches into his pocket and takes out the small, crud encrusted object. He begins to rub the gunk away. Gleaming gold appears. The more he rubs, the shinier it gets. Until he's left with a shiny gold coin. He holds the coin up to the light and he sees French words surrounding a Coat of arms and a date...1806.

Emil smiles. He can feel his luck changing as he bends down and picks up his sleeping son. Sitting in the chair, he gazes proudly at his son. Emil and his wife have already picked out a name. He looks at his sleeping son, the gold coin and his smile widens. "This is for you, Nicolo...little Nicky."

Chapter VII

"You've gone round the bend."

Jenny

Jenny is at ground zero. All the confusion is happening around her, but Jenny is paralyzed. Paralyzed by fear...or dread, she isn't sure. She looks at her dress...it's covered with blood, and she tries to wipe it off, but her hands...they're covered with blood also. She mutely looks at the mayhem surrounding her and picks up snippets of conversations.

"Lost a lot of blood."

"Where was the shooter?"

"Where did the shot come from?"

"Get Margot in the car."

"Looks like a through and through."

And finally, "Jennifer...Jenny?

It takes her a moment to realize someone is talking to her. She looks around vaguely and finally focuses on Uncle James, who's standing in front of her. She looks up at him with pleading eyes. "Is Dad...is he dead?"

James bends close and talks softly. "No chère...they've taken him to the hospital. We should go."

Jenny is momentarily relieved. Then she looks around frantically. "Margot...is she here? Where is she?

James puts a reassuring hand on the shoulder. "She's safe. She's already left."

He looks past Jenny to someone standing behind her. "Can you get her to the car, please?"

It is only then that Jenny notices strong arms holding on to her. Strong arms keeping her safe...protecting her from danger. She tries to look behind her, but still can't see, until the arms slowly turn her and her eyes lock with Robert's. Robert is there...taking care of her. He bends close to her ear. "Are you alright?"

Jennifer nods. "I think so."

Robert hugs her briefly and Jenny leans into it, lost in his arms. Suddenly, she pulls back and looks around, frantically. "My dad...I have to go to my dad."

Robert nods and tries to lead her away, but his way is blocked by Sergeant Durel. "Miss Chretien."

Jenny doesn't respond just tries to pull Robert to the car. Antoine tries again. "Miss Chretien...Miss Chretien, may I speak to you, please."

She shakes her head and tries to explain. "I have to go to my dad." She looks up at Antoine, imploringly. "I have to get to my dad."

Robert looks determinedly at Antoine. "Officer, can't you do this later?"

After a brief pause, Antoine nods, "Of course...we can speak later."

He looks directly at Jenny. "I'll be praying for your father."

Robert steers her away to the car. Jennifer looks back at the turmoil behind her before Robert puts her in the car. She is safe.

Daz and Diz

Diz and Daz sit amid musical instruments staring at ...nothing. He looks back to Daz. "Is he dead?...Johnny I mean."

Diz shakes his head. "I don't know. I don't think so. He was alive when they took him."

Daz asks the simple question. "How did this happen?"

"I don't know, brother."

Daz is beginning to get mad. "It was on our watch, Diz, and we didn't even see this coming." He looks over to Roger's casket. "What's going to happen to Roger? He deserves to lie in peace."

Diz stares at Roger's casket. "I don't know, man, but knowing Roger, I don't think he'll rest until this is done."

Daz and Diz share a long look. Daz is resolute. "Okay, then. Let's get busy."

Diz cocks an eyebrow. "Whatcha thinking?"

Daz sits back down and motions Diz to do the same. "Well let's ask ourselves some questions."

"Be my guest."

Daz surveys the area. "Okay, first, can we agree this is not a random shooting? That it has something to do with Roger's murder?"

"I think, for our purposes, it's safe to assume that it does."

Daz stares at Diz for a moment. "Okay, then, why shoot someone?"

"To keep them quiet…to keep them from telling what they know."

Daz smiles. "Right, but then, why shoot John. He just got here…he doesn't know anything."

Diz considers this. "So, maybe Johnny wasn't the target."

They both look at each other. "Margot."

They are proud of themselves, until Daz makes a face and stares off. "But what does she know?"

Jimmy

James sits staring at the floor in the waiting room in the surgical wing at Saint Patrick's Hospital. Johnny's been in surgery for an eternity and James just wants answers. He looks around and sees that Margot and Jenny are gone. Where are they? Did the doctor come in and he somehow missed it? They would have told him, wouldn't they?

He keeps reliving that one moment in time. The crack of the bullet, the acrid smell of gunpowder and the blood…all that blood…and Johnny lying there in all that blood. First Roger and now Johnny. He didn't protect them. He is the big brother, and he didn't protect them. He looks heavenward.

"God, look…Roger is dead. There's nothing I can do about that. What's done is done, but Johnny. You can't take him too. That's just…not fair. I still need him. I mean I never told him that, but I need him. Please, don't let him die. Not now…not for a long time." James looks around before adding: "Amen."

He makes a hurried Sign of the Cross and looks up in time to see the door at the far end of the waiting room open. He expects the doctor, but is relieved to see Margot and Jenny walk in. They didn't leave him, after all. They sit on either side of him, and both take his hand in theirs. Margot leans in close. "Have you heard anything?"

James shakes his head. Jenny smiles bravely. "I guess we would have heard by now, if things went badly."

Margot shakes her head. "That's what they say on medical shows just before someone walks in and says they're sorry, but they did all they could do."

They all freeze as the door opens and the doctor walks in. Without a word they stand and face him. For better or for worse, they will hear the news together.

"He's out of surgery. It went very well. It will be painful, but he should recover completely."

They didn't realize they were all holding their breath until all three exhale at the same time. Jenny hugs the doctor. "Can we see him?"

The doctor unwraps Jenny. "He's in recovery. You should be able to see him in about an hour."

James nods. "Thank you, doctor."

The doctor smiles and walks away as all three collapse into their chairs, look at each other and remember to breathe. Margot is the first to find her voice. "I'm so relieved. I don't think I could have taken another death."

Jenny shakes her head. "It all seems so random…I mean, why Dad."

James shrugs his shoulders. "We may never know."

Margot looks off. "I know."

They both look at her intently. Jenny needs answers. "Know what."

Margot focuses back on them. "They weren't shooting at John…they were shooting at me."

It takes a moment for that to sink in. James places his hand on her hand. "I think you're right, Margot, that's the only thing that makes sense."

Jenny turns to Margot. "This isn't good for you, Margot, but they must think you know whatever Uncle Roger knew."

Margot smiles grimly. "I wish I did, but I don't."

James stands resolutely. "That's the first order of business. Find out what Roger knew."

He thinks about that for a moment. "Well, the second really. The first is to make sure that Margot doesn't get killed."

With a determined expression he glares at the far door and strides off…a man on a mission. "And to hell with the doctors. I'm going to see my brother."

He pushes open the door and is gone.

Margot

Margot watches James stalk out followed by Jenny a few moments later. She doesn't know if she should tag along or not. After all John would not have been shot if not for her. She sits staring at her hands. That someone is trying to kill her is just sinking in. Every move she makes may be the wrong move. Every move that she makes may be her last. Every instinct in her body wants to run away and hide, but where would she go? There's no place where she'll be safe.

She needs to think this through. Maybe she should focus on what Roger knew. Perhaps she knows more than she thinks. Roger got really excited when he saw the brooch. He began talking about the family plantation and Jean Lafitte. Maybe he saw a connection between his family and hers. The more she thinks about it, the more likely it seems.

She needs to talk to James and John. Maybe they know more than they think they do. Before she can get up, however, Sergeant Durel appears beside her and slips into the seat next to hers. "Sorry to bother you, Miss Sallier, but may I speak to you for a moment?"

Margot doesn't have much of a choice. "Certainly, Sergeant, how may I help you?"

Margot doesn't know why she's being so polite. The police haven't been much help so far. Antoine squirms in his seat, just a bit. "Thank you. First, I think I should apologize." Margot raises an eyebrow. Antoine rushes ahead. "We were caught flat footed out there today and didn't do our job."

"Thank you, but you really should apologize to Mr. Chretien. He's the one who got shot."

Antoine takes a deep breath "I will, but there's something more I need to tell you."

Margot leans forward in her seat. "What is it, Sergeant?"

Antoine leans in close to Margot. "We received a letter from Roger Chretien dated the day he was killed."

A myriad of thoughts rush through Margot's mind. "What did he say?"

"He said that if something were to happen to him, you'd be in danger."

Margot can't do anything but point out the obvious. "Well, I guess he was right."

"Yes, he was…I want to let you know you'll have round the clock protection." Antoine points to Officer Duplantier standing against the wall. Duplantier grins and wave to Margot. Margot can't help waving back. Antoine glares at the young officer. "That's Officer Duplantier. He's got the day shift from eight in the morning to eight at night. We'll have a squad car parked outside Lagniappe House all night."

Margot nods as Antoine stands up. "I'll be in touch, Ms. Sallier."

Margot watches Sergeant Antoine walk to Officer Duplantier and have a brief conversation. From what Margot can see, it's more of a Come to Jesus Moment. She gets up to go to Johnny's room. She has a lot to tell.

Robert

Robert sits at the wheel of the Platinum Cadillac Mastercoach. It isn't often that a hearse is parked at the cemetery for such a long time, but it is his job to oversee the actual burial of Roger Chretien and Robert wants to make sure that Roger is, at last, laid to rest. Roger had to wait for the police to leave and the crime scene tape taken down. He had to wait among the overturned chairs and blood spattered ground. Roger had to wait on the living before he could be at peace.

Robert's mind keeps drifting to Jenny and what she must be feeling…doing. Before Roger was lowered into the ground, Robert had made sure to whisper to Roger that his brother was going to be all right, but he didn't know if that were true or not. Would John and James Chretien be, okay? Would Miss Sallier…would Jenny? Robert rests his head on the steering wheel. He should have protected Roger Chretien…he should have protected Jenny.

He looks up and starts the Mastercoach. He gives the gravesite one last look before pulling away from the curb. All the way back to the funeral home, Robert thinks about the shoulda', coulda' and woulda's. The logical part of his brain tells him he could not have prevented any of this, but there is a deeper part that tells him that he should have done it for Jenny.

These thoughts are spinning through his mind as he drives back to the funeral home…past the university…past the cathedral and pulls into the driveway and parks in the back where he will wash and wax the hearse in a sort of ritualistic cleansing.

As he sits there in the hearse, he realizes that he needs to speak to someone far wiser than he is. He turns off the engine, takes the keys and gets out of the hearse. He enters the funeral home and goes in search of his father. He finds Phillip Louragan in his small office next to the crematory and stands at the door while Phillip moves a stack of folders from the one other chair in the room and motions for Robert to sit.

He gives a sympathetic smile as Robert takes the seat. "Not a good day, Robert...not a good day at all. You must be exhausted."

"I am, but Pop, I should have handled it better."

Phillip looks understandingly at his son. "Robby, did you do you do your job? Did you give Roger Chretien a proper burial?"

Robert shrugs, but Phillip is having none of that. "You did son...in spite of everything that went on...in spite of a madman, you did your job."

Phillip gazes intently at his son and cocks his head. "But you know this already."

Robert meets his gaze and Phillip leans forward. "So, tell me, my son, what is really bothering you?"

Robert can't hold his father's eyes, who begins to smile. "Ah, it's the girl...does she know?"

"I don't know...sort of."

His father shakes his head. "Son, in my experience, there is no 'sort of' when it comes to women. You understand?"

Robert exhales deeply. "We just met...It's complicated, Pop."

Phillip lays his hand on his son's shoulder. "No, son, it's really not. Sometimes we make it more complicated than it needs to be." Robert isn't getting it. Phillip leans close. "Everyone in that family is concerned for everybody else and that's the way it should be, but you, Robert, can be concerned just for her. Be there just for her." Phillip leans back and smiles. "And that, my son, is how you win the heart of the fair damsel."

Robert is beginning to understand and grins. "Is that how you won Mom?"

"Well now, that is between me and my damsel."

Robert joins his father in a moment of remembering. Remembering the woman who loved and cared for them. Whose smile could brighten a room, but whose glare could ruin your week. A moment shared; Phillip considers Robert. "Where is your damsel right now?"

"At the hospital, I think…with her father."

"Then go to the hospital and be there for her…don't intrude but be there."

Robert nods and as he turns to go Phillip throws Robert his keys. "Take the Benz. She'll appreciate it after the day she's had."

Robert runs from the room and Phillip leans back in chair and grins.

Johnny

Johnny is still unconscious with his right shoulder bandaged and an IV dripping antibiotics and pain medication into his left arm. Lots of things are going on in Johnny's brain...images...memories...scenes. He and Jimmy are at the train station saying goodbye to Mom, Pop, and Rog as they wave from the Sunset Limited heading for LSU…Roger isn't home. He should have been home hours ago. Why can't he be more considerate and come home. They're all waiting for him…A picnic in a park, it's beautiful, but something is wrong. There're ants swarming all over, getting in the food. Mom is not going to like this, not one bit…They are on his arm, under his shirt biting him on the shoulder. He can't brush them off. "Can't anybody see? Can't anybody help brush the ants off."

He becomes aware of a voice calling softly. "Johnny…? It's time to wake up."

And now, more insistent. "Daddy…Daddy open your eyes right now."

Johnny's eyes pop open and he tries to focus on his surroundings, but it's too much and he closes them again. Jenny's voice is louder still. "Open your eyes."

Johnny opens one eye and focuses on Jenny, about three inches from his face. "What can you possibly want right now?"

Johnny opens his other eye and begins to focus on the people in the room…first Jenny, then James and finally on Margot. He tries to adjust himself in the bed and a searing pain shoots from his right shoulder down to his left foot. A strangled cry escapes from his lips as he tries to find a position that won't make him pass out. "Won't do that again." He looks around the room. "How did I get here?"

Jenny puts her hand on his. "You were shot, Daddy…at the cemetery."

Johnny tries to wrap his mind around this new information "The cemetery? Why would anybody want to shoot me?"

James comes in to focus. We don't think you were the target, Johnny."

Johnny is more confused as Margot takes James's place. "They were shooting at me, John. That's what we think anyway."

Johnny closes his eyes and tries to make sense out of all this. He gets a sudden thought and looks at his three visitors. "What about Roger? Is everything okay with Roger."

A horrified look passes between them. In all the madness at the cemetery, they forgot about Roger. James leans in and puts a reassuring hand on Johnny's good shoulder. "You need to focus on getting better. You leave everything else to us."

Johnny relaxes. "Okay…Now when can I go home?"

Jenny looks at her uncle. Who bends close to Johnny. "The doctor said maybe tomorrow."

Jenny adds sternly. "If you're very good."

Johnny nods and closes his eyes. After a few seconds he open them and glares at Jenny. "What does my being good have to do with it?"

James steps in. "Well, you know doctors…anyway get some sleep and we'll come spring you tomorrow."

Satisfied Johnny shuts his eyes and begins to drift off, until his eyes suddenly open. "Why did Margot shoot me?"

Horrified, Margot tries to speak, but Jenny puts a reassuring hand on her arm. "Go to sleep father. You've gone round the bend."

Johnny stares at Margot for a second before nodding and drifting off to sleep. The three gather their things and head for the door. James halts mid stride. He looks at Jenny and Margot. "We've got to make sure Roger's okay."

Jenny puts a reassuring hand on James' arm. "We will, Uncle James. We'll do it right away."

James nods and Jenny looks back at her father sleeping and turns out the light.

Antoine

Antoine sits in the corner of the waiting room. He's been a cop for a long time and the two things cops learn quickly are to be patient and be observant. As he scans the room, he sees…the kid from the funeral home, waiting nervously. "What is he doing here?"

He's about to walk across the room and find out when a door opens, and James and Jenny Chretien come out followed by Margot Sallier. As he watches, Jenny runs across the room and embraces him. Antoine scratches his chin. "Well, I guess I missed that one."

Antoine watches as Chretien and Sallier follow the girl to the boy. At first, they look concerned, but then, are relieved by his response. "Now, what is this about?"

All four head for the exit, but Antoine cuts them off. "I'm sorry to disturb you, but I must speak to you for a minute."

James and Margot share a look. James takes the lead. "Of course, sergeant, but only for a minute. As you can imagine we are very tired."

Antoine nods sympathetically. "I understand, but I do need to talk to you." He looks to include all of them. "If we could talk sometime tomorrow, it would be perfect…at your convenience, of course."

James produces a small smile. "We are picking up my brother sometime in the morning, but we should be free in the afternoon."

Antoine makes a note. "That will be fine. Sometime after lunch…I'll come to you."

James and Margot nod in agreement and the four of them head for the door. Antoine walks up to Duplantier. "Go with Miss Sallier and don't let anything happen to her."

Duplantier nods and salutes. Antoine glares for a second, then returns the salute. He watches Duplantier follow Margot out the door and shakes his head. "Sometimes, he's just like a puppy."

Panama City, Florida
November 20, 1985

At 3:30 in the morning, a 20-year-old Nick Disparte stands on the front porch gazing southward. The skies are gray and there's a fall chill in the air. Hurricane Kate is on the horizon. He sees the clouds gathering. He knows Papà wants to get one more day of fishing in before Thanksgiving. If they make it a quick trip, they should be back in plenty of time. Nick checks his watch...time to wake up the old man. He walks back in the house, makes a side trip to the kitchen to pour two cups of coffee...Italian roast just like Papà likes. He quietly enters his parents' bedroom and, careful not to wake Mama, he nudges his father awake.

Emil looks like an older version of Nick...same olive skin and dark hair. Emil is a little shorter and stockier. His hands are rougher with more callouses. This is his life...the life of a fisherman, but it's not what he wants for Nick. They must have a talk and it should be soon.

Nick finishes putting their gear in the back of the Ford truck. It's almost 30 years old and it may be time for a new one. Nick looks at the dents and rust...past time. It's time to talk to Papà. Nick goes back into the house and joins Emil in the kitchen. He picks up his cup and leans against the counter. "It's a little chilly out there today."

Emil cocks an eyebrow at Nick. "You going soft on me, bambino?"

"No, Papà...just worried about you."

Emil straightens up. "You don't worry about me Nicolò. I worry about you. Capiche?"

It's a stare down. Nick loses. "Yes, Papà, I understand."

They both finish their coffee and head for the truck. Emil checks the gear. He knows Nick did it right, but it's hard to break 40 years of habit. He slides into the driver's seat and tries to start the truck, but it sputters and dies. He tries again, and nothing. He feels Nicks' eyes. "It's just cold."

Nick blows on his hands. "Well, so am I, but I start right away. Maybe it's time..."

Emil cuts him off. "Not yet. It's younger that I am." He glances at Nick and tries one more time. The engine catches. He smiles to himself. "Maybe next year."

66

Nick smiles and they drive on in silence all the way to the dock and park, a light mist sprinkling the windshield. When Nick gets out, he finds Emil looking toward the south. It's beginning to look ominous. "I think we can beat it."

Nick joins his dad. "I think so too, but it should be a quick trip."

Nick and Emil grab the gear from the back of the truck and head for the Palermo. It's just minutes before they are heading out...Nick at the wheel. Emil stands behind him, Stephen King's Skeleton Crew in his hand, studying the sky before them. "I have a feeling, Nicolo...head south southwest. About fifteen miles out."

Nick nods and turns the wheel. He never questions his father's feeling. They are always dead on. Emil nods and heads below out of the cold to read his book.

The water's getting choppy, the light mist is turning into a steady drizzle. The Palermo is being buffeted by the constant breeze. Emil, an arrow marking the spot, puts King away and joins Nick on the bridge. "We're far enough out. Let's try our luck here."

The weather seems to be getting worse by the minute.

"I don't know Papà, maybe we should go in."

Emil looks off into the distance...the rain pelting his face. "Get the nets out. We'll leave in a half hour."

Nick nods and goes below to get the nets. When he comes up the wind is beginning to howl, and Nick is having trouble untangling the nets. Emil watches his son. "Here, let me help you."

As Emil struggles to Nick's side, the winch breaks loose, swings in the wind and catches Emil in the head. Nick watches, helplessly, as his dad loses his balance and topples overboard...a red pool of blood beginning to form on the angry sea. Horrified, his brain slips into gear and Nick rushes to the wheel, maneuvering the boat closer to his father. Nick grabs a pole and manages to catch Emil by the collar. He hauls his father's lifeless body aboard.

Time stops as Nick sits, cradling his father's head in his lap as blood pours out of the wound. He checks for a pulse...tears streaming down his face. What is he going to tell his mother? How will he explain this? He sees a yellowish glint on the deck. As he bends to pick it up, he sees it's that French coin. His father's cherished lucky charm. Nick smiles grimly. "Not so lucky now."

He looks up to see the storm baring down on him. He must go now. His one thought is to bring his father home to his mother. "Ti amo, papà."

Chapter VIII
"...the cheese stands alone."

Daz and Diz

It's 6:30 in the morning at Lagniappe House. The sun made an appearance about 20 minutes ago and Diz comes out onto the balcony with two cups of coffee and pokes Daz a couple times. "It's time to wake up, Cinderella."

Eyes closed, Daz frowns before he squints up at Diz. "It's Snow White, not Cinderella. I can't believe I have to explain damn fairy tales to you."

Diz rolls his eyes. "You want coffee or not?"

Daz tries to think of a comeback but takes a breath instead. "Yes, thank you. I would love a cup."

Diz hands a cup to Daz and sits on the swing next to him. Diz takes a sip and swings slowly. Daz points to a police car in the parking lot below them. "It was quiet last night. I didn't see them get out of their car once."

Diz chuckles softly. "How would you know? You can't see through your eyelids."

Daz is about to respond but takes a sip of coffee instead. He looks at Diz and frowns. "This can't be what we need to be doing. We can do so much more."

Diz and Daz swing some more. Finally, Diz, with a knowing smile, indicates the police on the street. "Do you think they might appreciate some coffee?"

Daz looks at Diz like he's lost his mind. "Should we bring them some beignets, too."

Diz nods excitedly. "You're right. That's a great idea."

Daz stops the swing. "When I said we can do more. I wasn't talking about opening a branch of Café Du Monde."

"Don't you get it. We need information. They have information..."

The light dawns, Daz begins to swing again. "So, we ply them with coffee…and beignets. That was a great idea I had."

Diz rolls his eyes. "You are a genius."

Daz nods in agreement. "Damn straight."

Johnny

The Chretien home is quiet. In some ways all the people who have inhabited this house have left their imprint. Not quite haunting it, but creating an atmosphere of love and security, of fear and pain, of all the joy and tribulation that make up a family. It waits for life. It's about to get more than it bargained for. The front door is closed and locked but even on the front porch, it begins.

"Dad, let me help you up the steps."

"Mr. Chretien, let me get the door."

"John, will you wait just a minute."

The front door opens to reveal an irritated John, arm in a sling, trying to maneuver through the door, wincing with every step. "Will y'all please let me do this? I know my body."

The others watch helplessly as he stumbles over the threshold. James reaches out to steady John sending pain radiating though his body. John stops, eyes clenched tight, waiting for the waves of pain to stop. He opens one eye and glares at everyone in the room. "I realize you're only trying to help, but please, let me do this."

James, Jenny, and Robert back off. They watch as John stands immobile, not sure what direction to go in. James shakes his head. "So, what now?"

Jenny tries to be helpful. "Maybe you should go upstairs. The doctor said you need to rest."

Trying to be supportive, Robert blurts out. "I can help."

Johnny raises his hand to stop the chatter. "I am not going upstairs. I'll be there and all the action will be here."

He looks around the room and focuses on the couch. He shuffles over to it. "Jenny, could you bring me coffee?"

He tries to sit but loses his balance and falls into the seat sending a jolt of pain through his shoulder. He looks at Jenny through squinty eyes. "And a pain pill."

Jenny rushes from the room. Robert feels the awkward moment between the brothers and scurries after Jenny. James sits in a chair across from Johnny and folds his arms. "Better now?"

Johnny glares at his brother. "No thanks to you."

They sit in silence until Jenny and Robert return with the coffee and medication. John pops a pain pill into his mouth followed by a healthy slug of coffee, scalding the inside of his mouth. It's all he can do not to spit it all out. Jimmy looks smugly at John. "Perhaps you should wait until the coffee cools off a bit."

John glares at Jimmy. "Thanks for the tip."

Jimmy glares back and Jenny has had enough. "Will the two of you stops it. You're acting like children."

The brothers look petulantly at each other. Johnny turns to his daughter. "Well, he started it."

Jenny throws up her hands. "You two can be so...juvenile. We need to focus. Sergeant Durel will be here soon, and we should figure out what we know and what we need to know."

The brothers nod reluctantly. James turns to Jenny. "Is Margot coming?"

Jenny gets down to business. "She'll be here in a bit...she's coming for lunch."

James rubs his hands together. "Well, that's our next order of business...lunch."

Jenny smiles at her uncle. At last, they have something to focus on. She looks from her father to her uncle. "Any suggestions?"

Johnny smiles for the first time since they got home. "I could go for some tamales. You remember, Jimmy? Pop always got them from..."

Jimmy completes the thought. "Old man Mancuso. Boy I could go for a mess of those."

Johnny nods his head enthusiastically. "I wonder if he's still around?"

Jenny rolls her eyes. "I think I need more than old man Mancuso."

Robert looks up, showing his phone. "Found it on Yelp...four stars. They're open now...a thirteen-minute drive."

Jenny throws up her hands in resignation and smiles at Robert. "Well, we'll be off to tamale land...how many should we get?"

Johnny grins at Jimmy. "A few dozen at least."

Jimmy rubs his hands together. "Yeah, get four or five dozen."

Jenny is dumbfounded. "Four or five dozen?"

Jimmy laughs "We want plenty of leftovers. Remember when we snuck down in the middle of the night and found Pop eating right out of the fridge?"

Johnny closes his eyes at this memory. "They are great cold."

Jenny looks at Robert, laughing. "Six dozen it is."

Jenny and Robert walk out the front door leaving Jimmy and Johnny, eyes closed, sitting back in genuine anticipation. This day has gotten a whole lot better.

Jenny

Jenny's driving the Focus while Robert's riding shotgun, navigating. He has the difficult job of letting Jenny think while keeping her headed in the right direction. He looks from his phone to Jenny. "In two miles you're going to want to turn left."

Jenny nods absently. She's trying to figure out how to keep her father and uncle on task. They can go from Uncle Roger's murder to who's the best cook, to who's the best brother, to who can remember the most obscure facts from their youth. Jenny must admit that sometimes it's very entertaining, but seldom gets them anywhere. Jenny begins to chuckle. Robert stares at her then he begins to laugh as well. "Can you please explain why we're laughing?"

Jenny tries to compose herself. "Well, at first I was just thinking about how goofy my dad could be, Then I remembered how when I was little, he used to sneak up behind me and tickle me and sing the Dayo song." Robert is perplexed until Jenny pokes him. "You know the Dayo song.' She begins to sing. "Day-o…Day-ay-ay-o, Daylight come and me want to go home." She looks at Robert and goes on. "Day, me say day, me say Day-ay-ay-o. Daylight come and we want to go home." Now she gets into the swing. "Come Mr. Tallyman, tally me banana. Daylight come and me wan' go home. Come Mr. Tallyman, tally me banana daylight come and me wan' go home."

She points to Robert, who after a beat joins in. "Day-o day-ay-ay-o, daylight come and me wan' go home."

By now they are falling over themselves, laughing. Robert, not to be out done holds up his hand. "My dad used to take me by the hand, and we'd run around the yard shouting out as loud as we could: Dance my mason, dance my chamber, house lemur, a treasure attend."

Jenny laughs, puzzled. "House lemur?"

Robert shrugs and nods…Jenny nods back and together they shout out:

"Dance my mason, dance my chamber, house lemur, a treasure attend."

Robert's voice cuts her off. "The street is coming up. You're going to want to get in the left turn lane."

Jenny makes the left turn. Her mind, however, makes a sharp turn to the right, because now there's Margot. She's not always on the same wavelength as her father and uncle but can have valuable insights that the guys frequently ignore. Robert nudges her.

"Turn right up ahead and then it should be on your left."

Jenny nods absently as her mind wanders. Adults can be difficult. She makes a right turn and left into an upscale Mexican restaurant. Robert looks up at a large sign in red, white, and green…Mancuso's. "I guess old man Mancuso is doing very well for himself."

Jenny shrugs. "My guess is that 'old man Mancuso' has turned the business over to the next generation. I hope the tamale recipe has been passed down or the guys will be very disappointed."

Margot

Margot is back at the dining room table surrounded by these quirky, smart, lovable, and sometimes frustrating people who have invaded her life. The table is covered in pages of the Times Picayune with tamales waiting to be eaten and corn husks from tamales past strewn across it. Margot finishes her last bite and wipes her hands. "I can't eat another bite. Where has this been my whole life?"

Johnny has been struggling to eat with his one good arm but has still managed to polish off a dozen. "This was Pop's go to place for a late-night snack."

As he reaches for number 13, he peers at his daughter. "I thought we said six dozen."

"We bought them out. If you want more, you should order ahead."

Johnny sees the sense in this and nods. James mumbles through the half tamale still in his mouth. "Did you see Old Man Mancuso?"

Jenny looks at Robert who avoids her eyes. Jenny returns to Uncle James. "I believe 'old man Mancuso' is no longer with us…we spoke at length with 'young man Mancuso'."

James shrugs. "In thirty or forty years he'll be 'old man Mancuso'."

As they push back from the table and move to the living room, Jenny grabs Robert's arm. "Whenever they get off track, we have to bring them back to the topic."

Robert looks at her dumbfounded. "And just how am I supposed to do that?"

Jenny kisses him on the cheek. "Just go with it. You'll know what to do."

Jenny bounces into the living room. Robert watches her, a smile spreading across his face. He touches the spot where she kissed him and follows her into the living room, taking a seat against the wall. Jenny looks at him, making a face. They are already off track. Johnny lounges back in his place on the couch. "I'm sorry James, but it wasn't Pop who made the Oysters Bienville it was Mom."

James shakes his head vigorously. "No, I remember, I was with pop when he made it. In fact, I chopped the spinach."

Johnny can't believe this. "That's Rockefeller, not Bienville."

James stops to consider this, while Jenny gives Robert a look. He squirms in his seat and blurts out. "I'm so sad your brother died."

Everyone turns and looks at Robert, who tries to make himself invisible. Then Margot clears her throat. "That reminds me, Roger said something, about a week before he died."

All eyes go from Robert, who sighs in relief, to Margot. James leans forward in his chair. "Go on. What did he say?"

Margot closes her eyes, trying to bring the conversation back. "We were talking about how funny it was that both our families are so closely linked to Jean Lafitte."

John and James look at each other, considering. James looks at Margot. "Right, we grew up on stories of Jean Lafitte and your family connection is legendary."

John is confused, "But we talked about that."

Margot nods but takes the cedar box out of her purse and lays it on the coffee table. "I know, but when I showed him this box with the brooch in it, it triggered something…he said it reminded him of something he read…or heard somewhere."

Still confused, John looks to James, who frowns at Margot. "Again, the story of the brooch is legendary."

Margot shakes her head. "It wasn't the brooch. It was the box."

James rubs his face. "That was all he said?"

They are at a loss, until Jenny pipes up. "Uncle Roger was an historian. He must have been doing research."

They pause to consider this. Then he doorbell rings.

Antoine

Antoine stands outside the front door. He hasn't quite decided if he should tell them everything he knows or not. He listens and hears scuffling on the other side of the door. He's about to ring the doorbell again when the door slowly opens revealing five people ringed in a semi-circle standing in the entry hall staring intently at him.

Antoine is a little unnerved, but walks in. "I hope I'm not early."

The group shares a look and John speaks a beat too soon and too enthusiastically. "Right on time, Sergeant, we just finished lunch."

He gestures to the living room and Antoine walk into it but realizes no one has followed him. He looks back, frowning, only to see the group huddled by the front door. He can almost hear what they are saying.

"Should we...everything...know?" "We don't... anything." "Let's wait...he...us what...knows."

Antoine watches as they nod and look up at him smiling. James takes the lead. "Sit down, Sergeant, anywhere."

Antoine looks around and sits on the couch. John's seat as it turns out, who looks around trying to find a suitable spot. "Well now, we'll find our seats and...sit down."

Everyone sits leaving John standing. James looks at John and chuckles. "It seems the cheese stands alone."

Johnny glares at his brother, but sits, gently, on the couch besides Antoine and looks at him expectantly. Antoine clears his throat. "Now, it seems to be the time when we share information. I'll tell you what I know, and you tell me what you know."

The group looks at each other considering. They nod to James, who turns to face Antoine. "To be honest, Sergeant, we don't really know anything." He looks to the others. "We have some ideas, but there is so much we don't know."

"Such as?"

Johnny jumps in. "We don't know how Roger died. We don't know where Roger died. We know Roger was found in this house, but we don't know who found him or how he got here."

Antoine glances at Margot with a big question on his face. Margot, looking sheepish, raises her hand. "I'm afraid I didn't mention that I found him." All eyes turn to her. It takes a moment for them to digest this bit of information. Margot shifts awkwardly. "I thought you had been told."

All eyes shift back to Antoine. "Okay, I didn't tell you everything, but to be honest we don't know much either." They just stare at him. He takes a deep breath. "All right, your brother drowned...in Contraband Bayou out by Prien Lake."

James starts to speak but Antoine holds up his hand explaining. "The water we found in his lungs match the water out near Prien Lake." Antoine looks at Margot and continues. "But he was found in this house. He had obviously been moved but at the moment we don't know by whom or why."

Johnny has a thought. "Where was he found?"

Antoine looks at Margot. "I found him in the upstairs study."

John looks from James to Jenny. "You mean where I'm sleeping...or trying to sleep now?"

James returns the look. "Yes, he was found in your room...get over it."

Antoine decides it's time to move on. "So, what do you know?"

After a shared look, James looks directly at Antoine. "Well Sergeant, you probably won't believe this..."

Johnny cuts in. "I'm not sure we believe it..."

They look to Margot, who shrugs and after a deep breath. "We think it has something to do with Jean Lafitte."

Sergeant Antoine looks at them considering. Finally, he reaches into his breast pocket, pulls out the gold coin and lays it on the coffee table. "So do I."

Jimmy

Jimmy leans against the front door after seeing Antoine out and rubs his face with both hands. That took an abrupt twist he didn't expect. He turns to the living room and just stands there. "Now what?"

Everyone stares back. Finally, Margot shrugs. "I guess it a good thing. The detective in charge is on the same wavelength as we are."

Johnny shakes his head. "Yeah, it means he's as crazy as we are."

Jimmy thinks about this for a minute. "Not necessarily." He looks around the room "Not that we're crazy, but that we continue down the path we were on."

John tries to find a comfortable position. "What path…we were on a path?"

Jimmy points to Jenny. "Jenny's path."

Everyone turns to Jenny. "Uncle Roger must have notes. He must have written stuff down, somewhere."

Finally. Johnny has a thought. "The room upstairs was ransacked."

He glares at everyone. "My room as it turns out…maybe that's what they were looking for."

They stop to consider, and Margot finally realizes. "They were. They did the same thing to my place."

Jenny rushes in. "So that means they didn't find it here and if they didn't find it there…"

She looks at Margot questioningly. "Then where is it?"

Robert

Robert is sitting on his bed in the living quarters above Louragan et Fils, when his father, wearing his Grateful Dead tee shirt, pokes his head in. "What's going on, Robby?"

Robert looks up considering. "I'm trying to do what you suggested. I'm there for Jenny…and that's working out okay, but the others don't know me."

Phillip tries to speak, but Robert rushes on. "And Jenny's father…I swear to God the man hates me."

Phillip laughs. "Well now, son, that's his job."

Robert rolls his eyes. "I know, I'll understand when I'm a father."

Phillip can't help smiling. "You are wise beyond your years."

Robert lays back on the bed. "Then why do I feel so stupid?"

Phillip chuckles. "Welcome to the club."

"Okay, what do I do…is there anything I can do?"

Phillip mulls this over. "Make yourself useful." He reaches into his pocket and pulls out a set of car keys. "The backup limo. From now on your job is to drive them wherever they need to go."

"But I have job here. I can't leave you hanging."

"Got you covered. Robby, go be a mensch."

Robert laughs and gets to his feet. "Okay, Pop."

Panama City, Florida
October 15, 1987

It is 5:00 am and Nicky sits in his brand-new Ford F-150 just steps from the dock where The Palermo is tied up. For just a moment he sits back and let's Pink Floyd's 'Learning to Fly' wash over him. He's glad he ponied up for the stereo cassette player...and the air-conditioning...and the Raven Black color is stellar.

He steps out of the warm cab to face a bracing gust coming from the north. Hurricane Floyd had missed them completely, but now the weather is cooler and the fish skittish. He hopes today is better than yesterday, but nothing can ruin this day. He's a dad, any day now, his wife, Victoria, is perfect and Mama is feeling much better after a nasty cold. The only thing missing is Papà. Nicky wishes he were here to see his new grandchild, but... Nicky lets this sudden feeling of loss wash over him...he's used to it. He grabs his gear and heads for his boat.

He senses that something is not quite right before he even reaches the Palermo. He can't explain it, and as he steps aboard, he drops his gear and grabs a grappling hook from the railing. Nick stands motionless, listening. His senses spreading out from stem to stern. He feels more than hears a motion behind and instinctively reaches out and grabs a collar scurrying by. The culprit struggles to pull loose. "Hey watcha doin? Let me go."

Nick turns him around and is face to face with a 16-year-old boy. "No...what are you doing?"

The boy is still struggling. "I ain't doing nothing, asshole."

Nick looks heavenward for strength. "First of all, it's 'I'm not doing anything, asshole.' and second you're on my boat."

The boy tries to pull away. "You're not my Mama."

Nick grabs his shoulders and takes a good look at him. "You got a Mama?"

The boy kicks out at him. "None of your business, dude."

Nick holds on. "Well, dude, again you're on my boat, so it's a little my business,"

He lets go of the boy who starts to run off. Nick calls out "You hungry? I mean you must be hungry."

The boy stops and slowly turns around, looking at Nick warily. "Watcha got?"

Nick goes about the business of getting the boat ready. "What I have is in the cooler. There's coffee in the thermos."

The boy peeks in the cooler and points to what can only be a sandwich. "What's this.?"

"It's a sandwich, my friend."

"I ain't your friend." He pokes at the sandwich. "What kind?"

Nick goes about his business. "The kind with bread."

The boy picks it up, opens it and takes a sniff. He looks suspiciously at Nick and takes a bite. "Not bad."

Nick smiles and slips into the captain's seat. "Pour me a cup of coffee."

The boy stops mid chew. "I ain't your slave."

Nick holds up his hands in surrender. "You're not my slave and I apologize. Would you...please...pour me a cup of coffee."

The boy makes a show of thinking about it but fixes a cup and hands it to Nick. "Are you good, now?"

Nick smiles back. "Peachy."

He starts the boat and turns to the boy. "Could you haul in the lines, please."

The boy stops stubbornly. "Hey, where you going? I ain't going nowhere."

Nick leans on the steering wheel. "Got something better to do?

The boy's trying to maintain his toughness. "See the Queen."

Nick puts the boat in gear and begins to pull away from the dock. "Tell Her Majesty 'Hi' for me."

As the boat gains speed, the boy has to grab a hold of a seat. "I ain't going fishing."

*Nick looks straight ahead, gaining speed. "**Not** going fishing. I'll pay you twenty bucks."*

The boy looks at Nick skeptically. "For what?"

"For fishing...you got a problem with that?"

The boy thinks about that and shrugs. "Guess not."

"Welcome aboard...you got a name?"

The boy is still holding on for dear life. "Drago...Vincent Drago."

Nick gives him the up and down. "I'll call you Vincenzo. Or maybe Vinnie...'Say Vinnie, How you doing?'...or Vincenzo...I'm not sure."

"Are you done, yet?"

"Nope…could you reach into the duffle and toss me the paperback?"

Resigned, Vincent reaches into the duffle bag and pulls out Steven King's Tommyknocker's and looks up at Nick.

"You reading this?"

Nick squints back at Vincent.

"Yeah, what about it?"

"Not as good at Misery."

Nick turns around in his seat to get a better look at Vincent. "You think so?"

"Absolutely…but neither of them is as good as Clancy. Hunt for Red October was awesome… Patriot Games not so much…but still okay."

Nick can't quite put this together. "An urchin who reads…never would have thought."

Vincent is offended. "Of course, I read. I ain't illiterate.

Nick considers this. After a moment he reaches into his pocket and pulls out his dad's gold coin and tosses it to Vincent. "My dad's lucky coin. Hold it and pray to the Virgin for a good catch."

Vincent examines the coin and looks up at Nick. "How much fish you want?"

"Why?"

"I got pull with the Virgin, but I like to be as specific as possible." He flips the coin back to Nick, who shakes his head in disbelief. What is he going to do with this boy and how is he going to explain it to Victoria?

Chapter IX
"Hey, let's look over there."

Johnny

Johnny is caught. The doctor told him to rest, which he ignores, and he wants to be where the action is, which he is, but now everyone is in this room to look through Roger' stuff. Margot is going through the desk...James is searching under the bed...Jenny is at the filing cabinet and what's-his-name is over there doing something.

Why is this a problem? Johnny just doesn't like people in his space. Of course, this isn't really his space. This is, after all, Roger's house and they did find Roger's body right there beside the couch. The very couch he's sitting on. "Are we going to be done soon?"

Jimmy eyes his brother. "What do mean, we? You're just sitting on the couch."

Johnny tries to come up with a good answer, but he settles for... "The doctor told me to rest."

"Right, the doctor told you many things, which you have heretofore ignored."

Johnny folds his arms and pouts. "Well, heretofore, you have been a pain in the ass...which you shall remain hereafter."

Robert pipes up. "It's really a shame your brother died."

Silently, the brothers turn as one to stare. Then across the room, Jenny calls out. "Hey, I think I found something."

Johnny turns to Jenny, who's reaching behind a filing cabinet, trying to reach something. "It's caught about halfway down."

It's almost in her hand. One more push and ...it falls all the way to the floor.

Robert rushes to her side. "Let's just move the cabinet away from the wall."

Everyone stares at Robert for a second before nodding in agreement. Even John is forced to agree this makes sense. They rock the cabinet back and forth and it slowly moves out enough for Jenny to reach her hand behind and pull out a manilla envelope. They stare at the envelope for a minute before Jenny tosses it to her father. Johnny catches it…with his bad arm. As he winces in pain, Jimmy takes it from him. "The doctor told you to rest…remember?"

Johnny glares back at his brother. "Well, go ahead, open it."

James opens the envelope and finds it stuffed with smaller envelopes and papers. He gives a handful to John, to Margot, to Jenny and reluctantly to Robert. They all find a spot…Surprise, surprise, Robert's spot is right next to Jenny's…and begin to go through their pile. One by one they stop, put the papers down and look up. Ever the accountant, James closes his eyes and shakes his head. "Taxes…last year's taxes."

Johnny takes a look around. "We've looked everywhere. We have to face it…it isn't here."

Everyone nods, except Margot. Her eyes are darting around the room. Finally, she turns to Johnny a smile spreading across her face. "You're right…it isn't here."

They all look at her like she's grown another head, but she just smiles back. "His laptop…it isn't here. It's always either here or at the university."

Johnny looks at Jimmy, who smiles back. "Of course, the university."

He looks at Margot. "Can you get us into his office?"

"Yes…I think I can."

Johnny gets up off the couch. "Well, let's go."

He looks around the room. "I guess we need to take two cars."

Robert clears his throat and holds up a set of keys. "I have the limo…there's plenty of space."

He looks around tentatively. Jenny kisses him on the cheek and Johnny scowls, briefly, before nodding. "Now, if everyone will please leave. I have to get ready to go."

Jimmy rolls his eyes and ushers everyone out.

Jenny

Jenny grabs Robert on the way out and hauls him into her room and shuts the door. She pulls him in for a passionate kiss. Robert is really getting into it when Jenny pushes his away. "Sorry, no time. We have to talk."

He draws her back in and begins snuggling her neck. She responds for a blissful moment but pushes him away again and sits on the bed patting the spot next to her. It takes Robert just a moment to realize the kissing portion of the morning is over. He sits down next to her. "Okay, chief, what's up?"

"I saw what you did back there, and I appreciate it…but now you need to change it."

"But I thought you wanted me to keep them on track."

"I do, but I'm thinking instead of bringing up Uncle Roger…you might want to refocus them on the search."

Robert thinks about that. "You mean, 'Hey, let's look over there.'?"

Jenny chuckles. "Yes, something like that."

"Okay, I can do that…I think."

Jenny kisses him softly. "I know you can…you've done great so far." Robert isn't so sure, but Jenny hugs him reassuringly. "Of course, you have…and you know what else?"

"What?"

She gives him the sideways glance. "I think my father's beginning to warm up to you."

Robert looks at her skeptically. "You think so? I didn't really get that."

Jenny pats him on the knee. "I do…by the way, thank you for the use of the limo. I know everyone appreciates it."

Robert smiles. "Well, thank my dad. It was his idea."

Jenny smiles back. "I will…the next time I see him."

Robert has a thought. "The limo doesn't have navigation; I may need your help there."

"But I don't know where I'm going."

Robert holds up his cell. "It's okay, it's all here. You just need to make sure I don't turn left when I should turn right."

"I can do that…I can even do the voice." She clears her throat and in a pretty good impression of the google girl. "Stay in the left lane…at the signal, turn left."

Robert hugs her. "Thank you, Siri,…or Alexis…whoever you are."

Jenny runs out of the room and calls out over her shoulder. "I'm just me. Catch me if you can."

Robert chases her out of the room and runs smack into, you guessed it, Johnny. Johnny glares at him. "I'm ready to go."

Robert fumbles over his words. "Okay, then…good…I'm ready too. We are all, ready…I guess."

Johnny continues to glare at Robert as Jenny rushes back and takes Robert's hand. She looks up sweetly at her father. "Daddy, play nice."

She leads Robert down the steps as Jonny looks after them. He girds his loins, so to speak. "I'll try."

Daz and Diz

A 1981 Autumn Red Corvette pulls into the Lagniappe House parking lot and circles the lot three times, like a dog before a nap. Diz is behind the wheel while Daz rides shotgun with a tray of three coffee au laits and a bag of beignets balanced on his lap. The Corvette comes to a stop outside the front entrance, engine throbbing. They look around the lot. Diz is getting annoyed. "The cops are never around when you need them."

Daz looks in the bag. "The beignets are getting soggy."

Diz glares at him, wiping powdered sugar off the seat. "You're getting stuff all over my silver-grey upholstery."

Daz glares back. "This is my car. This is my silver-grey upholstery."

Diz dismisses this with a wave of his hand. "Well, you're still getting stuff all over the seat."

Daz makes a big show of wiping off the seat. "Better now?"

Sarcastically, Diz grins. "Much. Now where the hell is Duplantier?"

"Well, Margot's car is gone too. He must be following her."

"Right, but where?"

"She probably went to the Chretien place."

Diz puts the car in gear and screeches out the lot, while Daz holds on for dear life. "Hey not so fast…this car isn't under warranty anymore."

Diz dismisses this completely. "What are you worried about? You're insured."

Daz looks at the outside rushing by. "I'm worried about you totaling my car. I'm worried about tickets. I'm worried about the amount of gas this gas guzzling behemoth is consuming…and frankly I'm worried about dying."

Diz shakes his head in disbelief. "You are not going to die."

He slams on the brakes and comes to screeching stop inches behind a line of cars at a stop light. Daz opens one eye. "You are insane, you know that?"

Diz just smiles back. "That's why you love me."

Daz just stares straight ahead. "I'm not even sure I like you."

Diz waves this off as he pulls up behind the squad car in front of the Chretien home. "No matter, we're here."

He gestures to the squad car in front of them. Daz tries to relax. "Okay so what now?"

Diz thinks for a moment. "Well, I guess we should deliver this before it gets any colder and soggier...and then see what information we can get."

"Alrighty then."

They get out of the car...Daz careful not to spill, and pile into the back seat of the squad car. Startled, Duplantier turns to them, reaching for his gun. "What are you doing? This is an official Lake Charles Police squad car here on official Lake Charles Police business."

Daz puts up his hands in surrender. "It's okay...we're friends. I'm Dazincourt Broussard and he's Dennis Dampier.

Dis smiles his most ingratiating smile. "My friends call me Diz."

He points to Daz. "His enemies call him Daz."

Daz frowns for just a moment at Diz, before taking the tray of coffee and beignets from him and turning back to Duplantier with a smile. "And we brought you coffee and beignets."

Diz snatches the tray back and holds it up. "See, it's from Stellar Beans...spared no expense."

Daz glares at Diz while taking a cup of café au lait and the bag of beignets and handing it to Officer Duplantier.' "The beignets might be a little soggy."

Duplantier takes the coffee and looks into the bag. He smiles, takes out a beignet and begins munching. "Not too soggy." He looks at them suspiciously while taking a gulp of coffee and munching a beignet. "Thank you...but why are you here?"

Diz and Daz exchange looks, and Diz takes the lead. "We know how tiring and boring a stakeout can be and thought you'd enjoy a mid-morning snack."

Duplantier nods and reaches for another beignet but stops to consider. "How'd ya'll know I'm on a stake out."

Daz jumps in. "Well first you're the famous Officer Duplantier and second, we're friends of Margot Sallier and we saw you there and then Margot was gone, and you were gone…and here you both are."

Duplantier nods at the logic. "Okay, but it's supposed to be a secret. I'm supposed to follow the suspect wherever she goes."

Diz is surprised. "Margot Sallier is a suspect?"

Duplantier thinks about this and shakes his head. "Not really…but it makes all this more …dangerous."

Daz rolls his eyes. "So, why are you here?"

Duplantier looks around to make sure no one can hear. "I'm supposed to make sure no one else is following her." He looks around again. "And between you and me, Sergeant Durel wants to know what they are up to."

Daz and Diz look around too. Diz frowns. "They?"

Duplantier whispers. "You know…the Chretiens. He wants to know what they know before they realize they know something."

Diz puts a reassuring hand on Duplantier's arm. "Well then, you carry on."

Duplantier draws them in close. "Remember, this is a secret."

Diz and Daz get out of the squad car and Daz looks back. "Our lips are sealed."

They shut the car doors, march up to the Chretien's house and ring the doorbell. When it opens Daz grins. "Have we got a story to tell you."

Robert

Robert walks out of the house and stops on the front porch, admiring the red Corvette across the street from the limo, wondering who it belongs to. Someday he's going to have one exactly like that. Mortician by day, 'playboy millionaire philanthropist,' by night. He looks at his reflection in living room window and grins. Tony Stark he ain't and his playboy days, real or imagined, may be over now. He hopes, anyway.

He notices the cop car sitting in front of the 'vette and debates giving him advanced noticed. Well, what's the harm? He raps on the side window and a startled Duplantier spills coffee all over himself. Robert, shaking his head, motions for him to lower the window. The window comes down and a powdered sugar dusted officer of the law glares back. "Can I help you with something?"

Robert smiles innocently. "I just wanted to give you a heads up...we're going to the university."

Duplantier returns a blank stare. Robert tries to explain. "The History Department at the university...Dr. Chretien's office...we're going there."

Robert walks back across the street, leaving a confused Duplantier staring after him. The front door opens, and everyone comes out...Jenny at the rear locking the door. Robert runs around to the passenger side and opens the door and Margot, James and John all get in. Daz gets in and just before Diz takes his seat, he quietly points a remote at the car and locks it.

Robert stares longingly at the car. "That is one awesome ride."

Diz looks at it proudly. "It is...if your good I'll let you drive it."

Daz stares at Diz in total disbelief. "That's my car."

Diz waves him off. "Whatever."

Daz looks back at the car. "And since when does it have a remote."

"About two months now."

Daz sputters. "How...why...what...but it's my car."

"Well, your car has remote, keyless entry...get over it."

Robert shuts the rear door and opens the front passenger side for Jenny before he runs around and gets into the driver's seat. He turns the key, the hum of the engine unnoticeable inside and the limo glides away from curb effortlessly, He turns to Jenny. "Do you know, where we're going."

She smiles back. "You can count on me." In her best Google Girl voice. "Proceed to the route...at the next signal turn left."

Robert grins and looks in the rear view and watches Duplantier make a U-turn, illegally by the way, and follow.

Margot

Margot sits back in the luxurious soft leather seat and closes her eyes. As she snuggles into the seat, Margot feels like she can relax. She is with family. Some, like Diz and Daz, she's had...well it seems like forever and others, like James, John, and Jenny, are new, but already feel comfortable.

She doesn't feel as alone or as scared as she did just a few days ago. She gazes at them. The brothers are exactly like Roger… and nothing like him… all at the same time. And Jenny…well Jenny is like a breath of fresh air. With them around, it's less painful to think about Roger…smiling at dinner or walking with her, hand in hand, along the Lakefront Promenade…instead of the ghastly image of him lying on the floor with that horrid flag draped over him…dead. She still wakes to that image at night when all the loneliness, sorrow and terror fill her soul. She closes her eyes tightly, physically bringing herself back from the edge of despair.

She feels a warm, friendly hand on hers and opens her eyes to see James looking at her intently. "You went to a dark place."

"How did you know?"

James leans his head back against the seat. "Because I've been there."

He smiles and squeezes her hand. Margot looks out the window to get her bearings and turns back to the others. "We're almost to the university."

John looks out the window. "Well first we have to get into the university…will that be a problem?"

Margot considers this. "I don't think so. I am there all the time…was there, I guess."

James smiles and squeezes her hand again. Margot smiles tentatively back. She reaches into her pocket and pulls out keys. "And I still have a key to his office." Margot looks at the university quickly approaching and leans forward to Robert. "The next street, Beauregard Drive, make a right and park in the second lot on your right."

Robert looks at Jenny, who does the voice. "At Beauregard Drive turn right, then park in the second lot on your right."

Robert and Jenny giggle, and John rolls his eyes. "First we have to make it through Security."

Robert turns right and glides to the security station. Margot motions for the window to come down. Robert pulls to a stop and Margot leans to the open window.

"Hi, I'm Margot Sallier. I'm here to pick up Dr. Chretien's things from his office."

The guard checks his clip board. "Sorry, ma'am, but you're not on the list."

Margot tries to clarify. "No, I wouldn't be. Dr. Chretien died and I'm here to collect his belongings."

The guard considers the limo and eyeballs the other members of the group. "I'll have to call this one in."

He disappears into the guard shack. James and John exchange looks. "Your guess is as good as mine."

The guard returns and glares at them. "Someone will meet you there. You know where to park?"

Margot smiles back. "Yes, sir, we do. Thank you."

The guard gives a brief nod, presses a button and the barrier rises. Robert pulls away and parks in the lot. A wave of…a combination of sorrow and terror washes over Margot, thinking about going through Roger's things yet again.

It isn't until the head of security meets them at Roger's building that she's able to focus. "Good morning. I'm Officer Charbonneau and I understand you're here to get into Dr. Chretien's office. I'm sorry for your loss, but I'm not sure I can let you in."

Margot is confused. "It's okay, officer, I have a key.

"It isn't that ma'am. The police came by…over a week ago and sealed it off. I don't know if they've been back to clear it or not. We can go up, if you like and check, but if there's still crime scene tape up, I can't let you in."

Margot nods and they follow him into the building and up the stairs. First Margot with James and John, then Diz and Daz, and finally Jenny and Robert bringing up the rear. When they reach Roger's office, there is no sign of any crime scene tape.

Charbonneau shrugs. "I guess, the cops came and cleared it. Again, I'm sorry for your loss."

They wait for him to go down the stairs before Margot uses her key and slowly opens the door.

Jimmy

James stands holding his breath…it's almost like he expects his brother to be on the other side of the door…sitting behind a desk, going through a stack of old books trying to answer a question that scholars have been puzzling over for centuries. At least that's the way he always pictures Roger. He said that to Roger one time, and he laughed saying he was only looking for recipes. James chuckles at the memory. When John looks at him with a raised eyebrow, he shrugs. "Just thinking about Roger."

"Me too."

As Margot swings the door open, they all stand staring. Desk overturned. Filing cabinet leaning on its side…drawers thrown across the room…papers everywhere. Books dumped in a pile. James stares at the devastation before him. Margot starts to go in, but James puts his hand on her shoulder. "Wait, perhaps we should take a moment and consider what we're going to do."

John, ever the attorney, steps up. "Well, let's ask ourselves…what do we know?"

James considers this for a moment. "We know this is Roger's office…we know that, at one time, there was crime scene tape, but now there isn't."

John accepts this but goes on. "Now, we have to ask ourselves…did this happen before or after the crime scene tape went up?"

James picks it up. "If it happened before… and the tape is down… it means this crime scene has been processed." He turns to John. "Way back in your dim and dark past you were an A.D.A. Does this look like a crime scene that's been processed to you?"

"Not unless the police are totally incompetent."

James concurs. "And Durel doesn't strike me as incompetent…stretched a little thin perhaps but not incompetent."

Margot frowns. "So, what do we do?"

John, considering all angles.

"On one hand, there is no crime scene tape, and the university gave us permission to retrieve Roger's personal belongings."

Margot's eyes narrow. "But…?"

"But…on the other hand we need to report this to the police right away."

This doesn't explain anything. James, bemused, takes over. "Before John runs out of hands, Margot, you need to understand that under no circumstances will an attorney give you a straight answer."

Jenny glares at her father. "Especially, this attorney…so what do we do?"

James explains their only logical course of action. He turns to Robert. "First… Robert, Duplantier is downstairs, right?" Robert is all ears. "You go tell him what we found." He turns to Diz and Daz. "Guys, when the police arrive, stall them as long as you can." The three of them stare at James, who smiles. "Well, go." Robert, Diz and Daz salute and they are gone.

Jenny watches them go. "But what do we do?"

James explains. "We go in and...have a little look see."

Johnny puts up his hand. "Being very careful not to disturb anything...too much."

Jimmy grins at his brother. "And be quick, we don't have much time."

Johnny smiles back and turns to Jenny. "Jay Bird, wait by the door and hoot when you hear the police coming."

Jenny hates that name but gives a thumbs up to her father, anyway. Margot waits for instructions. "Okay, what do want me to do?"

James thinks for a minute. "Look for the computer...it probably isn't here, but make sure."

James turns to John. "Go through the papers...you know what to look for...anything that has to do with...anything."

They all move into the office. James heads for the books. "I'll see what I can find over here."

Margot looks around at the overturned desk and filing cabinet...peering inside drawers that are strewn across the room. John, using a pen, turns sheets of paper over one at a time. "This is going to take forever...Roger hasn't thrown away anything since he was in kindergarten."

Margot looks up, frustrated. "I don't see the computer anywhere."

James scans the room, the edge of a book on the windowsill behind the curtain catches his attention. He leans over, trying not to fall into the pile of books and retrieves it using the tips of his fingers. He almost fumbles it, but at the last second, catches himself and manages to hold on. He looks at the book. A cursory glance, then more closely. "Hey...Pop's recipes."

John gives him a look. "Not exactly what we're looking for, sport."

James continues to peruse the book. "Maybe not, but I'm taking this."

Margot frowns. "I thought we weren't supposed to disturb anything."

James waves her off. "It's just a book of recipes."

Suddenly, from the doorway, Jenny calls out softly. "Cops."

Johnny frowns. "You're supposed to hoot."

Jenny gives him a look and rolls her eyes. "Hoot."

John and Margot hurry to the door, while James, hiding the book under his coat, catches his shoe on an overturned drawer. They all hold their breath as James regains his balance, just as they hear a frustrated Antoine. "I don't care whose car it is…get out of the way."

Antoine bulldozes his way to the office, while Diz and Daz stand at the top of the stairs, grinning. Antoine looks at the innocent trio standing in front of him and then into the destroyed office and then back to them. "Any of you go in there?"

John, innocently, looks into the office and then back to Antoine, holding up his right hand. "Sergeant Durel, I am deeply offended…I'm an officer of the court, after all."

Antoine holds his gaze, but finally gives it up. "And this was the way you found it? No crime scene tape?"

Margot steps up. "No sergeant, it definitely wasn't up. If you don't believe me, ask Officer Charbonneau. He was here when we found it."

Antoine scowls at her. "Believe me, Ms. Sallier, I intend to." He looks back to the room and his shoulders slump. "In the meantime, will y'all, please leave. I have work to do."

They scurry down the stairs. Johnny shakes his head. "Too bad we didn't find anything."

Jimmy looks behind him. "Are you kidding, I found Pop's recipes." He opens the book to a bookmark. "Pop's recipe for crawfish bisque. This recipe is legendary."

Diz rubs his hand together. "I've heard tell."

Daz shakes his head. "Yeah, you it heard from me."

James looks at the recipe. "Then it's decided…tomorrow we make crawfish bisque."

Diz speaks up. "We'll bring the crawfish." How many do you think we'll need…five…six dozen?

Daz glares at his friend. "You are not putting six dozen live crawfish in my car." Diz waves him off.

Jenny doesn't understand. "Don't we have something more important to do."

Johnny puts his arm around his daughter. "Jenny dear, magical things happen when you make crawfish bisque."

Antoine

Sergeant Antoine Durel stands looking into Roger Chretien's office. It was not more than a week ago that he stood in this very place. He had taken the computer, sealed off the office and left, without a second thought. He would come back later and do a more thorough investigation. Well, somebody had already done a more thorough search and it wasn't him. He turns to his CSI team. "Okay, have at it." A suspicion suddenly blossoms in his mind. "And if you find any indication that the two Chretien brothers have been in this room I want to know about it."

The two investigators stare at Sergeant Antoine and then stare at each other. Finally, one of them gets the courage to speak, "Sure, Sarge, as soon as we know something, you'll know."

Antoine watches them, then shaking his head, he barks. "Duplantier…is Officer Duplantier anywhere around.?"

A rather timid voice from the hallway calls out. "I'm here, Sarge."

"Well, come here."

Duplantier does as he's told and stands before Sergeant Antoine. "Didn't I specifically tell you to make sure no one got into this room."

"Yes sir, you did."

Antoine squints and points to the office. "Then explain this."

Duplantier tries to sort it all out before speaking. "Well, you see, I tried…but you told me to follow Miss Sallier. So, I tried to do both. I'd follow Miss Sallier and then I'd think I should be here, so I'd come here…but then I'd feel guilty and go back to Miss Sallier and she'd be gone, and I'd have to try and find her." He looks up at Antoine. "She goes a lot of places, Sarge."

Antoine shuts his eyes and nods. "I know, son…this one's on me."

Duplantier stares back. He knows he should say something…but what? "I guess I should get back…Miss Sallier won't follow herself."

Antoine doesn't know what to with that. "No, officer, you're right. You'd better go."

Duplantier salutes and is gone. Antoine can only shake his head and watch him leave. Unexpectedly, a voice calls out. "Sarge, found something here."

Antoine turns to see one of the investigators waving his cell phone. "Sarge, I found a print on the windowsill and sent it into AFIS...got an immediate hit."

Antoine expects more...but doesn't get it. "The print...who does the print belong to?"

"Oh right...it belongs to James Chretien."

Antoine stares daggers...no ICBM's... at no one in particular. He knew it...he knew they'd been in here. They'd have to have a 'Come to Jesus' talk very soon...very, very soon.

Panama City, Florida
October 3, 1995

Nicky stands in his living room considering the rain through the picture window. The driveway is flooded, but he doesn't care. Hurricane Opal is going to hit, just west of them, and he's not going anywhere. A Category 4 storm is nothing to ignore, and he plans to stay right where he is, He's not going to risk his life, that's the way his father died... besides fishing has been good and he can afford to stay at home for a couple of days. It gives him some time to spend with Joey. It's hard to believe that he's almost eight. Soon, it'll be time to take him out...to learn the business.

Nick has no illusions. He knows Joey may not want to fish, but he needs to know the business. He smiles to himself...Joey will have to know enough to keep Vinnie honest. Nick turns when he hears someone behind him. Joey is there holding out a cup coffee. "Here, Papà. I brought you coffee."

Nick looks seriously at his son. "Is it the way I like it?"

Joey closes his eyes to get it right. "Yes sir, black...two sugars."

Nick regards his son seriously. This is a game they play, and they both have their part. "Italian roast?"

Joey, a grin on his face, is about to answer when a voice calls out from the kitchen. "What else would we have in this house?"

They both look back at Victoria coming out of the kitchen with a cup of Atole de almendra. She hands the cup to Joey who takes sniff, smiling. "Thank you, mamà."

She smiles at her son and lovingly ruffles his hair, then she puts her arm around her husband's waist and gazes at the falling rain out the window. "So, what are my men doing this morning?"

Nicky smiles at his son. "We were just trying to decide...to fish or not to fish...what do you think, Joseph?"

Victoria sternly puts her hands on her hip, "If either of you set foot out of this house today, I will never let you back in."

Nick raises his hands in surrender, "I promise, we will not leave this house today...maybe never."

Victoria waves him away. "If you're still here day after tomorrow, I'll throw you out." She leans in and kisses her husband on the cheek. She points out the window at Vincent slogging his way to the front door. "Here comes the third musketeer."

Joey cranes his neck to see and runs to the door just as Vincent opens it. He comes in dripping water and, takes off his coat and hat, hanging them up neatly next to the door. The first person he sees is Joey...he makes a funny face and in his best Harrison Ford voice. "Hey, Short Round." Joey giggles and Vincent turns to Nick and Victoria. "Buongiorno, zia y zio. Come sta?

He kisses Victoria on the cheek. She smiles at her "adopted" nephew. "We are all fine, Vincent." She looks at him conspiringly. "You have an important job to do...keep these two inside."

"I'll do my best, but you know those two..." He looks toward Joey. "Particularly that one...always up to no good."

Victoria laughs. "Well, just make sure they both behave."

Vincent smiles and Victoria kisses her husband on the cheek and goes back into the kitchen...calling over her shoulder. "Vincent, want some coffee?"

"No, thank you, zia."

Nick grabs hold of Joey and hugs him tightly. He looks up at Vincent. "So, the day is ours. What shall we do?"

Joey brightens. "Basketball."

Nick laughs. "We'd have to be ducks to play today, son."

Joey pouts for a second. Vincent has other ideas. "Nick, can I see the coin you father found...the lucky coin?"

Nick looks at him quizzically. "You like that coin...want to pray to the Virgin?"

Vincent is puzzled. "Pray...? Why, we're not fishing. I don't want anything."

Nick frowns for just a second. "Vincenzo, we don't just pray when we want something...Sometimes we just want to say 'hi'."

Vincent thinks. "I suppose...but I just want to see the coin."

Nick reaches into his pocket and flips the coin to Vincent. "You ask to see the coin more and more often...any reason?"

Vincent turns the coin over and over in his hand. "Just curious. You ever wonder if there's more?

"Not really...I mean, I'm sure there are more. Thousands of ships have sailed in these waters...a lot of wrecks. That coin could have been carried by the currents a thousand miles."

Vincent still stares at the coin. "I suppose, but wouldn't it be great to find a ship load of these on the bottom of the Gulf?"

Nick turns to Joey. "Want to hunt for sunken treasure, son?"

Joey thinks about it but shakes his head. "I'd rather play basketball."

Nicky laughs, the coin forgotten. Vincent, however, continues to stare at it...mesmerized.

Chapter X
"Jambalaya, Crawfish pie, File gumbo"

Diz and Daz

It's 8:00 AM and the sleek red Corvette skims through the streets of Lake Charles like the Flash. Daz is once again holding on for dear life. He doesn't know how Diz does it every time...rock, paper, scissors is not that complex. The law of averages says that he should be able to drive his car sometime.

He's sure Diz cheats...he doesn't know how...but anyway, here he is, once again, in the passenger seat with a tray of coffee and a bag of beignets in his lap. Plus, this time, he has five pounds of crawfish meat, with fat, and a bag of shells at his feet. The 'vette pulls up behind Duplantier outside of the Chretien home. Daz holds up the tray. "A little help here."

Diz looks over at Daz, smiles and takes the tray. "Certainly...by the way you need gas."

Daz glares at Diz as he climbs out of the car, muttering. "Of course, I need gas. If you didn't drive like we were at Indy, maybe I wouldn't need gas every five minutes...at least I'll be able to drive my own car."

Diz hands the tray back to Daz. "I can do it if you want...just give me your card."

Daz continues to glare at Diz as he brings the coffee and beignets to Duplantier, who rolls his window down. Daz curtsies as he hands him the coffee and beignets. "Here's your morning fix."

Duplantier peeks in the bag, takes a sniff and smiles. "Thanks, guys."

Diz retrieving the crawfish, waves him off. "Think nothing of it. By the way, we're making crawfish bisque. If you want, maybe we can save some for you."

Duplantier tries to speak around a mouthful of beignets. "That'd be great, thanks."

Diz, with a flourish of his hand. "You are most welcome."

As they walk to the front door, Daz rolls his eyes. "Sometimes you are so full of crap."

"True…but we might still need him."

Daz rings the doorbell' "Yeah, yeah…but share our bisque, I mean really?"

Robert opens the door. In a soft voice. "Thank God, you guys are here, Mr. Chretien…James…Mr. James…Jenny's uncle…has been storming around the house since 6:30 this morning waiting for you guys."

Diz rolls his eyes. "J.T's Fish Market didn't open until 7:00."

Robert opens the door all the way and lets them in. Margot rushes over and takes the crawfish from them and rushes them into the kitchen. "Crawfish is here."

A disembodied voice from the kitchen. "It's about time."

Johnny walks down the stairs. "Never mind my brother, he's kind of highly strung." All they hear are pots and pans being banged about. Johnny raises his voice. "Brother, dear, would you mind coming out here for just a minute?"

More banging of pots until James appears at the kitchen door. "What can you possibly want? I'm busy here."

Johnny looks heavenward for strength. "Well first, get a grip. And second, why don't you say, 'good morning' and perhaps a 'thank you' to our friends who were so kind to get up early and bring us the crawfish?"

James, looking like a three-year-old who just got caught having a tantrum, scowls at Johnny, and then at Daz and Diz, and Robert and Margot. Jimmy turns all red. "Have I been acting like a jerk?"

Margot holds up her thumb and forefinger, a little bit, Johnny puts his hand over hers, spreading them wide. "A big, huge one,"

James looks around the room and gives a collective. "I'm very sorry." He turns specifically to Diz and Daz. "Thank you for getting the crawfish. We couldn't do this without you."

Daz and Diz smile back and are about to speak, when Jenny appears at the top of stairs, still in her robe, hands on her hips…obviously annoyed. "What is going on down there?"

John looks at Jenny and then back to Daz and Diz. "As you can see, the Chretiens are not morning people."

He looks specifically at Robert and lowers his voice. "Something you may want to remember for future...and I do mean future...reference."

After a moment spent glaring at Robert, he goes on. "James and I will go into the kitchen, make coffee, and try to get our collective selves calmed down. Margot, will you please get with Jenny...and Robert and lay everything we have regarding Roger's murder out on the dining room table."

Then to Daz and Diz. "I know you guys just got here, but would you mind running out and getting...beignets, donuts...or something."

Diz and Daz share a look. Diz nods. "We know just the spot."

Diz flips the car keys to Daz, who is stunned. "Me drive?"

"Who else? It's your car." He turns back to the others. "We'll be back in a few."

He reaches for the doorknob when a loud banging comes from the other side of the door. "But first, I'll see who's at the door." More loud banging on the door. He looks through the peep hole and back to the group. "Uh oh."

Antoine

Diz opens the door, mid bang, to reveal a very irate Sergeant Antoine and a less irate more terrified, Officer Duplantier. Antoine marches into the room. "This ends now. Your meddling days are over. You are no longer going to participate in this investigation in any way."

He looks at everyone one by one. "Is that clear?"

Officer Duplantier raises his hand. Antoine looks heavenward. "No, Duplantier, not you."

Antoine continues to glare. "But the rest you...no more interference."

More virtuous people you have never seen. Jimmy spreads his hands in total innocence. "Whatever do you mean, Sergeant?"

Johnny cuts in, helpfully. "Coffee?"

Antoine glares at him. "I don't want coffee."

His eyes dart to Diz and Daz. "Or beignets."

His eyes go back to Jimmy. "Or any crawfish bisque...what I want is for you to mind your own business."

Jimmy is dumfounded. "What brought this on, Sergeant?"

99

Antoine closes his eyes in total disbelief. "Did you go into your brother's office yesterday?"

James begins to puff up. Antoine just rolls his eyes. "Didn't you tell me that you didn't go into your brother's office?"

James looks quickly at John. "Well, I might have said…"

Antoine cuts him off. "Would it surprise you to know that we found footprints on the floor that I'm guessing we'll find come from…" His eyes sweep the room to include James, John, and Margot. "You three…inside the room?"

It is time for the lawyer to speak up. John clears his throat. "Oh, I see what problem is here. There seems to be a misunderstanding."

Antoine raises an eyebrow. "Oh really?"

"Certainly, when we got to the office, the crime scene tape was down, and the head of McNeese security said we could go in. So, we did…until we realized that something was not right."

James jumps in. "We said to each other, we said the Lake Charles Police Department would not search a room like this. It would be more precise…more methodical…not all willynilly."

Margot rushes to agree. "That's exactly what we said."

John wraps it up. "And that's when we notified the police."

James is in total agreement. "That's what happened…I'm sorry for the confusion."

Antoine just stares. "So, you're saying that, as soon as, you realized something was wrong, you left the room and notified Duplantier." Antoine cocks his head. "Okay then, but give me all the information, next time…when I ask."

James smiles at the detective. "Certainly, sergeant we shall be an open book."

Antoine nods once. He turns to leave and makes it halfway to the door before it's his turn to pull a Columbo. "Oh, one more thing."

He turns to James. "Could you clarify something?"

James smiles in all innocence. Antoine smiles, disarmingly, back. "Could you explain how your fingerprints were found on a window ledge in Roger Chretien's office?" James looks to John for help, but Antoine goes on. "Next to, what is certainly, a missing book. Dust or actually the lack of dust, clearly indicates that a book…or something with the shape of a book was removed from the office…can you explain that?"

John tries to explain. "Oh, I see the confusion."

Antoine looks at him with total disbelief. "Really…I'm the one confused…again?"

"No, no, no, you're not confused as much as our answer was…incomplete."

Antoine cannot wait to hear this. James decides to jump in. "Yes, well…as I was leaving, I saw a book that I thought I recognized…Completely unrelated to anything impacting this case…in any way." Antoine just waits. "It looked like…and it turned out to be…our father's recipe book."

Margot tries to help. "Yes, sergeant, I can verify that…It's a book of recipes. It's in the kitchen…let me get it." She rushes from the room, before Antoine can say anything. Antoine glares at everyone, including Duplantier, in turn. Margot rushes back in and hands the book to Antoine, who opens it and flips pages. "You're sure this is the book you took?"

James in all innocence. "Absolutely."

Antoine's eyes narrow. "You're sure?"

James nods, resolutely. "Hand to God."

Antoine is not totally convinced. "I don't trust any of you."

John completely understands. "Yes, Sergeant, but please believe me, we only want to find out what happened to Roger."

Antoine shakes his head. James tries to speak, but Antoine cuts him off. "Please believe me when I tell you that everything…and I mean everything…we've learned about the killer indicates he's very dangerous."

James looks excitedly at John and Margot. "You've learned something?"

Antoine can't believe this. "Don't you get it…I'm trying to protect you here. Go back to your crawfish bisque and let me do my job and so help me, I'll protect you…even if I have to throw all of you in jail for obstruction of justice…Do you understand?"

James and John surrender. John speaks for both of them. "Of course, we understand, Sergeant…if by any chance we come across any additional information we will turn it over to you immediately. You can count on us."

Antoine doesn't quite trust any of them but decides to let it go. "Officer Duplantier will continue to be on station…to protect and serve. If you need anything…learn anything…or innocently stumble across anything…please tell him immediately."

James, Margot, and John exchange glances. Margot speaks for them. "We will, Sergeant, immediately."

Antoine turns on his heal to leave when James tries to speak. Antoine raises his hand in dismissal and continues walking. "No, I don't want any crawfish bisque, even if it's your dad's recipe…and Officer Duplantier doesn't want any either."

An extremely disappointed Office Duplantier follows his boss out the door.

Johnny

Johnny can't help flinching when the front door slams. He turns to the others and shrugs. "Well, that's that…now, where were we?"

He looks at Diz and Daz. "You were going to pick up beignets."

Then at Margot, Jenny, and Robert. "And you were going to lay out everything we know on the dining room table…while James and I were going to make coffee.

Margot is confused. "But I thought we agreed…"

John shakes his head. "All we are going to do is review what we have…and if we have anything pertinent…we'll turn it over immediately."

James nods in agreement. "Of course, we'll have to determine exactly what is pertinent and what is not."

John agrees, smiling. "Let's meet back here in fifteen."

Everyone sets upon their appointed tasks. John motions for James to follow him into the kitchen. "So now what?"

"We review what we have and go from there. In the meantime, crawfish bisque."

He checks his watch. "Only two hours behinds schedule."

When Diz and Daz return. James gathers them all in the kitchen, prepares coffee for all of them and waits for them to get situated…but before he can speak, Johnny takes a bite of a beignet, powdered sugar floating around his face like a cloud. "Oh my God, this is wonderful."

Margot takes a bite. " Stellar Beans…have you tried their…?"

James clears his throat. "I'm sure that everything this Stellar Beans has is absolutely grand, but if we don't focus, we'll never get the crawfish bisque ready for dinner."

John takes one more bite. "My brother is of course right…as always."

James ignores the slight dig and Johnny looks at Margot, Jenny, and Robert. "You three, start going over whatever we have…and try to sort it into categories."

As they leave, he looks at Daz and Diz. "And could the two of you stay here and help with the bisque." Diz rubs his hands together. "We'd be delighted."

"Okay then, how much crawfish did you get?"

"We got five pounds of crawfish…with fat and shells…enough to make about 80 heads."

John can hardly contain himself. "So, why don't you guys concentrate on the heads."

He points to the counter. "There's the food processor…and onion, garlic, cloves, and breadcrumbs."

James adds his two cents. "Eggs are in the fridge…use three pounds of the crawfish and John and I will use the rest for the bisque."

He looks to John with a big grin on his face. "Let's get to it then."

Diz and Daz scurry off and begin chopping onions and garlic. John is momentarily frozen in spot. James gives him a nudge. "I'll start the water and chop the onion, celery, and green pepper… you take care of the roux."

Johnny gets with it. "The roux…of course the roux. You do the trinity and I'll do the roux" He looks at the flour and oil on the counter beside the stove and frowns. "Jimmy, toss me the book…I want to get the ratio of flour to oil right."

Jimmy is busy measuring out two quarts of water into a four-quart pot and adding bay leaves and cloves. He absently tosses the recipe book to John, who watches the book turn three times in the air. On the third time around something small and black flies out and lands on the floor. Johnny catches the book with his good hand and bends down to see what flew out. He looks up at James. "Jimmy, you may want to take a look at this."

Jimmy turns the pot of boiling water down to simmer and squats down looking where John is pointing. "What do we have here?"

He picks up a very small thumb drive and looks over at John. "Well, now, this is…interesting."

John calls out to those in the dining room. "Hey guys…you want to come in here? We may be going in a slightly different direction."

Jenny

Jenny looks up from the dining room table where they have separated what they have into two piles...relevant and not so much. In the relevant pile is Margot's cedar box with the brooch inside. Jenny supposes that the one other relevant thing is the gold coin Sergeant Antoine found...but of course Sergeant Antoine has that on his dining room table.

Well, she decides. any direction is better than the direction they're going in. They all file through the kitchen door and find a beehive of activity. Definitely more fun in here. Her dad is at the stove stirring a pot, Jenny takes a sniff, making a roux and Diz and Diz are cutting up the celery, onion, and green pepper...while her uncle is holding a very small thumb drive. James waits until they are all gathered around...all but John.

"John, will you come over here, I need your input."

John is still stirring. "I'll be there in a second...the roux is almost ready...turning from a dark cherry to mahogany."

James hesitates; first things first. "Okay, take your time."

John stirs the roux a few more times. Finally satisfied, he dumps the chopped onion, green pepper, and celery into the pot. The pot sizzles while a glorious fragrance fills the room, as John adds the garlic, turns the fire down and puts on the lid.

"Now you have five minutes,"

James checks his watch and nods. He holds up the thumb drive again. "This fell out of Pop's recipe book."

Margot cocks her head. "You think it's important?"

"Yes, I think it could be...might be.... must be. Why else would it have been hidden in Pop's book?"

John considers this. "I agree, it's too much of a coincidence."

He looks at his watch. "Time." He stirs the pot and looks over at his brother. "Jimmy, pour a quart of the boiling water into this."

Jimmy measures out a quart and pours it into the pot. Johnny mixes it together. "Okay, then...we'll bring this back to a boil and then down to a simmer."

He turns to Daz and Diz. "How are the heads coming?"

Diz speaks up. "Stuffing's done...oven is pre-heating and we're going to start stuffing heads."

Johnny rubs his hands together. "Excellent."

Jenny, however, isn't sure. "Daddy, I don't care how magical it is...I'm not eating crawfish heads."

Johnny grins at his daughter. "They're not really heads."

Jenny examines the operation skeptically. "Then why are they called heads?"

Johnny looks at Jimmy, who looks at Diz and Daz, who look back at Johnny. He turns to Jenny and shrugs. "I don't know."

James tries to bring them back. He holds up the thumb drive. "Let's talk about this...are you guys finished sorting through things?"

Jenny speaks up. "There really isn't much."

James hands her the drive. "Well, maybe we'll get lucky with this."

Margot hesitates. "Shouldn't we tell Sergeant Durel what we found?"

James looks to Johnny, who averts his eyes, looking heavenward. James is in perfect agreement. "Well, first of all, we haven't actually found anything yet. So, it's really our duty to go through this ourselves first...before we bother Sergeant Durel. After all, he's extremely busy. So, once we go through the drive, we'll share any relevant information...if any."

Johnny grins. "Right, if any.

After an almost too long a pause, everyone agrees.

Robert

Robert sits at the dining room table, chin in hand, watching Jenny and Margot go through the thumb drive. All he really wants is to spend time with Jenny...lovely Jenny...pretty Jenny...sexy Jenny...I dream of Jenny with the light brown hair. Well, of course, it's a darker brown, with hints of red...it's the most beautiful hair in the world.

Robert suddenly realizes that he's just sitting there staring at Jenny and can't pull his eyes away from her. He can't, that is until their eyes meet and her face lights up with her lovely, shy, incandescent smile. He smiles back. "Hey."

She cocks her head. "Hey back."

Meanwhile Margot is becoming more and more frustrated. To begin with, she doesn't know what she's looking for. So, she's just randomly opening files. When she looks up from the computer screen and sees Robert and Jenny making googly eyes at each other, she sits back and folds her arm. "I'd say, get a room." She glances at the closed kitchen door. "But that may be wildly inappropriate." Finally, Margot clears her throat. "I don't want to break up this love fest, but I could really use your help here."

Robert and Jenny pull their eyes away from each other and focus on Margot, who frowns clearly exasperated. "There are just so many files. I didn't expect to find one labeled Lafitte's treasure...Well, I guess I hoped I would...but there's so much stuff here and it doesn't seem very logical. It seems kind of random...or at least part of it does. There's a folder for each class he teaches...now that makes sense, but other stuff...like letters of recommendation or an article he was working on...here is a folder about a cruise we were thinking of taking...why make a copy of this and then hide it. It doesn't make any sense to me, and Roger always made sense."

Robert pulls the laptop in front of him and begins scrolling through the drive. The more he scrolls the more random it appears. He's very puzzled. "I see what you mean."

He motions for Jenny to look closer. She leans in, their heads almost touching and studies the screen. Margot just stares at the two of them, heads together, in their own little world. "This is certainly over my head." No response. "I think I'll get some coffee." Still no response. "I don't suppose, either of you want anything."

Margot huffs, gets out of her chair, and opens the kitchen door, letting the magical aroma of the crawfish bisque into the room. Suddenly, Robert sits back...his eyes wide...a moment of inspiration. "Wait a minute...maybe it seems random because it's meant to seem random."

Jenny doesn't see it. Robert tries to explain. "Okay, so maybe your uncle knew he was being followed...and he had some information he didn't want to fall into the wrong hands...so he puts it...somewhere...in some document or file on his desktop...copies the whole desktop onto the thumb drive and hides it in your grandfather's book."

Jenny begins to understand. "So, it's not as random as it seems...but Uncle Roger wanted it to seem random."

"Exactly right."

Jenny smiles, but stops, a frown forming on her lovely face. "But we still don't know what it is...or where it is for that matter."

"You're right…but we've learned two important things…Roger definitely had important information he wanted to hide…and it's somewhere on this thumb drive."

She looks intently at Robert. "So, what you're saying is that…we've learned something…and nothing all at the same time."

Robert holds his hands up in surrender. "Yes…but at least we know 'something' exists…maybe."

They look at each other and smile begins to form…that turns into a giggle…that turns into a laugh…then an all-out, fall down, eyes streaming, snort inducing guffaw that turns into a kiss…a deep lingering kiss…that goes on and on…and on, until Margot, coffee cup in hand, swings open the kitchen door…letting in even more of that wonderous smell…comes back in and takes her seat. She takes a sip of coffee and looks, innocently, at Jenny and Robert. "Any progress?"

Robert and Jenny share a look and bust out laughing. Robert turns to Margot. "Well, yes and no."

Margot

Margot sits, toying with her coffee, while Robert goes on and on about evidence that is both there and not there at the same time. Jenny occasionally chimes in, trying to clarify points that Margot isn't really listening to, anyway. She tries focus but her mind keeps racing from finding Roger's body…to Johnny being shot…to Diz and Daz helping James make crawfish bisque…to Robert and Jenny, blissful in their own world. It's like she is at the bottom of a well and observing everything through the round hole at the top. She doesn't seem to fit anywhere.

Two weeks ago, she was in love with her best friend and now he's gone. She listens to his brothers in the kitchen and Jenny and Robert at the table…and it's all wrong. She doesn't know how she can feel lonely with all these people around…but she does.

As she sits, the tantalizing aroma of the crawfish bisque fills her senses. She rises slowly from the table and wanders into the living room.

Suddenly everything changes. She feels at peace. This room is all about Roger…about them, Their first kiss happened in this room… Roger said he loved her, for the first time in this room…they planned their future in this room. The more she looks around…at their picture on mantle… the furniture they bought, together, the more she realizes that she is not alone. Roger is and always will be in this room. She sits in his favorite chair, her eyes closed, reveling in Roget's presence. She finds herself listening, needing to hear Roger's voice…and it comes. "I love you."

And a little closer. "I miss you."

And finally. "Please help me."

She opens her eyes and finds her cheeks wet with tears. "How can I help you?"

"Follow my trail."

Her mind whirling, not sure what just happened. She feels so close to Roger, but she knows it wasn't really Roger speaking. She also knows something that she can't quite bring into focus. Some question that has gone unasked…but what?

So lost in thought is Margot that at first she doesn't hear Jenny calling her name. Finally, she gets up from the chair and stands in the doorway that separates the living room from the dining room…reluctant to leave her memories behind.

Jenny, her face aglow, looks up from the computer screen, "We found it, Margot. We found the file Uncle Roger was protecting."

Then James's booming voice calls out from the kitchen. "Set the table, because dinner is almost ready."

Jimmy

Jimmy stands at the stove, surrounded by Johnny on his right and Diz and Daz on his left taking one last taste before declaring it officially done. Each in turn dip their spoon into the rich, dark reddish brown, creamy bisque, and savor the complex flavors. Eyes closed; Jimmy lets the bisque roll through his mouth enjoying the first burst of flavor to the last afterglow of the cayenne pepper. He opens his eyes and declares: "It's done."

Jimmy and Johnny transfer the bisque from pot to tureen and bring it into the dining room. It's an almost religious procession. Entering the dining room, Jimmy finds the table set with ma mère's good china. He smiles as he sets the tureen down in the middle of table and takes his seat.

Jenny and Robert, eager to share what they found begin to speak. "You won't believe what we found."

Jimmy, however, cuts them off with an up-raised hand. "There's plenty of time for that…for now, Pop wrote out the blessing we always said before we ate a bisque." He turns to Johnny. "Will you do the honors mon frère."

The others bow their heads as Johnny prays. "Bless us, Oh Lord, and these crawfish that we are about to enjoy. Bless those who caught them and those who prepared them and give crawfish to those who have none." He smiles and looks at the others, "Officer Duplantier." Before he continues… "Bonne santé, bon amis et mas famille, et le bon Dieu, who hears our prayer. Amen."

They take a moment to breathe in the enticing aroma, before bringing a spoonful to their mouths. Diz shakes his head. "I always thought that those who said your pop's crawfish bisque was the best ever were sale menteurs, but now I see they weren't dirty liars at all."

Margot takes another spoonful. "It is certainly wonderful, but I can't help thinking, that if you let a woman into the kitchen, it might even be better." She looks at the men around the table. "I mean a dash of estrogen makes everything better." She looks at Jenny. "Am I right, chère?"

Jenny looks up from toying with the crawfish heads. "Totally."

James smiles. "You are right, as always."

Margot smiles in return, but Johnny is more interested in watching Jenny take careful sips of the bisque. "Are you still thinking about heads? Remember, they are not heads, just shells stuffed with crawfish stuffing."

He picks up a head, expecting his daughter to follow. She does, reluctantly and watches her father scoop out a spoonful of stuffing. She does the same. He takes a bite and savors the moment. She isn't sure at all, so she takes a small nibble. Johnny watches as his daughter eyes get big and she finishes off the spoonful, going back to finish off the stuffing in the shell. Johnny hangs the empty shell on the rim of the bowl. "And that's how you eat crawfish bisque."

For a while, there is no sound in the dining room except the clinking of spoons against China bowls and soft yummy sounds…except from Johnny who is singing Jambalaya under his breath in between spoonsful…"Jambalaya, crawfish pie, file gumbo, cause tonight I'm going to see ma chère amio."

Finally, James puts his spoon down and pushes away from the table. He looks around the table, stopping at Johnny who is still eating and singing. Johnny stops with a spoonful halfway to his mouth and salutes Jimmy with it. "As good as Pop's…almost."

Margot shakes her head. "Well, I don't know about Pop's bisque, but this is the best I've ever had."

Daz pipes up. "Should we fix a bowl for Duplantier?"

James agrees. "I think he deserves it…What do you think Johnny?"

"I agree totally…besides, it has the added attraction of pissing good Sergeant Durel off."

James looks around the table. "All in favor say aye."

There are raucous 'ayes' from all parts of the table and Robert stands. "I'll fix it and bring it out to him." Robert walks to the kitchen and Jenny gets up to follow. "I'll help."

As they walk into the kitchen together, John calls out. "Don't forget what you're in there to do…and don't take a lot, we don't like him that much."

Jimmy smiles and shakes his head as Jenny and Robert hurry out of the kitchen with a plastic container filled with the crawfish bisque. Johnny makes a show, craning his neck to make sure they haven't taken much. "I have my eye on y'all."

James smiles wistfully. "You know, I can't help thinking how much Roger would have enjoyed this." He looks to John. "Why didn't we do this when Roger was alive?"

John looks at the floor. When he speaks it's in a soft rasp. "I don't know. Didn't have time? Why didn't we make time?" Then to Margot. "We should have made time."

Margot nods silently. James ends the uncomfortable silence. "Okay, so what did you guys find on the computer?"

Jenny and Robert come back inside, giggling. Margot nods her head in their direction. "I couldn't find anything, but Jenny and Robert did."

Robert defers to Jenny. "We found the file…buried in the folder for Uncle Roger's current class, inside another folder that was inside another folder…you get the idea…Anyway, we eventually found a folder labeled 'Lafitte.' Inside the folder we found a lot of files. Several of them were about Lafitte himself…legends…dates…War of 1812…and of course Lafitte's treasure."

Jenny continues. "There's stuff about Lafitte and the Chretiens and Chretien Point…Also, Lafitte and the Salliers."

Margot picks up on this. "Does it say anything about the brooch and cedar box?"

Jenny shakes her head. "It mentions the brooch, but not the box."

James is anxious to find something that will help them. "Anything else?"

Robert turns to Jenny, who turns the computer around so that everyone can see. "Here is a document labeled 'Notes.'"

She clicks on the document and a single spaced, bulleted list appears on the screen. "At the beginning, this list is just interesting facts from the other documents, but when you get near the bottom you find this...

- Bayou Contraband
- Prien Lake
- Chretien Point
- I think I'm being followed."

James frowns. "Being followed? Does it say anymore?"

Jenny, slowly, shakes her head, "Not about that, but the last entry is interesting. It says 'Lafitte – 167."

Margot sits back. "What can it mean?"

They all look perplexed until Diz has a thought. "Maybe Roger was in a hurry...and he left out a number...maybe it's a date."

Daz gets on board with this idea. "Sure...maybe it's a wine. 1967 is a great year for Chateau Lafitte Rothschild."

Diz can only shake his head while James rubs his forehead. "First, I agree it is a fine bottle of wine, but that's not it. Roger was too precise for that. If he said, 'Lafitte-167' that's what he meant."

He looks around the table. "Any ideas?

There is silence until the spark of an idea lights up Jenny's face. She picks up her phone and googles. The room is silent...waiting. Finally, she looks up and smiles. "I was right...Lafitte is a place...a town. On highway 167."

James thinks about this new information. "So, did Roger go there or was he killed before he could go?"

Johnny takes just a moment. "I don't think it matters. We need to go."

Diz and Daz look at each other and shout out. "Road trip."

Robert smiles at Jenny. "The limo will be gassed and ready to go."

Margot has a thought. "We should plan on staying overnight in New Orleans."

Jenny, ever the organizer, nods. "Right, how many rooms will we need."

She looks at Robert, but Johnny has his own idea. "Well, Jenny and Margot can share a room, Diz and Daz, and James and me."

He looks pointedly at Robert, who squirms, just a bit. Daz waves him off and looks to Diz, who gives him a barely perceptible nod. "We'll take care of the New Orleans details."

He and Diz can't help but chuckle and say together. "We know a guy."

Vincent steps aboard the Palermo at precisely 5:30 AM. He believes in a strict regimen and since becoming captain of the Palermo, this is when his day begins. Nick now has three boats, and he spends most days in the office which is fine with Vincent. As long as he delivers the fish, Nick doesn't bother him and this leaves him time to do, precisely, what he wants to do...find Lafitte's treasure.

After years of secretly charting wrecks, figuring out current patterns and learning all about salvaging sunken ships, Vincent is ready. He looks up at the cloudless sky as it turns from red to blue. This has been a strangely quiet hurricane season. The water is still, glassy and the gulf floor should be clear and current free ...perfect for what he has planned. His scuba gear is safely on board and his tanks full. Finally, this could be the day when he begins to stand on his two feet.

He appreciates everything Nick has done for him, but Vincent knows he's no fisherman. He was meant for something bigger. Nick has no vision...his whole life is fish...and Joey and Victoria. Nick doesn't understand that he wants more. Vincent doesn't want to stink from sweat and fish. He wants to be his own man. Vincent takes a deep breath, relishing the sensation ...the rush he feels. This is the day he quietly disappears...vanishes into the vast depths of the Gulf of Mexico. He is unstoppable.

Then the unthinkable happens. Vincent hears the sound of footsteps on the dock. Footsteps that Vincent recognizes all too well. He sees Nick and Joey walking toward the boat, waving to him. The last thing he expected...or wanted. He waves back and helps them aboard. Nick gratefully takes his hand. "Thanks, Vincenzo."

He in turn reaches back to help Joey. "Thanks, dad. Hey there, Vinnie."

Vincent puts on a smile to mask his frustration. They are not supposed to be here. "Hey, Short Round."

Joey makes a face. "I'm not short anymore."

Vincent laughs. "Shorter than me."

Joey cocks his eyebrow. "Yeah, but I'm smarter and better looking."

Vincent smirks. "Right...anyway, I thought you were down at FU."

Joey is starting to get just a little pissed off. "That's UF."

Nick tries to smooth things over. *"Joey's up here doing research for his dissertation. He's almost Dr. Joseph Disparte."*

It's a stare down between Joey and Vincent. Vincent tries to hold the look but, finally, has to look away. *"Anyway, you guys just caught me. I was ready to take off."*

Nick smiles, trying to recapture some of their old camaraderie. *"We thought we'd tag along...just like the old days."*

This is not what Vincent wants to hear. He sees the treasure slipping through his fingers. He watches them get settled. Nicks looks up. *"Why don't we head to that place I took you, the first time we went out."*

Vincent thinks for a moment and nods. *"Whatever you say, boss."*

As the Palermo pulls away from the dock, Joey closes his eyes for some much-needed rest, while Nick takes out his copy of Benjamin Percy's 'Red Moon' and at once becomes immersed in this strange tale of werewolves in modern history.

Vincent stares out at the gulf as they slice through the water...a plan beginning to form. This might work after all. The disappearance of a father and son is the story everyone will be talking about. He will be all but forgotten.

How will he manage it? He sees a grappling hook on the deck, and he knows there's a speargun with his scuba gear. Vincent will have to catch Joey by surprise and take care of Nick quickly. He regrets what he's about to do, but they have forced him into this. Vincent clutches the wheel and is almost in a trance as they rush to their fate.

As they near the spot where he first learned about the treasure, Vincent looks back at Joey and Nick, both napping. He silently grabs the speargun and picks up the grappling hook. He has to act fast before he loses his nerve. He swings the hook, catching Joey just below his left temple impaling his skull. He turns, almost in a trance, and fires the speargun at Nick, hitting him in the chest. Nick opens his eyes and stares at Vincent in total disbelief before collapsing on the deck.

Vincent hauls the bodies to the railing and dumps them in the gulf. As the bodies disappear into the crystal-clear waters of the gulf, he is already thinking about the small Mexican village of Dzilam de Bravo...the legendary pirate...and the fabled treasure, his obsession.

114

Chapter XI

"And he was a pirate after all."

Jimmy

As usual James is up at 5:30. It'll take at least three and a half hours to get to Lafitte and they have be on the road no later than 7:00. That won't be a problem for anybody but John. How he can sleep the day away James can only imagine, but John needs to be up now. This could be fun after all. He remembers how Pop used to do it. He quietly opens Johnny's door, throws back Johnny's covers and shouts in his loudest voice. "Wakey, wakey, eggs and bakey!"

Johnny sits bolt upright in his bed, a look of confusion and terror on his face. Jimmy had forgotten that Johnny had been shot just a couple of days ago and maybe he should have been more considerate. He lowers his voice a dozen decibels. "Get dressed. We're leaving in an hour."

He gets a grunt from Johnny, and satisfied, he moves from room to room making sure that his performance had awakened Margot and Jenny. After closing Jenny's door, he has an afterthought and opens it again. "Make sure Robert will be on time." He closes the door and then opens it once again. "A half hour if he wants breakfast."

As he sees it, he's responsible for keeping this group on track. For the first time they are on Roger's path. "What could Roger have expected to find in Lafitte?" James had always considered Lafitte tourist trap. A kind of like a year-round version of Lake Charles' Pirate Festival. Was Roger just grasping at straws? "I guess we'll find out."

Jimmy makes coffee and puts out croissants and fruit. Done, he pours a cup of coffee and leans against the sink as everyone begins to straggle in. Robert is the first to arrive completely put together, not a hair out of place. "Good morning, Robert."

Robert smiles. "Good morning, sir. My father sends his regards."

Jimmy smiles back. "Please send my regards back to your father."

He points to the food. "Please help yourself and if you wouldn't mind, could you take coffee and a plate to Officer Duplantier, and tell him where we are going. Wouldn't want him to get lost."

Robert laughs. "Will do...by the way the car is all gassed up and I have the route planned."

Robert goes about getting coffee for Duplantier. James watches, fondly. "Thank you, Robert. I am very grateful you are here. If there is anything you need, just ask."

Robert nods and coffee cup in hand heads for the door, pauses and turns back. "Well sir, there is one thing," He lowers his voice. "Could you please put in a good word with your brother...I don't think he likes me very much."

James throws his head back and laughs a good laugh. Wiping the tears away he shakes his head. "Son, he likes you...he doesn't want to like you...but take my word. He likes you fine."

Robert considers this and finally smiles and nods, taking the coffee out to Officer Duplantier. James doesn't have long to wait for the others. First Jenny, then Margot and finally Johnny. They all come in silently and James waits for them to get food and coffee. As he's about to speak, Robert returns with Diz and Daz in tow. "Look who I found."

Diz glares at Robert. "Kid's taken on our job."

Daz shrugs. "Well, at least, Duplantier is well fed and watered."

James clears his voice. "Well, now that you're all here...plates full and coffee sugared and blowed, as Pop would say. I thought we should discuss the plan for the day." They all grunt and continue to eat and sip coffee.

James takes this as agreement and continues. "We need to figure out why Roger was going to Lafitte."

Eyes half shut, John mumbles around a mouthful of croissant. "I vote 'wild goose chase.'"

Margot shakes her head. "I don't think it is a wild goose chase, I mean, I think this is the trail Roger wants us to follow."

James considers this. "Possibly...probably...I hope it is, but between now and the time we get to Lafitte we need to find out all the information we can about Lafitte...both the town and pirate."

He looks at Robert. "Before we go, I think we should acknowledge the debt we owe to Robert." He lifts his coffee cup to Robert. "We would be up the...bayou without you."

They all lift their cups. Diz and Daz together. "To Robert…long may he wave." Jenny kisses him on the cheek, while Margot silently lifts her cup and smiles. James turns to see John glaring at Robert. Johnny feels his big brother's look and raises his cup. "To Robert."

Robert looks at both brothers and bows slightly. "Thanks, y'all. I wouldn't be anywhere else."

There is a brief pause. Then, James checks the time. "We leave in five."

Antoine

An hour later, Antoine pulls up in front of the Chretien house. He's finishing up a call and notices that Duplantier isn't there. He sees the Prius, Fusion, and Corvette, but no limo. He rubs his forehead. "Great, where are these people now."

Antoine sits absolutely still, then keys the radio. "Duplantier… Duplantier, I need you to check in."

He gets nothing back but static. "Duplantier, I need you to check in…immediately."

Static…He tries a different way. "Dispatch, this is Sergeant Durel. Come in."

Nothing. "Dispatch…is anybody there?'

Nothing. Antoine shakes his head. "For God's sake will somebody answer me."

Nothing…finally. "Sorry, Sarge…I was in the can."

Antoine looks heavenward. "Son, I don't need to know where you were…I don't want to know where you were. I just need some information."

"Right, Sergeant, how can I help?"

Many things pass through Antoine's mind, but he settles on…"We can start with…answering the damn radio when I call…but I really need to know if you've heard from Duplantier."

"Yes, sir, he called in about an hour ago and said he was following Ms. Sallier and the Chretiens to Lafitte,"

Antoine sits up at this revelation. "Lafitte?...There's nothing in Lafitte…Did he say why they were going to Lafitte?...Never mind, I'll take care of it…Out."

Antoine takes out his phone and punches in a number. He closes his eyes while he waits for Duplantier to answer. After six rings a happy Duplantier answers. "Hellooo."

117

For a moment Antoine stares at his cell phone. "Officer Duplantier...this is Sergeant Durel."

Silence on the other end. Antoine can only imagine Duplantier sitting up at attention. "Yes, sir, sergeant sir."

Antoine feels sorry for Duplantier...he really does. "Officer, where are you right now?...and please don't say in your car."

A long pause, Officer Duplantier tries to come up with an answer that won't get him into more trouble. "On highway 10 about four and a half miles west of Lafayette."

"Very good, Duplantier...succinct and informative. I understand you're on your way to Lafitte. Do you have any idea why?"

"Well, sergeant, the answer is yes...and no."

Antoine was afraid of this, but Duplantier continues. "I am now in Lafayette, turning onto the road to Lafitte because I'm following Ms. Sallier to make sure she's all right and the Chretiens to find out what they're up to. However, I have no idea why we're going to Lafitte."

Antoine chuckles. "Okay how many are on this...road trip?"

"All of them, sir."

"All of them?"

Duplantier wants to be clear. "Yes, sir, all seven of them."

"But you have no idea why...put yourself in their shoes, Duplantier. Why would you go to Lafitte?"

Dead silence for almost a minute. "Well Sergeant, I have always wanted to go there myself...I'm interested in Jean Lafitte, and I'd like to find out more about him."

"That makes sense to me Officer Duplantier. They are on a fact-finding mission...Good job, officer."

Duplantier revels in this compliment, but Antoine won't let him off that easily.

"You do realize that you still have a job to do. You can't just sit in your car...I want you to hear what they hear and see what they see."

"But then I'll blow my cover."

Now it's Antoine's turn to be confused. "Cover? You have no cover. They know you're there. They have always known you're there...they bring you treats."

Duplantier considers this. "You're right, sarge. I'll stick to them like glue."

"That's exactly what I want...but Duplantier I want you to report in every half hour...report to me directly. Every half hour, do you understand?

He can almost see Duplantier saluting. "Yes, sir, I understand perfectly."

Antoine disconnects. He's a very happy man. Let them search for buried treasure as much as they like. It will keep them entertained while he does the real work. While he answers the real question. "Who killed Roger Chretien?"

Margot

Margot sits in the back of the limo next to James and John, across from Diz and Daz...both pair, heads together speaking intently about...something. Robert and Jenny are in the front seat, one piloting them on this journey of discovery, the other searching the internet for some clue. She doesn't know what they will find in Lafitte but she, at last, is following Roger's path. She reaches for her Coach Hobo bag and feels the bulky shape of the small cedar box inside. Is there some link between the box, brooch, and Roger's death? If so, what?

Margot's reverie is interrupted when a very agitated Jenny turns in her seat. "Hey, did you know what a horrible person Lafitte was. He was despicable...he stole...raped...pillaged." She refers to her phone, "He robbed slave ships of their cargo...and did he return them to their homes...did he set them free?" She looks at them in outrage. "No, he sold them and kept the money."

She glares at her father. "I thought you said he was a hero."

Johnny finally comes up with, "He helped us win the Battle of New Orleans against the British."

Jenny's glare softens. "Well, okay there is that."

Johnny tries to take it to the next step. "And he was a pirate after all."

Jenny erupts all over again. "You think that excuses his behavior."

Johnny meekly shakes his head and Jenny continue the glare out her window. Jimmy has never seen Jenny explode like that and he doesn't ever want to experience it again. He turns to the others. "Did anybody else find out any information?"

Silence until Jenny slowly raises her hand. "There's talk that Jean Lafitte had a journal."

John exchanges looks with his brother, afraid to say anything. "And?"

"And …There some debate over whether it's real or not." She looks up from her phone and shrugs. "I mean, it has Lafitte dying…in the 1850's…in Alton, Illinois."

Johnny can't contain himself. "Alton, Illinois? He… literally… wouldn't be caught dead in Alton, Illinois."

Margot interrupts. "John, we need to keep an open mind…I have a feeling we will find out something important in Lafitte. Anyway, I hope so."

Margot sits back and closes her eyes. She needs to find out something that will help explain Roger's death. She must have dozed, because the next thing she knows Robert is calling out as the limo passes 'Welcome to Lafitte Louisiana, Population 1,014.' "We have arrived. Where do you want to go first?"

Jenny turns around to face the others. "I think we should start at the visitors center…it's up here on Jean Lafitte Boulevard across from the Jean Lafitte Historical Park."

Margot, craning her neck, tries to take it all in. She has a very good feeling about this. Robert turns right onto Jean Lafitte and left into the parking lot. Duplantier pulls into the spot next to theirs.

They all pile out of the limo and stretch their backs. James looks around. "Anybody see coffee? I could use a cup right about now."

John shrugs. "Maybe inside."

They walk up the path to the front door as Duplantier shows up beside them. James raises one eyebrow. "Can we help you, Officer Duplantier?"

Duplantier looks down at the ground, embarrassed. "Sergeant Durel said I should follow you…see what you see…hear what you hear."

James and John look at each other. John begins to smile. "You mean spy on us."

Duplantier would like to deny it but knows he can't. "Well, yes sir, in a manner of speaking…with your permission."

James looks at Margot, who crosses her eyes, briefly, and back to Duplantier. "In a matter of speaking and with our permission? And what would you do if we said 'no?'"

Duplantier tries to come up with an answer, but James waves him off. "Never mind, officer, you are most welcome to join us."

He gestures for Duplantier to proceed them through the door. He walks through the door holding it open for the others to follow. They all congregate around the front desk. The man behind the desk does not even acknowledge their existence. Unsure how to begin, Margot takes a shot. "Excuse me…" Still no response so Margot tries again. "We're trying to find out some information about Jean Lafitte."

The clerk stops what he is doing and looks up at the big sign over his desk: JEAN LAFITTE HISTORICAL PARK INFORMATION DESK and back at Margot. If eyes could say "DUH" his would say it… very sarcastically. Margot pushes on. "Specifically, we're looking for information on his treasure and his journal."

The clerk looks up and huffs. All big, Duplantier steps forward and flashes his badge. This is obviously unnecessary since he is, after all, wearing his uniform. The clerk in clearly unimpressed.

"Aisle 3…on the left…halfway down."

Duplantier puffs out his chest…another thorny problem taken care of by the LCPD. They all head to aisle three and look on the left about halfway down and begin paging through books. Johnny holds up a book. "Found the 'Alton, Illinois' journal."

James doesn't look up. "Anything worthwhile?"

John continues flipping pages. "His brother Pierre may or may not have had a wooden leg."

Jenny shakes her head and looks at Robert. "We found out more in fifteen minutes on the internet."

James looks up and down the aisle. "Well let's get the journal and some stuff about the treasure…it may prove useful."

John acknowledges the remote possibility and walks to the clerk to pay. Margot stares at the books in front of her, frustrated beyond belief.

"There's got to be something, somewhere in this town, that's useful."

Diz puts his arm around Margot. "Yeah, but where?"

Johnny finishes paying for the books, and they all follow him out the door. "Well, that was a bust."

As they pass a beautifully tended garden, an African American man, with shears in his hand, stands up. His age…somewhere between fifty and ninety. "Pardon me, folks." Everyone turns and looks at him.

The man puts down the shears and brushes dirt from his hands. "Y'all looking for information on Jean Lafitte?"

Margot looks to the others and then back to the man. "Well, yes, sir, we are."

The man looks from the visitor's center and back to them. "And I take it, you didn't find much there."

Margot shakes her head and smiles. "Not really, no."

The man extends his hand. "I'm Theodore, by the way."

Margot steps forward and takes his hand. "It's a pleasure Theodore. I'm Margot. She gestures to the rest of the group. "This is Officer Duplantier, Diz and Daz, Jenny and Robert, and James and John."

Theodore clears his throat. "There's an elderly woman, and I mean a hundred or so, living on the edge of town. Talk is she's a relative of Jean Lafitte...Zora something...niece, probably great niece or great great...anyway you might try there."

They all perk up at that, but Theodore isn't finished. "I'd be careful though...she doesn't cotton much to strangers."

John narrows his eyes. "And how do we find this...person?"

Theodore scratches his head. "Well, you take this road...Jean Lafitte... East about three miles...when it turns into a dirt road, follow that a couple more miles and there it is...at the end of the road...you can't miss it...a big Keep Out sign right in front."

Margot looks to the others and back to Theodore. "Can we say you sent us?"

Theodore thinks hard about that. "You can try...we don't always see eye to eye...you might wind up with a load of buckshot."

Glances all around, finally, Margot replies. "Well...okay. Thank you very much, Theodore."

The others mumble. "Yes, thank you." "We're so grateful." And such, as they make their way to the car. Theodore nods, picks up his shears and gets back to work.

When they are all safely inside, Robert backs out and with Duplantier following heads back to Jean Lafitte Boulevard. At the crossroads, Robert pauses, both brothers pointing in different directions. Jenny closes her eyes and in a soft voice says just one word. "East." Robert turns left.

John leans forward. "Did we learn anything there?"

Diz rubs his eyes. "We learned that we might learn something...if we can avoid being shot."

This thought hangs in the air, while the limo moves too fast and too slow at the same time, toward their destination, until they reach the end of the road and a modest cabin behind the 'Keep Out' sign. Robert comes to a stop and turns off the engine, as Duplantier pulls up next to him. Complete silence. Everyone silently dares the others to get out first.

Daz clears his throat. "Rock, paper, scissors?"

For just a moment, James actually considers this solution, but shakes his head. "No, but we need to figure out what we want to ask."

Margot speaks up. "Maybe the journal...and about the brooch and cedar box." James reaches for the door handle. Duplantier, weighing all the possibilities, decides to remain in the squad car. John glares at him as they pile out of the limo.

An old, weathered woman come out onto the front porch. They hear the unmistakable sound of a shotgun being cocked. Zora stands her ground. "Can't y'all read?"

John, ever the mediator steps forward raising his hands. "Yes ma'am, we can. We just want a little information."

"The only information you need is back the way you came."

"We'd just like to ask a couple of questions about Jean Lafitte."

Just a glare and John takes a step back. "It's very important."

Still the glare. John throws a Hail Mary. "Theodore sent us?"

The only response is the raising of the shot gun to her shoulder. John backs off and mumbles under his breath. "Alrighty, then."

It's a stand off until Margot steps forward. "I realize this is an imposition, but someone very close to us has been murdered and we think it might have something to do with Jean Lafitte and his treasure."

The gun stays up and Zora talks around it. "You know how many yokels I've had to run off because of 'Jean Lafitte and his treasure'?"

Margot continues. "I'm sorry, please let me introduce myself. I'm Marguerite Sallier...and these gentlemen are James and John Chretien."

A long pause, finally Zora, lowers the shotgun ever so slightly.

"Sallier and Chretien...together?" Margot, James, and John nod.

Zora squints. "Who got himself killed, Sallier or Chretien?"

James steps forward. "My brother, Roger Chretien."

Zora raises the shotgun. "Chretien...figures. Chretiens always getting into trouble."

She turns to Margot, finally lowering the shotgun. "Okay, missy, speak your piece."

Margot takes the cedar box out of her bag and holds it up. "I've got this brooch and cedar box, that was given to my great, great, great grandmother by Jean Lafitte, and we were wondering…"

Zora cuts her off. "Come." She turns abruptly and walks back into her cabin. Calling over her shoulder. "Just Sallier."

Margot looks at her companions, then follows Zora into the cabin. She enters the dim room and while her eyes adjust, Zora closes the door behind her. Startled, she watches the old woman pass her and take her seat in an ancient rocking chair. The chair groans with every rock as Zora gestures to the chair beside her.

As Margot takes her seat, Zora holds out her hand. Margot, reluctantly, hands the box over to her. The old woman stares at the box before opening it and taking out the brooch. Zora gently feels the indentation on the side of the brooch and traces the crack with her finger.

Finally, Zora stops rocking and turns to Margot. "Ask your questions."

Sitting there, Margot doesn't know where to begin. "When my…when Roger saw this for the first time, he got excited. He didn't say much, but he began looking for information about Lafitte's treasure…even going out into Contraband Bayou. Three weeks later he was dead. There must be a connection."

Zora looks intently at the box while she rocks. "You're right. This box got your friend killed." She puts the box on the table next to her and gets up. Both the rocking chair and her back creaking. She disappears into the recesses of the cabin and returns with an armful of books. "These are Uncle Jean's journals."

Margot leans forward with wonder. "So, they do exist."

Zola nods, but Margot's brow furrows. "So, he really died in Illinois?"

The old woman makes a rude noise and shakes her head. "Non." She searches for the right book. "There are things you need to know about my uncle."

She finds the book she wants and thumbs through it until she finds the right section. "Premier, my uncle trusted women far more than men. So, he left clues with the two women he trusted most…your great, great, great grandmother and the mistress of Chretien Point. I'm sure it never occurred to him that the two families would meet."

She looks up at Margot. "Et seconde, he had a fascination with puzzle boxes."

Margot stares at Zola. "Puzzle boxes?"

"Mais oui, they were all the rage in Paris."

Zora picks up the box and with three deft moves of her arthritic fingers, a small drawer pops open revealing a neatly folded piece of paper. The old woman takes the paper out of the drawer, unfolds it and after examining it hands it Margot. There are two lines.

"Near the muddy banks Christians gather." and "Regarde vers l'nterieur ou ils demeurent."

Margot looks up. "But what does it mean?"

Zola hands the box back to Margot. "Qui, ma chère, est votre problème."

She stands and ushers Margot to the door. As they walk onto the front porch, Zora's gaze falls upon Robert. She points a bony finger at him. Robert's eyes dart back and forth, finally, pointing to himself. "Me?"

"Qui d'autre?"

Suddenly, Robert becomes very uncomfortable. The words barely make it out of his mouth. "Robert…Robert Louragan."

One eyebrow on her weathered face rises. "Why are you here, Monsieur Louragan?"

Robert shifts his gaze to Jenny. Zora smiles in understanding. "Ah, I see, Louragan and Chretien together again."

Confused Robert looks at Jenny and then back to the old woman. "Together again? What do you mean?"

"For that you should ask your father."

Robert is even more confused. "What does my father…you know my father?"

Zora cocks her head. "We have met…Now I must say au revoir…to the Salliers, Chretiens and the Louragans." She looks at Diz and Daz, and Duplantier standing by his squad car and waves her hand. "Et, les autres…I must go now, it is time for my dodo."

They all look at each other, confused. Zola shakes her head. "Nap."

She disappears into the cabin. The rest just stand around, unsure what to do next. James huffs. "Well, I guess this is us…leaving." He turns to get back in the limo. The others stand waiting for…something.

Finally, John ushers them to the cars turning to Robert. "How far to New Orleans?"

Robert, his mind elsewhere, takes a moment before answering. "Thirty miles or so...forty, forty-five minutes."

Johnny shakes his head like he's just waking up. "Anybody feel the need for coffee."

They all raise their hands. "Robert, if you'd be so kind...find us some coffee." Robert nods and opens the door for Jenny, runs around to the driver's side, and gets behind the wheel. When everybody is buckled up, he puts the limo in drive and heads for New Orleans...by way of coffee...trying to digest what he just heard.

Robert

Robert finds himself driving the limo on Highway 90 and isn't exactly sure how he got there. He must have stopped for coffee because they all have it...and it's still hot. Jenny is beside him and he hears conversations taking place in the backseat.

"Near muddy banks Christians gather." "What can that possibly mean?" "Don't get me started on the French." "Jenny can take care of that."

That just washes over him. It's just white noise...he keeps seeing a bony finger pointing at him and hearing the words. "Louragan and Chretien together again."...and what did the old woman mean by... "You should ask your father?" Ask him about what?

Robert's eyes have gotten are all squinty and his brows so furrowed there's not enough room for a dime between them. He slowly realizes he has a death grip on the steering wheel. He takes in a deep breath and slowly lets it out, trying to relax, peeling his fingers from the steering wheel. His mind though is still going a mile a minute. He's not naïve. He's grown up in Louisiana. He knows the history...he knows the present. His father has instilled a pride...a pride in rising above the past and focusing on the future. Never...absolutely never...forgetting the past.

He knows his ancestors were kidnapped from Africa and sold into slavery. He knows there are those who still see him as less than. Those who have not had the education he has had...not had the opportunities that he has had and don't have the future he has. Still, his family was owned by someone else's family. He glances in the rear-view mirror...was that family the Chretiens?

126

He is suddenly very conscious of driving them around in limo…like a…servant. 'Find us some coffee.' Another 'S' word immediately comes to mind, but he pushes it down. And what of his father? The woman had said, "You should ask your father."

Ask my father about what? Is it some deep, dark secret, he's ashamed to tell me? Are we somehow related to the Chretiens? Is that what he meant, at the mortuary, when he told the Chretiens, 'We are family?' He never tried to discourage me from pursuing Jenny. In fact, quite the opposite. He encouraged it…gave me advise on how to win her heart.

He turns and looks at Jenny and can't help wondering if she sees him in a different light. Did the old lady's words have the same impact on her? Did she already know? Is that why her father hates me?

He must look at it logically…find out the truth. He looks ahead and tries to focus on driving…focus on what's real. Still, he can't help wondering.

Jenny

Jenny is absorbed in trying to decipher the message from the box. This shouldn't be difficult, but she is distracted. She's never seen Robert like this. At first, she thought he was just concentrating on driving…but that's not it. He hasn't looked at her…not once since they got in the car.

She instinctively takes his hand. He doesn't pull it away, but it's stiff, like he doesn't want to be touched. By her…or just generally? What has changed? Was it something she said? Someone else? Then it clicks…the old woman pointing her finger at him. What did the woman say? "Louragan and Chretien together again." What did she mean? "Together again."

The answer comes as a jolt. Is it possible? Could Robert's ancestors have been at Chretien Point? A horrible thought. Did her ancestors own his ancestors? Jenny is an intelligent girl. She knows her history. She marches in all the right marches. She has a 'Black Lives Matter' tee-shirt at home, but right now she knows it's not enough. She never thought about her family actually owning slaves. She glances over her shoulder at her father…at her uncle. Not once have they ever talked about this…with her anyway. Do they ever talk about it…do they ever think about it?

127

There's some commotion in the back seat and Diz leans forward and taps Robert on the shoulder. "Robert, up here you're going to want to take the Camp Street exit. Stay on Camp until you get to Gravier make a right. We're going to Chez Gray it'll be on your right. If you get to Magazine, you've gone too far."

Robert stares ahead and mumbles. "Got it."

Jenny glances at Robert and squeezes his hand. He turns and squeezes her hand giving her a tight smile. She holds on, tightly. Would they ever be okay again?

Diz and Daz

Diz and Daz lead the pack into the opulent lobby of Chez Gray, all wheeling their overnight bags...some wheels squeakier than others. Margot, Jimmy, and Johnny enter right behind Diz and Daz, pausing to take in the sophisticated yet intimate ambience. Jenny and Robert follow, tentatively holding hands and speaking in hushed tones. Bringing up the rear is Officer Duplantier, who clearly feels out of place.

Standing in front of the main desk is Adrienne Gray, a tall, elegant African American woman with the most beautiful emerald green eyes. She embraces Diz and Daz...how do they know her?... and turns to the others. "Welcome to Chez Gray."

Duplantier can't take his eyes off her...she is the most beautiful woman he has ever seen. "I am Adrienne Gray, the owner, general manager, and ma mère, of this establishment. I've taken the liberty of assigning rooms on our 'Executive Floor.' I hope you will be comfortable."

She begins handing out key cards. First to Diz and Daz...then to James and John. She envelopes their hands in hers. "I am so sorry for your loss."

She turns to Margot and Jenny embracing them both in turn. "I am here if you need me." Finally, to Robert and Officer Duplantier.

She looks at Robert, then at Jenny and raises one eyebrow. Her gaze wanders to Johnny and back to Jenny. "Ton père?" After a quick look at her father, Jenny nods and Adrienne, looking between Jenny and Robert, shrugs in understanding. "Quelle dommage."

Adrienne turns her attention to Officer Duplantier, who still can't meet her gaze. She glides to him and takes both his hands in hers, kissing him on both cheeks. "Thank you for your service, Officer Duplantier."

There is a long moment before Duplantier can look her in the eye and when he does, he is turned to stone like a hapless sailor in the presence of Medusa. Robert nudges him and finally he manages to mumble: "Thank you."

Adrienne smiles sweetly at Duplantier before turning to include the rest. "I have taken the liberty of making a reservation at our rooftop restaurant, Gravier by the Seine at 7:30. Our chef, Francois Ruffin, specializes in Nouvelle Cajun cuisine and will take very good care of you."

She turns her gaze to Duplantier once more. "But I hope to join you later for a drink."

Officer Duplantier is mesmerized by the sight of her floating across the lobby. After she is gone, Diz and Daz turn to the rest. Daz smiles. "And that, my friends, is Adrienne Gray."

James looks at them with newfound respect. "How do you know her?" Diz shrugs. "She's a guy we know."

"A guy?" James shakes his head. "Definitely not a guy."

Margot and Jenny share a look and roll their eyes. Margot breaks the spell. "Better get to our rooms. Don't want to be late for dinner."

Johnny

Johnny takes the elevator to the top floor depositing him in the lobby of Gravier by the Seine. The maître d', an attractive young woman named Sandy, according to her name tag, is the first to greet him. Johnny is about to speak when Sandy ushers him to a table, set for eight, in the center of room. "Good evening, Mr. Chretien, your table is ready."

Johnny sits and a waiter, he can't see if it's Tod or Tom, places a napkin on his lap and waits for instructions. "Would you like anything while you wait for the others?"

Johnny is about to shake his head, when he reconsiders, clearing his throat. "Water, please." He thinks for a moment before gesturing to the entire table. "All around...the others will be here shortly." Tod or Tom, he still can't tell, nods, and hurries off.

Margot is next, pausing at the front desk before Sandy shows her to the table. As soon as she sits...she barely has time to say, "This is lovely," before a group of servers descend on the table with goblets of water, baskets of freshly baked bread, butter, tapenade, and a charcuterie board. As fast as the whirlwind appears it dissipates just as quickly.

Even Margot is out of breath when she turns to John. "My." Johnny nods in agreement. "My, indeed." He offers a crudité with pâtè du foie gras to Margot before preparing one for himself. He pauses mid chew. "This is amazing." Margot agrees as she helps herself to a cracker with gorgonzola cheese. "It certainly is."

Sandy approaches this time with Jenny, Robert, and Officer Duplantier in tow. As they sit a flock of servers descend on them placing napkins in their laps, before disappearing into the kitchen. Jenny looks to Margot. "My." Margot agrees. "That's what I said."

Johnny takes another bite, looking at Robert and Duplantier. "So, how's your room?" Robert barely looks at him. "Nice."

John wonders what's up with Robert when Duplantier begins to speak. "It's great. I've never been in a place like this before. Everything is perfect...and that Miss Gray...isn't she wonderful? I mean you don't just meet people like that all the time."

John hasn't heard that much from Duplantier...ever. He begins to speak but stops...he looks at Officer Duplantier like he's seeing him for the first time. "Uh...Officer Duplantier...what are you called when you're not...you know...being Officer Duplantier?"

Duplantier stops with a buttered piece of bread halfway to his mouth. He grins. "Howard...my name is Howard."

John smiles back and puts out his hand. "Howard...I'm John."

Duplantier is momentarily confused but takes John's outstretched hand. "I know."

Johnny is about to speak when James appears. He smiles and sits before turning to John. As he begins to speak John holds up his hand and gestures to Duplantier. "James, this is Howard."

At first, James doesn't know what he's talking about...then he smiles and extends his hand. "Good evening, Howard...I'm James."

Duplantier is more confused than ever but shakes James' hand. He's about to speak when Diz and Daz arrive, following Sandy. When they reach the table, Diz faces the maître d'. "Thank you, Sandy."

Daz bows to the ladies. "Good evening, ladies...Good evening, gentlemen."

Diz grins at Duplantier. "Hey, Howard." Howard waves. "Hey, back."

Diz and Daz sit, but there is no flurry of activity. One lone man appears tableside. He grins at Diz and Daz. "Welcome, I am François Ruffin, and this is Gravier by the Seine. I'm always happy to share with special friends, what the Good Lord has blessed me with. With your permission, I have taken the liberty of preparing a special dinner for you."

Daz rubs his hands. "What have you got for us, François?" François grins at him. "I thought we'd start with petite tarte aux ecrevisses, cream of jambalaya soup with andouille…"

Diz turns to the others. "So far, we have jambalaya, crawfish pie…file gumbo?

François chuckles and shakes his head. "For the entrée I thought I'd prepare a pan seared trout with crab reduction, on a bed of polenta aux champignon, and petits pois, paired with a bottle of Chateauneuf du Pape, 2016."

James and John look at each other like they've died and gone to heaven. François goes on. "For dessert I thought we'd have Banana's Foster with Café Brûlot to end."

As he finishes, François takes a step back allowing the wait staff to serve the first course. John cuts a small wedge from the tart. From the instant he cuts into the flakey crust to the moment he puts the fork into his mouth, Johnny knows he has been transported to another time, another place.

Very little talking takes place as one dish is more exquisite than the last. Finally, the table is cleared to make room for dessert. John takes the cedar box and note out of his pocket and places them on the table. After a moment he speaks. "I think we all agree that the first part, 'Near the muddy banks, Christians gather.' Refers to Chretien Point. While the second part seems to say that whatever we are looking for will be found in the house itself."

James huffs. "That's a problem right there. I mean, what do we do? March up to the front door and announce we're searching for something that may have been left by Jean Lafitte?"

John replies, "I don't know, maybe."

This conversation is interrupted by the servers bringing eight chilled silver dessert dishes filled with ice cream and placing them on the table. Duplantier is about to say, 'They have one too many,' when a second server places another chair next to him. He's beginning to get that tingly feeling when Adrienne places her hands on his shoulder.

Duplantier struggles to stand, but Adrienne gently pushes him down into his seat. She sits next to him and speaks with that voice that sends the quivers up and down his spine. "I told you I'd be back later, Cher."

Duplantier is saved from becoming a puddle on the floor by the arrival of Bananas Foster and Café Brûlot. François joins them and the next twenty minutes is devoted to pleasant conversation, that is only interrupted when both Adrienne and François are called away. The rest are unwilling or unable to move.

Finally, John rises. "We won't solve anything here. We need to go to Chretien Point...I don't know how, but we'll find our answers there."

They all agree, and Daz and Diz get up. James gets to his feet and holds out his hand. "Thank you, this was incredible."

Both Diz and Daz smile at this. As they walk to the elevator James raises his voice. "Any other friends, we can meet."

Diz grins over his shoulder. "A few."

James laughs. Robert gets up from the table. "Good night. I'll see y'all in the morning."

Robert walks off with Howard, formerly known as Officer Duplantier, trailing after. Jenny is about to follow when John holds her back. "What's going on with Robert? He doesn't seem himself." He gets a knowing look. "Did you two have a fight?"

Jenny kisses her father on the cheek. "I love you, Daddy, but you really don't get it." Jenny begins to walk to the elevator, but after a few steps, stops and turns back. "We need to talk, daddy...soon."

Vincent Drago sits outside Chez Gray in a blacked-out Chevy Suburban...waiting. He thinks back to the day in the gulf when he died with Joey and Nick. It must have been so sad for Victoria. So sad it's almost laughable. Everyone thought it was the end when, in reality, it was the beginning...for him anyway. That was the day his life changed...his life began.

Nick and Joey had sacrificed their lives for him, and he would always be grateful for that. They lacked his vision...his purpose in life. Their life was fish, but he had set a wider net. He thanks the Virgin every day that they came aboard the Palermo when they did. At first, he thought it was a disaster, but she laid out the plan so vividly before him. Some people had to be sacrificed for the greater good.

He had made it to shore with nothing, but he learned many things after his death. First, how easy it is to steal from people...they're so stupid they practically give whatever you desire. Second that Lafitte's treasure is not on the bottom of the Gulf of Mexico, but in Louisiana...Southern Louisiana.

He remembers when he discovered there might be a connection between Laffite, the Salliers and the Chretiens. Imagine the synergy he felt when he discovered a Chretien, and a Sallier were actually following the same path. He was perfectly willing to give Roger Chretien a chance, but when he found out about the brooch and cedar box it was time to take control back.

Vincent had confronted Roger Chretien in the bayou, but he was a fool and couldn't see the bigger picture. Chretien couldn't see that the treasure was destined for him, belonged to him by right and so Chretien had to go.

He looked for the evidence at Chretien's home and Sallier's home, then at Chretien's office but it was no good. Then the idiot brothers got involved. Looking back, it was a mistake to shoot the brother. That just brought out the police and he's been playing hide and seek ever since.

Then the Virgin showed him this was part of a bigger plan. All he had to do was lie low and let all the pawns do the leg work...and here he was with the treasure almost in his hands. By this time tomorrow it should be his. And that brings him to the third thing he learned. Killing got easier and easier the more times you do it. It will be very easy this time.

Chapter XII

"...it's a pretty spectacular bump."

Daz and Diz

The elevator door to the lobby slides open and out comes Daz, wheeling his overnight bag behind him. He takes a look around the lobby and heads for a cluster of four leather Queen Anne wingback chairs. Two of them have a view of the front desk and after careful consideration he picks the one closest to the elevator. Just as he is snuggling in the elevator pings and the door slides open to reveal a very disgruntled Diz. He marches over to Daz dragging his overnight bag that has one very wobbly wheel. "Didn't you hear me yell 'hold the elevator'?"

An innocent Daz looks up at his friend. "Oh, were you speaking to me?"

Diz is trying to control himself and at the moment, losing. "You were in the elevator."

A look of surprise, almost genuine, passes over Daz's face. "I had no idea...my bad."

Diz glares at Daz as he drags his bag, banging Daz on the shin, to the seat next to him. "You did this on purpose. I know you did. You know damn well that's my favorite chair...has she come out yet?" Daz shakes his head. "Not yet...maybe soon."

Their eyes never stop moving as the elevator pings again disgorging James and John. They wheel their bags over and take the seats across from them. After a long moment, John can take it no longer. "What are you doing?"

Diz, eyes never stopping, is clearly bothered by this intrusion. "Waiting."

John looks at James, who takes shot. "Waiting for what?"

Daz explains the obvious. "Her."

They hear the elevator ping but don't acknowledge Robert and Howard as they walk up. Adrienne come out of a side door and glide over to them…never taking her eyes off Officer Duplantier. She envelopes his hands in hers, gazing into his eyes. "And how did you sleep?" Duplantier tries but can't seem to get his brain and mouth to work together.

Jenny and Margot exit the elevator. Adrienne gives Duplantier's hand one last squeeze and goes to meet them, guiding them off to the side. The guys watch the ladies engage in a very intense conversation. Finally, they turn to the guys, and laugh. Adrienne waves giving a special flourish to Duplantier and disappears into a side door.

Margot and Jenny wheel their bags over. Diz stands blocking their way. "So, what was that about?"

Margot smiles sweetly. "She was just saying goodbye and how much she loves you guys."

Diz smiles back. "Of course, why wouldn't she. We're lovable."

Johnny points to his watch.. "It's getting late." He wheels his bag toward the parking elevator. Duplantier follows with Margot and James close behind. Jenny falls in line beside Robert and takes his hand…he smiles, tentatively and they get on the elevator.

Duplantier holds the door while Diz and Daz take one last look. They are rewarded when Adrienne comes out and waves. They bow to her, and she bows back. She is, after all, their guy.

Jenny

Jenny sits quietly in the passenger seat as Robert pulls the limo out of the parking garage and heads to Interstate 10 toward Baton Rouge before turning to the back seat. "We need someone to go on the internet and find out who owns Chretien Point and what we're likely to find when we get there…and come up with a plan."

Johnny, after all he's her father, can't stop himself. "Isn't that what you usually…"

Jenny cuts him off right there. "Maybe so, but not this time."

She reaches over, in front of Robert, and pushes a button sending a glass divider sliding up between the front and back seats. Jenny turns, facing Robert. He chooses to concentrate on driving. Jenny clears her throat…still nothing.

Finally, she leans forward, inches from his right ear and whispers those four words that all men dread. "We've got to talk."

135

Robert's shoulders slump and he expels an entire lungful of air, he didn't realize he was holding. Resigned, he nods, eyes still glued to the road ahead. Jenny folds her arms and waits for Robert to make the first move. At last, he can't put it off any longer. "What?"

Jenny gives him...the look. "You know darn well what. So...what's going on mister? You haven't spoken more that twenty-five words to me since yesterday."

Robert clearly doesn't want to talk about this. "It's complicated."

The...look...intensifies. "So. It's complicated."

Robert drives, weighing all his option. Shaking her head, Jenny can't wait any longer. "It's about what that old woman said...isn't it?

Resignedly, Robert nods. "Yes. Well, that's where it began...my thinking I mean."

Jenny nods and smiles, just a bit. "Yes, thinking always gets us into trouble."

Robert briefly smiles back before turning serious. "Growing up...black...in the south, there are somethings you just have to deal with." He glances at Jenny to make sure she's following. "There are so many feelings that you have. You have to deal with the fact that somewhere in your past your family was owned by someone...and that there are some people today who won't let you forget it."

Jenny squeezes his hand, urging him to go on. He pauses, briefly. "You push it down...try to rise above, but somewhere, deep inside you feel anger and fear...mistrust... self-doubt, all jumbled together. And it never, really goes away...it's just a part of you."

He continues to stare straight ahead, while Jenny holds on to his hand ...tightly, afraid to let go. "But yesterday, I was surrounded by people who owned my family...the actual people and I didn't know what to do. And then, I realized here I was driving y'all around...and began feeling like a servant...a slave and wondering if that's the way your father and uncle saw me...if that's way the way you saw me...see me."

Jenny sits frozen because she doesn't know how to respond. She wants to scream that isn't the way she sees him...or her uncle...or her father, but she also knows that somewhere in the past, her family would have seen him exactly that way. Seeing the pain on his face, she knows she has to respond.

"I...I'm so sorry Robert. I mean, I never thought...I mean I always knew that my family owned slaves, but it wasn't me...it was somebody in my deep dark past…" This is sounding lame…even to her. "I did…stuff…to reassure myself that I wouldn't have done that. I marched…I protested…I wore Black Lives Matter shirts, thinking that, somehow those things absolved me from the past."

She brushes away a tear. "But yesterday, when I saw your pain. I didn't know what to say. I still don't…because my family caused that pain. To you…your family…to all the innocent people we thought it okay to buy and sell. I can't tell myself that I'm not responsible…that was the past. Because right now…right here…it's in the front seat, like a wall between us."

Robert looks directly at Jenny and squeezes her hand. "Exactly, like a wall. I want to tear it down, but I don't know how. We can't let it come between us…to define us, but we can't ignore it…pretend it doesn't exist."

Jenny looks forward. "So, what do we do?"

Robert shrugs. "Don't know. We're still at the beginning of…us and we can't let this be the thing that ends us. Every relationship has bumps."

Jenny can't help but smile. "You have to admit, it's a pretty spectacular bump.

For the first time, Robert actually smiles back and nods. "A pretty spectacular one…a story to tell the grandkids."

He sneaks a look at Jenny, who grins back. Robert looks at the road ahead…then back at Jenny. "You know this conversation isn't over…it never will be."

Confusion is written all over her face. Robert tries to explain. "As much as we come to care about each other…even love each other. As much as we think alike on almost every issue. There are things about me that you will never understand…can never understand."

Jenny thinks about that before she looks up at him. "You're right, of course…but I will try. I'll always be willing to try."

Robert smiles and reaches in front of him, pushing the button that lowers the divider. Jenny turns to face the back seat. "So, what's the plan?"

Margot

Margot looks up from her phone and shares a quick look with Johnny and Jimmy…then at Daz and Diz. "We don't exactly have a plan yet…we aren't even close to a plan…but we do have some information."

Jenny smiles urging Margot to go on. "Well, we know that the property is currently owned by a Mr. Hilton John Brodie, but we can't find any information about him."

Jenny frowns but Margot goes on. "In the past, Chretien Point has been a Bed and Breakfast, a private residence…it's been rented out for weddings and banquets."

Jimmy breaks in. "There have even been plantation tours. But after this man bought it, there is no indication that any of that is going on…so we can only assume that Mr. Brodie is using it as his private residence."

John tries to lay it out logically. "Okay…so we arrive. Do we just march up and knock on the front door?"

James considers this option. "And what do we say? We're here looking for clues to a pirate treasure?"

Johnny cranes his neck looking through the rear window. "Do you think we should call Duplantier and let him know what's going on?"

James gives him a look. "And just what do we tell him is going on?"

Johnny is about to speak when Jenny interrupts. "Found it on Google Maps…The plantation is on Chretien Point Road. The street curves…almost ninety degrees, just after we pass it.. I think we should pull over just after the curve and decide what to do."

Margot taps Jenny on the shoulder. "How long before we get there?" Jenny points off to the left. "We just turned onto Chretien Point Road. The driveway should be on the left and the road curves just ahead. We should be there in about ninety seconds."

They watch the open front gate as they pass, wondering what lies on the other side. Margot looks back at Duplantier on their tail. "Robert, pull over as soon as you make the turn." The limo curves to the left and Robert pulls onto the shoulder as Duplantier pulls in behind him. They begin to pile out of the limo and stretch their legs and backs with accompanying cracks and groans. Margot looks over at the squad car but there is no movement from inside.

Margot nudges Johnny. "Could you see what's going on with Howard?"

Johnny

Johnny approaches the LCPD squad car peering through the windshield, seeing Duplantier, head back, eyes closed. He turns back to the others. "I think he's asleep...maybe dead." He taps on the side window and Duplantier opens one eye. He pushes a button and window slides down. There is a brief conversation, and the window slides up. Johnny stares at the closed window for a moment before walking, slowly, back to the others. Johnny, with a puzzled look on his face, stands quietly. James lets impatience get the better of him. "Well...?"

Johnny looks back at the car before turning to James. "He's listening to music. He's listening to Holtz...Gustov Holst...The Planets."

This is not what they were expecting. James starts to speak, but Johnny holds up his hand. "He's on Neptune...he says he just got to the good part, and he'll be out as soon as he's done."

James turns to the rest unable to comprehend what's going on. Diz and Daz look at each other and nod. Diz puts a comforting hand on James shoulder. "He's right. I know the spot he's talking about...trust me, it's worth waiting for."

Daz steps up. "It's the last movement. He'll be out in a minute."

As is on cue, they hear the squad car door slam shut and Duplantier saunters over. They can't help but stare at him. They are beginning to look at Duplantier in a whole new light. He gives them a slightly goofy grin. "I was meditating." The light gets brighter. He gazes into another world. "I was thinking...I'm thinking of getting a cat." And there it is...Duplantier is back.

It takes John just a moment to recover. "Okay...well, we're here...now what?"

Daz speaks up from the back. "Why don't you go up to the front door and ring the bell?"

James scoffs at that, but John chews on that for just a moment. "Maybe he's right. I mean think about it...we're Chretien's...this was our family's plantation."

Jimmy thinks about this and smiles. "So, we just drive in?"

Johnny nods. "We just drive in." He points to Duplantier. "Besides...we have Johnny Law with us.

Duplantier grins. "I've never been called 'Johnny Law' before…I like it." Duplantier freezes, having an epiphany. "I'm going to name my cat Johnny Law."

They all, briefly stare at Howard, before Johnny gets down to business. "Okay, everyone back in the car. We'll just drive in like we own the place."

Robert arrives at the front gate. "We just drive in?" Johnny nods. Robert pulls slowly into the oak covered drive and follows it until, through the leaves a red brick, plantation home, in the Classical Revival style, begins to emerge. Robert rolls to a stop as they gape at mansion before them.

James looks to John. "What now, oh wise one?"

Johnny points to a road cutting off to the right. "Robert, take that road. Let's see where it takes us."

Robert nods and slowly glides down the lane. Everyone is watching the house on the left. Everybody but John, who's looking to the right. He begins to frown as a group of buildings begin to materialize. As they move closer, John grabs James' arm and points to the buildings ahead. Johnny taps Robert on the shoulder. "Robert, could you pull up over here and stop for a moment."

Robert pulls over and John continues to stare at the group of buildings… getting out to have a better look. James slides out of the car and joins him. The closer John and James get, the more vivid the scene before them appears and slower they walk. John stops, staring at twenty or so dilapidated, weathered small wooden cabins in front of him. He half turns to James and whispers to him. "I don't remember this from the time we were here before. Do you?" Not taking his eyes from the scene in front of him, James nods, remembering something from the dim past.

John thinks back to the old lady in Lafitte. She said something to Robert. He didn't pay attention to it and the time, but now it comes flooding back. "Louragan and Chretien, together again." He turns slowly to Jenny and Robert behind him. His eyes lock with Jenny's seeing her pain and anguish, He turns slightly to Robert and sees him, ramrod straight staring stoically at the scene, frozen in time, in front of him.

John looks back, his mind reeling. Men, women, and children crowded into these tiny cabins…working endless hours in the fields. His mind leaps to beatings…rapes, families torn apart. Did they…did his family do these things? Did his family do this to

Robert's family? Johnny is physically sick…leaving his shame and disgust on the ground. James moves to his brother's side helping him to stand upright. The others gather around him…everyone but Robert who still can't tear his eyes away from the images before him.

Suddenly a sound…a sound that's becoming all too familiar, the sound of a double-barreled shotgun being cocked. They turn as one to face the barrels pointed directly at them. Behind the gun stands a casually dressed African American man, in his mid-eighties, staring back at them. "Who the hell are you and what are you doing here?"

Jimmy

James tries his voice…the problem is that it's somewhere down around his left ankle. He holds up one finger, waiting for his voice to get somewhere closer to his mouth. Finally, the voice, a little squeaky, appears. "I will be happy to tell you who we are if you'd, please, lower your shotgun."

The man's eyes…and the barrel of the shotgun, focus on James. "Name first…shotgun second."

James clears his throat and shoots a quick look at Johnny. "I'm James Chretien. My brother…"

The gun lowers a fraction of an inch. "Are you a good Chretien or a bad Chretien."

This stumps James. He looks to Johnny for help, but he just shrugs. Margot is a little offended on the Chretiens behalf and takes a half step forward. "They're the best Chretiens I know."

The shot gun now points to Margot…who takes a step back and slightly behind Johnny. "I'm not sure I like your tone, missy."

His focus returns to James. His eyes narrow. "Who's your papa?" James has to take a moment to remember. He finally gets it out. "James…James Henry…Chretien.

The squinty eyes get squintier. "He's dead." James is getting a little annoyed. "I know that…what I don't know is if he's a good Chretien or a bad Chretien."

The shotgun lowers, the squinty eyes get less squinty, and a small smile touches the corners of his mouth. "A good Chretien…and he had a better disposition than you, but nowhere as good as your Mama, Marie Alma."

His courage returned, John steps forward. "Well, maybe they didn't have a shotgun pointing at them."

The smile broadens as the old man steps forward with an outstretched hand. "You must be Johnny."

Johnny shakes his hand and glances at Jimmy…trying to figure this guy out. The man turns to Jimmy. "And you of course, are Jimmy." A shadow passes over the man's eyes. "Sorry to hear about your brother…your dad spoke highly of you boys." He reaches out to shake Jimmy's hand. "I'm sure you don't remember me. We met once, sixty or so years ago. I'm Etienne Bastineau." A light dawns…Jimmy looks at Johnny and back at Etienne…Mr. Etienne.

He turns to Johnny, grinning ear to ear. "This is the old man I met when Pop brought us here when we were kids."

Etienne can't help but take offense at that. "Sonny…I was younger than you are now."

Jimmy rushes to apologize. "I'm sorry, sir. It's just that it's been such a long time."

Etienne waves him off. "And you thought I'd be dead by now."

Jimmy tries to come up with some kind of response, but Etienne just goes on. "You can call me Etienne if someone will introduce me to the ladies."

Johnny steps forward and pushes Margot toward Etienne. "This is Margot Sallier." Etienne's smile just gets bigger. "My, Sallier and Chretien…I guess I should have expected this…this is indeed an honor, Miss Sallier."

Margot blushes and takes his outstretched hand. "It's a pleasure to meet you…Mister…Etienne."

Etienne nods and turns to Jenny. "And who is this lovely young woman?"

Johnny puts his arm around her shoulder. "This is my daughter, Jenny."

Etienne takes a step back to admire her. "Ah, the granddaughter…you know my dear, you look remarkably like Fèlicitè, your great, great…and so on." Jenny turns pink and Etienne cuts off the remark forming on Jimmy's lips. "I've seen pictures…I'm not that old."

Diz and Daz step forward. Daz puts out his hand and Etienne takes it. "Dazencourt Broussard, at your service."

142

Not to be outdone Diz steps up. "I'm Dennis Dampiere." Etienne smiles at two musicians and bows. "The famous Diz and Daz. I have heard you play. This is quite an honor."

They step aside and push Duplantier to the front. Daz introduces him. This is Officer Howard Duplantier from the Lake Charles Police Department." Etienne shakes his hand. "A police escort...this gets curiouser and curiouser." His eyes move past Duplantier and rest on Robert. "And who is this?"

Robert isn't sure how to respond but takes a step forward. "I'm Robert...Robert Louragan." Etienne's eyes get bigger and bigger. He pushes his way through the others and embraces a very uncomfortable Robert.

"I can't believe it...Chretien, Sallier and Louragan...here together." He looks away pondering. Then to himself: "Qu'est-ce que cela signifie?" He looks back to Robert and kisses him on both cheeks. "And how is your father?"

Now Robert is even more bewildered. "You know my father?"

Etienne chuckles softly. "Of course, my boy."

Robert has to think about this revelation. "You'll have to excuse me...I only found out yesterday that my family were slaves on this plantation."

Now it's Etienne's turn to be bewildered. "No Robert you're wrong. Make no mistake, there were slaves on this plantation...many slaves...too many slaves." He turns to James and John. "For which your family needs to atone." Then back to Robert. "But your family weren't slaves. Your great, great, great grandfather was indeed taken from his village, but the slave ship he was on was wrecked during a hurricane off the coast of Martinique. He was found, washed up on shore...half dead...by Jean Lafitte."

Robert and Jenny exchange looks, and Etienne goes on. "Lafitte carried him back to his ship, where he was nursed back to health. That's when Lafitte named him Chanceux Louragan...Lucky Hurricane." He smiles at Robert. "Robert, your great, great, great grandfather was not a slave...he was a pirate and more. It is said that without your grandfather and his intricate knowledge of the bayous, the United States never would have beaten the British at the Battle of New Orleans."

This is a bit much for Robert. Etienne pats Robert on his shoulder. "Talk to your father."

Etienne turns his attention back to James. "So, what brings y'all here?" James looks at Margot, who takes the cedar box from her purse and hands it to Etienne. He examines the box and looks up. "Where did you get this?"

Margot takes it back. "It belonged to my great, great, great grandmother, Catherine. Jean Lafitte gave it to her."

Etienne nods. "Of course, the brooch."

Margot goes on, "We met a woman in Lafitte…"

Etienne nods knowingly. "Yes, Zora…she must have approved of you since you're still alive."

After a quick look at James, Margot hands Etienne the paper they found. "I showed her the box…she opened a secret compartment and we found that."

Etienne examines it closely. "And this brought you here…and you think it might have something to do with Lafitte's treasure? I have long expected something of the sort, but don't know how I can help…As far as I know, nothing of the kind has been found."

James and Margot exchange looks, and Margot turns to Etienne with tears in her eyes. "Etienne, Roger Chretien was murdered for this treasure, and this is the only clue we have."

James rushes in. "We were hoping that perhaps we could look around inside…to see if anything…" His voice trails off.

Etienne puts a comforting hand on Margot's arm. "Of course, you are welcome. The Brodies are away…in Europe I believe…but I can't hold out any hope that you will find anything."

James shakes Etienne's hand. "We understand…If you will just point us in the right direction."

Etienne smiles. "I will do better than that…I will take you." With that, Etienne heads off toward the house.

Robert

As the others follow Etienne, Robert and Jenny hang back. Robert is dumbfounded. A pirate? He truly doesn't know what to do with that information. I mean…a pirate? Robert looks to Jenny, bewilderment all over his face. "A pirate?"

Jenny can only shrug. "So, it seems."

Robert rubs his face. "Well, I don't know how I feel about that."

Jenny caresses his cheek. "It doesn't change the way I feel about you…not in the least."

Robert looks at Jenny and smiles. He takes her by the hand and follows the others, while singing softly to himself. "Yo ho, yo ho, a pirate's life for me."

Etienne unlocks the front door and as the door swings open, his cell phone buzzes. He retrieves it from his pocket and looks at the display. Holding up his hand he mouths. "Mr. Brodie." And goes off to speak privately, while James and John crane their necks to get a look at their ancestral home.

Diz pokes his head between them and shatters their reverie. "You know, this room was used in 'Gone With the Wind." Both James and John take a step back and gape at Diz.

John looks back into the foyer. "What?"

Daz pushes Diz out of the way. "They built a copy of this room." He points to the staircase. "Scarlett was at the top of the stairs looking down at Rhett." In his best Vivian Leigh voice. "But where will I go? What will I do?...Fiddle DeeDee" Diz steps forward channeling Clark Gable. "Frankly, my dear, I don't give a damn."

Etienne saunters back and smiles. "I see you've gotten History of the Film 101."

Their heads swing to Etienne. Margot can't contain herself. "You mean that's true?"

Etienne looks at Diz and Daz and back to the others. "Absolutely."

Diz and Daz, all puffed up, look at the others as if to say, 'told you so.' Etienne shakes his head, walks into the center of the foyer, and spreads his arms wide.

"Entres vous, dans ma maison." He steps back as John and James enter, followed by Margot, Diz and Daz, and Duplantier. Each swiveling their heads, trying to see everything.

Robert begins to follow when Jenny pulls him back. "Did you hear what he said?"

Robert looks at her, puzzled. "I think so." After a look. "I thought so."

Jenny's eyes light up. "You told me about a game you and your father played." Robert nods but...what? Jenny goes on. "What was the first part?"

Robert thinks for just a moment. "Dance my mason..."

Jenny nods emphatically. "And what did Etienne say? Dans ma maison...in my house." Robert gets it and Jenny kisses him quickly. "You were speaking French and you didn't even know it."

145

She turns to the others and calls out. "Daddy." Johnny, a little miffed at being interrupted. "What?"

Jenny pushes Robert ahead. "Go on Robert, tell them about the game."

Robert looks at everyone staring at him. "Well, when I was little my father, and I would play this game. We'd shout, dance my mason, dance my chamber, house lemur, a treasure attend."

Both John and James take a step backward. Jenny just shakes her head. "Don't you get it? Dance my mason…dans ma maison. In my house." She turns to Robert. "What comes next?" Robert thinks. "Dance my chamber." Jenny grins. "Sure…dans ma chambre…in my room." She looks at Robert and pokes him. It takes a moment for Robert to get it but, finally blurts out. "House lemur."

This puzzles Jenny…puzzles them all. Until Margot smiles. "House lemur…'haut sur le mur' … high on the wall." Both Robert and Jenny share a looks and grin. "Un trésure attende. A treasure attend." They say in unison.

Jenny turns to her dad. "In my house…in my room…high on the wall…a treasure attend."

Johnny beams at Robert and claps him on the back. "You just may have solved the puzzle."

Robert isn't so sure. "But this isn't my house."

Jenny, shaking her head dismisses that. "Don't you see? This is from the child's point of view. In my house…in my room."

Robert gets it. "Sure…in my room." He looks at Jenny and they both grin. "The nursery."

Suddenly, Johnny has a thought and turns to Etienne. "There is a nursery, right?" Etienne smiles and points up to the second floor. "Follow me."

They troop upstairs and Etienne leads them to a closed door. He turns back to them, somewhat embarrassed. "You'll have to excuse the mess. This has become a kind of junk room."

He opens the door to reveal a room with old furniture and clothing piled high in the center. Its faded robin's egg blue walls are in need of a new coat of paint. Etienne shrugs. "This room is scheduled for a redo…overdo for a redo."

James turns to Robert. "So, you said 'high on the wall."

Robert nods, as he cranes his neck looking up. They are all disappointed. They were expecting some big reveal and all the have is cluttered room in need of a coat of paint. Robert stops...he points to a corner of the wall, near the window.

"Margot, you see where the wall meets the crown molding. Isn't it a slightly different shade of white, then the rest?"

They all look, and James slowly nods his head. "I think you're right, Robert." He turns to Etienne. "Has the crown molding ever been replaced?"

Etienne looks at the ceiling and shrugs. "Don't know."

James cocks his head. "Can we check?"

Etienne takes his time staring at that one piece of crown molding. "I suppose...if you put it right back...in one piece."

Jimmy looks at Johnny, who refuses to make eye contact. Jimmy clears his throat. "Of course, not a problem."

Johnny finally looks at James. "You know what is a problem?"

Jimmy shakes his head and Johnny spreads his arms. "We don't have any tools."

James huffs and looks to Etienne who shakes his head. Disappointment clouds all their faces...all except Howard, who grinning from ear to ear. "I got a crowbar in the trunk."

Etienne's face goes white. James looks at Duplantier and shakes his head. Howard stares at James who makes a 'it's only this big' gesture with his hands.

Duplantier frowns for just a moment before he gets it. "Don't worry, sir...it's a very small crowbar."

Before Etienne can say anything, Duplantier hurries down to the squad car. James turns back to Etienne and smiles. "It'll only be a minute." Changing the subject, Margot smiles sweetly at Etienne. "So, Etienne, how long have lived here?"

Etienne knows when he's being played but decides to go along. "All my life...I was born here...and after a while I knew more about this place than anyone. So, every time a new owner came along, they'd ask me to stay."

He's interrupted by an out of breath Duplantier who comes running in with a forty inch crowbar. Etienne glares at James. "Please be careful."

James looks for something to stand on and hauls an old wooden chair over to the corner. He stops briefly to check with Etienne, who shakes his head but gives him the go-ahead. As Duplantier begins to step onto it, Etienne can't bear to see what's about to happen and slips out of the nursery.

With a last glance at James, Duplantier slips the end of the crowbar under the piece of crown molding and slowly pushes it down. At first nothing…but then with low groan the piece of wood slowly comes away from the wall, revealing a small opening. They all stare at it…finally Johnny can't take it anymore. "Well?"

Duplantier looks at him and then back to the hole. "I ain't putting my hand in there."

Johnny glares back. "What are you afraid of?"

Duplantier continues to stare at the hole. "Everything."

Robert urges him forward. "Come on, Howard. You can do it." They all begin to chant, softly. "You can do it…you can do it…you can do it."

Duplantier closes his eyes to gather strength and reaches up…slowly…and puts his hand in the hole. He pauses for a moment fully expecting to be bitten by something…but nothing. He begins to feel around, his fingers reaching out and touching…again nothing. Until his fingertips lightly brush against…something.

He opens his eyes and looks up as his hand, moving ever so slowly closes around the object…holding his breath until he brings it out from the wall. A small cedar box They all exhale.

Howard hands it off to Robert, before he turns and bangs the piece of wood back into place. Robert, hands it to James, who, hands it to Margot. Duplantier climbs down and Johnny calls out to Etienne. "You can come back now." Etienne pokes his head in and stares at wall. Johnny smiles and points to the corner. "See, good as new."

Robert turns to see all eyes on Margot as she tries to remember how to open the box. After a couple of missteps, Margot presses the right places in the right order and a small drawer pops open. Margot looks up at the others before pulling out a folded piece of yellowed paper. After glancing at it she hands it to James, who lays it flat on a table, as everyone gathers around to see. "Out of the Water." And "Des Apparitions Fantomatique Apparaissant."

They all turn as one and look at Jenny, who shrugs. "Something about ghostly apparitions appearing. So far it doesn't mean much to me."

James turns to Etienne. "Thank you so much." He holds up the box. "I hope you don't mind if we take this."

Etienne smiles. "As far as I'm concerned you were never here."

James hands the box to Margot, who puts it in her purse with Catherine's box. Johnny ushers them out of the room, down the stairs and onto the front porch.

As they walk to their cars, Etienne calls out. "Please come back and let me know how it all turns out."

Johnny calls back. "We will."

At the last minute, Robert runs back to Etienne and takes his hand. "Thank you so much."

Etienne nods but reminds Robert. "Make sure you ask your dad."

Robert laughs. "Oh, I will."

He runs back to the limo and slides in. They all wave as Robert makes a U-turn and follows the drive back to Chretien Point Road followed by Officer Duplantier. Nobody notices a black Suburban pull out into the road behind them.

Antoine

Cranky and frustrated, Antoine sits at his desk flipping the gold coin. It's been hours since he's heard from Duplantier. He put himself on time out, because he yelled at a rookie because his tie wasn't the right length...and he told the captain to get out into field and do something. So, he is cranky...and worried.

He's tried to get a hold of Duplantier or James Chretien...or John Chretien...or Margot Sallier but keeps getting voice mail. He'd put out an APB, but he's secretly thinks they are all somewhere shucking oysters...or enjoying a crab boil, or some such nonsense.

He's about to hurl his grandmother's antique, demitasse cup against the wall, when his cell phone begins to vibrate sending it wobbling all over the desk. He grabs for it and sees the name Duplantier appear on the screen. He tries to keep emotion out of his voice as he answers. "Durel."

"Hey, Sergeant, it's me Howard."

Now Antoine is really confused. Who the hell is Howard and why is he using Duplantier's phone? Then it clicks.

"Where have you been...OFFICER DUPLANTIER? I've been trying to reach you for hours."

Dead silence...finally. "Sorry, Sarge. No cell service...just got your messages."

"And just where the hell have you been."

149

Duplantier is afraid to say the wrong thing. "We were at the Chretien Plantation." Antoine shuts his eyes in total frustration. Duplantier is quick to explain. "The old lady in Lafitte found the clue in the box."

Antoine holds his head in his hands. "What old lady?"

Duplantier is about to answer when Antoine cuts his off. "Never mind...where are you now?"

"Highway 10 about an hour out from Lake Charles. We should be there in about...an hour. But Sarge, I think someone might be on our tail...it's a black SUV, maybe a Suburban...or Escalade."

Antoine rifles through papers on his desk, until he finds what he's looking for...a report mentioning a black Suburban. "Okay, officer, hang tight. I'm going to get...a Chretien on the line."

Antoine finds the number and runs from his office while dialing. The phone connects to James Chretien. "Chretien, here."

Antoine slides into his car, buckles up and screeches from the lot. "Durel...I'm on the line with Duplantier...he says you're being followed."

There is a moment of silence while James puts the phone on speaker. "I don't see anything?"

Duplantier checks the rear-view mirror. "It's a black Suburban coming up fast behind me."

Johnny cranes his neck. "I see it. About three car lengths behind Duplantier."

Antoine merges onto Highway 10. "I'm on my way...calling for back up. Don't do anything stupid."

Officer Duplantier is all business. "You can count on me Sergeant Durel."

These are the last words Sergeant Durel heard Officer Duplantier speak, because suddenly, Antoine's speaker is filled with the sound of metal against metal...a screeching, tearing, almost animal sound...then James. "Sergeant...the Suburban hit Duplantier... sending him over the median into oncoming traffic...it doesn't look good."

Antoine tries to think of something to say...then James continues. "Now he's coming for us...ROBERT PULL OVER." A loud screeching sound, a horrendous crash followed by screams and then...nothing...the phone is dead. Antoine looks at his phone...horrified, before putting on the lights and sirens. He's got to get there before...

It's about 20 minutes before he nears the scene, he has to drive on the shoulder to see anything...wrecked cars strewn across the highway, ambulances, firetrucks, State Police ...and Duplantier's squad car, mangled beyond recognition. He looks across the median at an overturned limo, a black SUV on its side near the median, a firetruck and two ambulances. He rubs his face. Ambulances...at least some made it out alive. He looks back at the squad car. His hope is dashed when the coroner's wagon pulls up beside it.

Highway 10
Between
Lafayette and Lake Charles

The last thing Vincent remembers is the rush he felt when he sent the squad car careening over the median into oncoming traffic and the beautiful sound of mayhem when it skidded to stop in the center lane. Then all Vincent could think about was smashing the limo and those people inside. All those people who were standing in his way. He increased his speed ramming the limo again and again until it became airborne landing on its roof on the side of the freeway.

He had only a moment to revel in the sight, when his SUV, taking on a mind of its own, slid back into traffic lanes tumbling over three times before coming to rest against the median. He tries the door, but it's jammed. There must be a way...if only he could concentrate. He thinks of climbing into the backseat and trying the back door, but suddenly his arms are so heavy, and the world is getting dimmer and dimmer...until there is nothing.

Part Three
Hurricane Category 5
Catastrophic Damage

Chretien Point
60 Years Ago

*I*t's a beautiful spring morning and James Henry Chretien chooses this day to bring his young family to Chretien Point for the first and last time. As he surveys the grounds great memories of fishing in Bayou Bourbeau with his dad and pápère flood his memory. But James shakes his head...it's not the same since they passed. All the magic seems to have died with them.

Now it's all the cousins who own the property and old family rivalries and insults, real or imagined, have resurfaced. The only thing they could all agree on was selling the property and James Henry has decidedly mixed feelings about that.

On one hand it is the last tangible link to his pápère and on the other are family issues and the plantation's decidedly checkered past. He hopes to put the family's stain of slavery behind him so his children will never have to bear that burden. He can make new memories with his boys.

Eight-year-old Jimmy Chretien doesn't care about any of this. All he sees is plenty of room to run and play, if only he can escape from his mom and dad...and his two very annoying little brothers. Actually, Roger isn't the problem, he's in a stroller, but Johnny. He has to take Johnny with him wherever he goes. Who knew a five-year-old could be such a pain?

He stealthily looks at his mom, who's busy with Roger and Johnny, and his dad, who is busy talking to some stranger...now is the time to make his move. He slowly steps away until he's sure he can make his escape. Keeping his head down, Jimmy sprints around to the side of the house and doesn't look back until he's out of earshot. Now he can discover what mysteries this place holds.

He's heard his dad talk about the plantation, but he had no idea this is what he was talking about. He could run forever and not ever see or hear his brothers. He wanders down to banks of the bayou and spends some time skipping rocks, before taking off his shoes and wading in cold water This place is great. Jimmy notices some mysterious buildings behind a low stone fence and hatches a plan.

He runs, low to the ground, before throwing himself on the grass and leaning with his back against the fence, He counts to ten before peeking over the other side. There doesn't seem to be anyone there, but you never know if some bad guys are hiding somewhere...maybe in those buildings.

Before he can spring over the fence a voice comes from directly behind him. He freezes and slowly turns around until he faces a very stern man. The same man his dad was talking to. "And just what are you doing, young man?"

Jimmy has been taught to be polite to his elders, but he doesn't want to blow his cover either. "I'm...investigating."

The man tries to maintain his stern look but can't keep a smile from touching the corners of his mouth. "Investigating, eh?"

Jimmy nods very seriously. "Yes, sir."

The man cocks his brow. "I'm Mr. Etienne and to whom do I have the honor of speaking?"

Jimmy hesitates just a moment before standing and extending his hand. "I'm Jimmy...Jimmy Chretien."

Mr. Etienne smiles, taking Jimmy's hand. "Ah Jimmy Chretien, I'm very pleased to meet you. Your father was just talking about you. He says you're very smart."

Jimmy beams. "Yes, sir, I am."

Etienne smiles. "Well, your mother and father are looking for you. Perhaps we should return you to them."

Jimmy looks longingly over the fence, before turning back to Etienne. "Yes, sir."

Jimmy reluctantly follows Etienne back to his parents and his annoying little brothers. Etienne calls out, "I'm returning your errant son to you."

James Henry looks sternly at his son before turning to Etienne. "And where was the boy?"

Etienne looks briefly at Jimmy before answering. "Near the slave quarters."

James Henry shares a look with Etienne before looking down at his son. "I told you not to wander off."

Jimmy can't meet his father's eyes." Yes, sir."

His dad ruffles his hair. "Well son, why don't you spend some time with your brothers. I'm sure your mother could use a break."

This is what Jimmy was trying to avoid, but he can't argue with his father's logic. "Yes, dad."

He picks up Roger and takes Johnny by the hand to play, what he thinks of as, baby games.

Etienne watches Jimmy walk off before turning back to James Henry. "You may want to have a talk with Jimmy. There is going to come a time when the boys are going to need to understand everything that happened here."

James Henry looks at his sons and nods, but that is for another day.

Chapter XIII
"Making friends are we, brother dear."

Jenny

Jenny finds herself, once again in the St. Patrick's Hospital waiting room. She sits, shoulders slumped. They had all been so pleased on the way back to Lake Charles. Although it was just another clue, they all had felt they were getting closer. Closer to the answers they were looking for. And then…what? She doesn't really remember much…except sound. The sound of metal against metal, of cars screeching, of voices screaming around her. Then the car tumbling over and over…and then the sirens.

Where is everyone? Is anyone hurt? Is anyone dead? All these thoughts are jumbled together. Jenny, remembering her first aid classes in Girl Scouts, runs a quick triage on herself. No bleeding or open wounds…no apparent broken bones…no head trauma…aches and pains, but nothing life threatening. Jenny nods to herself. But what about everyone else? What about Daddy and Uncle James, or Margot and Diz and Daz? Her mind freezes. What about Robert? He was driving. Does that make him more or less likely to be hurt?

Jenny leans back in her seat. She tries to remain calm, catching images as they fly by until one image remains. She is in the front seat, looking over shoulder at Duplantier's SUV behind them. She watches as he's rammed one…two…three times sending him skidding across lanes. She tries to block out the almost animal sounds of brakes screaming, cars careening and the shrieking as the oncoming traffic engages in an almost balletic dance of destruction.

Jenny finds herself eyes closed, standing in the middle of the waiting room with tears streaming down her face. People wander by, walking around her muttering.

"What's her problem."

"Some people have no sense."

"I should call security."

Jenny makes her way back to her seat and collapses into it. She is only aware of the here and now and an overwhelming sense of loss and loneliness...as if she is the only one left if the world. Nothing matters except having those people she cares about... loves... surrounding her.

Jenny shakes her head, finally coming out of the darkness. She needs to find out what's happening. She needs to send out good thoughts into the universe. She needs to pray.

Eyes still closed, Jenny is vaguely aware of the sound of a door opening and click of the latch, when it closes. She senses a presence and opens her eyes to see Margot standing in front of her, arms resting on crutches.

Margot

Margot doesn't remember anything until she's loaded into the back of an ambulance, while paramedics immobilize her right leg. After that it's all a blur of people talking about her and around her, but not to her.

"It's a mess out there."

"More ambulances coming,"

"One person bought it."

She prayed a fervent, but very selfish, prayer that no one she knows 'bought it.'

Once inside the E.R. she is whisked to a curtained off cubicle where she lays on a gurney and listens to the bustle and murmured conversations just beyond her curtain. When the doctor finally arrives, she's freezing cold, in intense pain and afraid all of her friends are dead. She is rolled to have an Xray, a CT, and an MRI. She is poked and prodded, given a steroid shot and a pair of crutches and told she's good to go. Now here she is, armpits already becoming sore, hoping to get some information, "Hi, Jenny."

Jenny looks up with a vacant stare...then. "Margot...are you okay? Have you seen my dad? Robert? Anybody?"

Margot is about to speak when Jenny finally notices the crutches. "But you're hurt...here let me help you." Jenny taking the crutches and helps Margot into seat beside her.

Margot searches for a position that accommodates her leg without being a hazard. She turns to Jenny. "Tell me what's going on. I heard someone died."

Jenny begins to panic. "I don't know...I hadn't heard that...What if it's Daddy? Please don't let it be Daddy...or Robert...or anybody." She looks up at Margot. "Thank God it isn't you."

Margot puts a reassuring hand on Jenny's shoulder. "Waiting is hard, but we don't know anything yet."

Jenny exhales and puts her head back. "That's what I keep telling myself. But now...now I'm hoping it's someone I don't know that's dead." She looks up at Margot becoming a frightened eleven-year-old girl again. "Does that make me a horrible person?"

Margot shakes her head emphatically. "Of course not." She pauses to consider. "Well, if it does, then I'm one too, because that's all I've been thinking."

Margot sits back and looks around the waiting room. "No word on anybody?"

Jenny shakes her head. "You're the first I've seen,"

Margot looks from Jenny to the E.R door. "How long were you in there?"

Jenny follows her gaze. "Not long, they took an Xray and once they found out I didn't have any broken bones...or head trauma, they let me go." She looks back at Margot. "I've been sitting out here ever since...trying to remember what happened." She looks up at Margot. "How about you...do you remember anything?"

Margot shakes her head. "Not much...mostly sounds and panic." She closes her eyes. "Mostly panic." She opens them and studies Jenny. "How about you?"

Jenny stares off into space. "The same...except I have a vivid image of Officer Duplantier's squad car being rammed again and again...and then a black SUV coming right at us."

Margot reaches out to embrace Jenny. At first Jenny is stiff almost resistant until she relaxes into Margot's comforting arms and, finally, begins cry. Margot holds Jenny as her crying goes from a soft whimper, to all out, shoulders shaking, sobs. Margot holds on to Jenny until she reluctantly pulls away. Margot holds out a tissue and Jenny takes it gratefully. "I'm sorry about that."

Margot waves her off. "No need to apologize. I'm sure I'm only about fifteen minutes behind you." Jenny smiles at that. "You'll probably be a lot more ladylike than I am."

Margot gives her a gentle elbow poke. "Are you kidding. I'm going to need as many arms and tissues as I can get."

She gets an actual laugh from Jenny at that. Margot sits clutching Jenny's hand. Now there is nothing to do but wait and watch for the next person to come through the doors…and she doesn't have long to wait. The door swings open, and Daz comes through followed immediately by Diz.

"Are you sure you didn't hear anything about Margot?"

Daz stops dead in his tracks. "I didn't hear anything…see anything…feel anything…or had any psychic visions about anything having remotely to do with Margot." He looks at Diz who is pointing off to the left. He follows Diz's finger until he sees Margot and Jenny sitting, watching them. He looks back to Diz. "Until now."

Diz and Daz

Margot stands, using Jenny and the crutches for support, while reaching out to embrace both her friends as they rush to greet her. Diz is the first to find his voice. "Margot, I'm so happy to see you." He looks over at Jenny. "And you of course, but Margot, I was so worried."

Daz helps Margot sit down. He looks smugly over at Diz. "I told you she was okay."

Diz can't believe his ears. "You did no such thing."

Margot raises her hand to silence them. "It doesn't matter…you're okay…I'm okay." She looks to include Jenny. "We're all okay."

Diz and Daz pull chairs together forming a kind of survivor's circle. Diz grabs Margot's hand, who in turn grabs Jenny's, who grabs Daz's. Diz takes a hard look at Margot. "Are you sure you're, okay?"

Margot closes her eyes for just a second, takes a deep breath and returns the look. "Yes, I'm sure." She narrows her eyes. "What about you guys? They did give you permission to leave, didn't they?"

Diz nods, but Daz shrugs. "Not exactly…more like they told us leave."

Diz continues to nod. "I believe their actual words were…get out."

Margot looks heavenward and rubs her eyes. "What did you guys do? I mean you weren't in the same room, were you?"

Diz shakes his head. "No, there was some old guy between us."

Daz gives him a look. "Older than you? I don't think so."

Diz considers this. "Well, maybe not, but you have to admit he was making some weird noises."

Margot's look intensifies. "What did you do?"

Both Daz and Diz look away quickly. Finally, Diz looks back. "Nothing...really."

Margot shifts her gaze to Daz, who still avoids it. "I mean, we were in those cubicles for a long time...with nothing to do."

Diz nods. "That's right, nothing to do."

Daz spreads his hands. "So...we found...something to do."

Diz looks at Jenny. "Do you have any idea how many musical instruments you can make in an ER? The suture tray alone offers almost unlimited possibilities."

Daz breaks in. "And the cardiac monitor offers that steady beat."

Diz breaks in on Daz's break in. "Until a certain nurse came in." A quick look at Daz. "Then there was an abrupt change in tempo."

Daz acknowledges that. "True, but it worked for the song.

Diz grins and together, in perfect two-part harmony. "Won't come back from Dead Man's Curve."

Margot looks at Jenny and shakes her head. "Yes, you may have crossed the line a bit there."

Diz and Daz share a look and a shrug as Margot gets down to the matter at hand. "Do you have any news?"

Daz squints. "No...except it was a bad accident."

Jenny is clearly frustrated. "So, no news on my Dad or Uncle James...or Robert?"

Sadly, neither Diz nor Daz can offer any words of encouragement. Diz reaches out to Jenny. "I'm sorry."

Before Jenny can respond, Phillip Louragan rushes in and almost runs through the other door into the ER. All color drains from Jenny's face and she collapses into a chair. Margot sits beside her and takes her hand. Jenny squeezes it tight. "Oh, Margot."

The waiting room doors open again and James strides out looking perplexed. He makes a beeline to the others, not seeing the drama playing out before him. He looks back at the door. "Just saw Louragan. Is Robert okay?"

He turns back to the others just in time to catch an armload of Jenny. "Oh, Uncle James. I'm so glad you're not dead."

Jimmy

James closes his eyes and hugs Jenny back...not a perfunctory Thanksgiving or Christmas hug, but a real hug. "Oh, Jenny, me too."

James runs his hand through his hair. "You know it's odd. I don't remember any details from the accident, and yet it's all I can think about."

Jenny reaches out to him. "Me too...but I remember sounds. Horrible...awful sounds."

James squeezes her hand and Jenny looks up at him with a tearful face. "Oh, but even worse is sitting here not knowing. We know that somebody died...but we don't know who." She looks pleadingly at James. "I'm so afraid that it's Daddy...or Robert." She looks back at the ER door. "And then we saw Mr. Louragan race by...and Oh, Uncle James, I'm so afraid it's Robert...I mean he was driving..."

James enfolds her in his arms. "I know Jaybird."

Jenny peeks up at James. "You haven't called me that since I was nine."

James shrugs. "It seems like an appropriate time to start again. Don't you agree?" Jenny buries her face in his chest and nods. James holds on tight. "I'm here. We're all here no matter what happens."

They sit quietly for a moment, lost in their own thoughts, until Margot's focus returns to James. "So, when you were in there, you didn't hear anything?"

James shakes his head. "Not really. It was crazy in there. I was in this cubicle between two drunks, and they wouldn't be quiet...they finally threw them out when they started singing Dead Man's Curve. Out of tune I might add."

Slowly, Daz turns to James with a look that could kill and in a deadly tone. "We Were Not Out Of Tune!"

Just then a familiar voice. "Will you let me do this? I am perfectly able to do this myself." The door bangs open and just as noisily bangs shut.

Another voice is heard. "No...I cannot do that...This is hospital policy... please believe I am going to win, and you are going to lose...if I have to tie you to this wheelchair." A very disgruntled orderly wheels a very unhappy John, arm back in a sling, into the waiting room.

162

He spies a cluster of people all standing, staring in his direction. "Does he belong to you?" Both Jenny and James nod at the same time. From halfway across the room, the orderly gives the wheelchair a last mighty shove and watches Johnny glide away.

"You might want to do us all a favor and...put him out of his misery."

John rolls to a stop right in front of James who can only shake his head. "Making friends are we, brother dear?"

Johnny

Jenny is the first to embrace her father with tears streaming down her face, careful not to jostle his bad arm. "I'm so glad you're all right."

Johnny holds on to his daughter. "They wouldn't tell me anything about you. I didn't know if you were...safe or not. I was so worried."

Jenny smiles through the tears. "I'm okay, Daddy...really."

James pushes the wheelchair into the circle and sits beside his brother. "So, what's up with the arm?"

Johnny looks back at the ER door and scowls. "Some nonsense about my overusing my arm after I got shot. They want me to wear this sling for three weeks...that's two and a half weeks longer than I wore it the first time. My arm is just as good as it ever was." He demonstrates by waving his arm around then doubling over in pain.

When Johnny can focus again and has some control over his voice, he looks over at Jenny. "Remind me to pick up my prescription for pain medication at the pharmacy."

Jenny shares a look with Uncle James, who just shakes his head, then turns to Johnny. "Oh, yay...you were so much fun the last time you were on pain meds."

Jenny sits staring at the floor...she knows that there's still one person missing. "Did you hear anything about Robert?"

Time stands still for Johnny. Every nasty thought he ever had about Robert, parades through his mind. He sees Jenny's anguish and knows he has nothing that is going to help her. He shakes his head. "I'm sorry, Jenny. I didn't hear anything." When his little girl needs him the most, Johnny has nothing to make it all better.

A light glimmers when they hear the ER door open and turn to see Phillip Louragan motioning them in.

Robert

Jenny is the first one through the door, but as they follow Phillip through a labyrinth of corridors past curtained off cubicles and then private rooms, she finds herself dropping back until she's bringing up the rear with her dad and Uncle James. The further they go the tighter her grip on Johnny's hand gets until Phillip stops outside a room and motions them all closer.

In a voice one step above a whisper Phillip starts to explain. "The doctors all say Robert will be fine, but he did suffer a concussion from a nasty knock to the head and they want to keep him overnight for observation." There is a collective sigh of relief. The death they all heard about was not one of them.

As Jenny makes her way to the front, Phillip looks through the door. "He's in and out of consciousness and isn't always coherent when he's awake. He doesn't seem to remember the accident...not yet anyway."

Jenny looks from Phillip into the room seeing Robert hooked up monitors and tubes running into his arms. "Can we go in?"

Phillip hesitates, his gaze never leaving Jenny's face. "He's been asking for you, so yes you can go in, but I don't know how lucid he's going to be." With a quick look at her father for moral support, she nods to Phillip and enters the room.

As she enters, she is first aware of the steady beep-beep-beep of the heart monitor. She closes her eyes and listens to the strong and steady beat. Jenny moves closer to the bed just as Robert moves slightly and lets out a low, soft moan. Jenny sits in a chair beside the bed and reaches for Robert's hand. At her first touch Robert slowly opens his eyes and after a moment, smiles briefly and softly utters "I love you," before nodding off.

Jenny sits watching Robert breath...in and out...thinking about what Robert just said. She's been aching to hear those words, but this isn't the candle lit, soft music, romantic vision she had in her mind. She smiles briefly before letting out a huge sigh. This is a stark reminder of the difference between reality and fantasy.

Phillip pokes his head in and Jenny gestures with folded hands against her cheek that Robert is sleeping. Phillip nods ushering the others in while reminding them to be quiet. They form a semi-circle around Robert's bed watching him sleep...sending up silent prayers of thanksgiving that Robert is all right. A nurse quietly enters, checking Robert's vitals and just as quietly leaves the room.

Suddenly Robert's eyes fly open, and a strangled cry comes from deep inside. He frantically tries to remember where he is. Jenny holds on to his hand and Phillip rubs his brow, trying to calm him. Finally, Robert relaxes, laying back against the pillows, gazing up at the faces surrounding him. "I know something happened, but I don't know what,"

Phillip looks intently into Robert's eyes. "You were in an accident, son, but you're safe now."

Robert focuses on Jenny. "Was anybody hurt? Jenny looks briefly at the others before turning back to Robert. "I think there may have been many injuries...even one death...but luckily none of us were seriously hurt."

None of them hear Antoine enter the room, but they see Robert's gaze shift from them to the doorway. They all turn and focus on the silhouetted figure standing just inside the door. "You're wrong Miss Chretien. One of you is...in fact he's dead."

Antoine

Margot is the first to realize the meaning of those words and turns a horrified face to Sergeant Durel, who nods grimly. "Yes, Miss Sallier, Officer Duplantier, was the fatality you heard about." He looks around the room at the shocked, soundless faces before him. "He died protecting those he was sworn to serve. He may have been a nuisance to you, but he was one of my officers and I allowed this to happen."

John and James share a pained look as James runs a hand through his hair. "We're to blame sergeant...we should have listened to you, instead of insisting we do things our way."

Antoine shakes his head. "No, Mr. Chretien, It happened on my watch and I'm the only one responsible."

Guilt begins to settle on the room. Memories of sarcastic remarks and cheap shots taken at Officer Duplantier's expense...all the impatience and ridicule that he experienced at their hands. But there are other recent memories too...Duplantier and Adrienne Gray...Duplantier and classical music...and a cat...and with his hand in a wall. The man they had come to know much too late.

Johnny looks around the room and gives voice to their thoughts. "We're so sorry. He had become a friend" He looks helplessly at Antoine. "Is there anything we can do?"

Sergeant Durel shakes his head. "Keep his grieving parents in your prayers. They're good people." With a final look at their distraught faces, he turns to leave the room.

A small voice stops him, and he looks back to see a distressed Jenny standing before him. "If it's not too much trouble, Sergeant could you tell us about the accident?" She looks at the others. "We really don't know what happened."

Antoine stares deeply into her eyes before deciding. He finally turns all the way back around and plants himself, looming large in the doorway. He turns to James. "Do you remember the last conversation we had...you, me, and Duplantier...where he said he was being followed?"

He is met with a blank stare until a light begins to shine in James' eyes. "Yes...yes, I do."

Antoine nods. "It was a black Suburban coming up fast. He tried to avoid it, but it kept ramming the squad car until Duplantier lost control and skidded across two lanes, over the guard rail and into oncoming traffic. Then the driver came after you, clipping you on the left rear of your limo sending you tumbling into a ditch on the side of the highway. He tried to get away, but lost control of his vehicle, slid across two lanes of traffic and ended on his roof in the median. When we got to him, he was unconscious...and still is."

James is trying to wrap his head around this. "So, he's in this hospital...now?" Antoine nods and points up. "Two floors up."

Johnny rubs his eyes in disbelief. "Do you know why he did this?"

Antoine is very matter of fact. "Well, I'm pretty sure that he killed your brother." Antoine thinks for a minute before deciding to tell all he knows. "His name is Vincent Drago, and he was a commercial fisherman working out of the Florida panhandle...until a few years back when he was reported lost at sea along with two other fishermen. Now we think he killed the other two and faked his own death."

Margot rubs her eyes. "Does this have to do with Lafitte's treasure?"

Antoine nods. "That's my guess...of course we'll know more when he regains consciousness."

Chretien Home
55 Years Ago

It's a balmy July evening in Lake Charles. The temperature is hovering around 78 degrees and mosquitoes are humming, crickets chirping, cicadas buzzing and bullfrogs croaking. A perfect night for a campout in the back yard with smores, scary stories a little singing and stargazing.

Thirteen-year-old Jimmy, 10-year-old Johnny and 7 years old Roger are lying on sleeping bags staring up at the night sky, while Pop lies in their midst pointing out Jupiter and Saturn, which 'Sky and Telescope' has said are Perfectly Visible on this particular July 25th.

He points out the constellation of Orion and the two brightest stars, Rigel and Betelgeuse, Orion's belt and the sword hanging from it. He turns slightly to his left and points to a cluster of stars just to the left and slightly down from Orion.

"Does anybody know the name of that constellation," Roger blurts out. "It's the Big Dipper."

Pop looks at his youngest son, beaming. "Vert good, cher." He turns to the older boys. "Now, do either of you remember its Latin name."

Jimmy is the first to call out much to the chagrin of Johnny. "Canis Major."

James Henry nods but is looking for one more thing. "Meaning?"

This time Johnny gets there first. "The greater dog...one of Orion's two dogs, Canis Major, and Canis Minor."

Pop can't help but be impressed. "Someone has been doing their homework."

Just for a moment Jimmy glares at his younger brother until Mom arrives with a pitcher of sweet tea and a plate of cookies.

Marie Alma looks down, lovingly, at her husband and sons. "And just what preposterous stories are you filling their heads with."

Pop returns the look. "No, mon amour, they are schooling me in astronomy."

She sits next to her husband and pours the tea, passing it around to her family. "Has he told you yet about his famous discovery?"

The boys in wide eyed wonderment shake their heads. Mom and Pop exchange smiles...this is a tale often told. Pop looks seriously at his sons.

"Well, this happened a long time ago...so long that even grand-mére forgot the date." The boys giggle...it always begins the same way.

Pop lays back down, pulling his wife next to him. She snuggles in as he points, once again to the night sky. "Okay, so you see the Big Dipper?" The boys nod. "Now follow the tail as it curves around and just off the tip...you can't see it with the naked eye...is the twin star your Mama is talking about."

Little Roger pipes up. "I think I can see it Pop."

Jimmy and Johnny roll their eyes but Pop kisses his youngest son on the head. "Good eyes son. Anyway, it was on a night much like this one, Dennis Ryan and I were in this very back yard looking through the telescope."

Jimmy points to a telescope covered to protect it. "You mean that one?"

Pop nods smiling at his son. "That very one. We were looking up at the sky...you know trying to spot something no one had ever see before. We were taking turns looking through the telescope when we saw something just off the handle. The more we looked...there weren't as many lights like today...the more we were positive that we could see twin stars. Well, we searched all the star charts, but we couldn't find any mention of double stars in that location." The boys look on in wonderment, hanging on every word. "So, we wrote it up and submitted it to the American Association of Star Observers."

Jimmy is anxious for his dad to go on. "So, they named the double star after you and Dennis Ryan?"

James Henry scratches his head. "Well sort of...they wrote back in a very official letter that the double star had been reported before but had never been named...so they named it after Dennis and me. So up there, just off the tip of the handle is a twin star named Chretien and Ryan."

The boys punch each other. "Wow."

Pop looks from his wife to his sons. "Now, would you rather hear about Jean Lafitte and Ghost Island or the Ten-Legged Jibberjacker?" Roger is the first to shout out. "Jean Lafitte." Pop smiles. "Then Jean Lafitte it is."

Roger smiles satisfied and Pop settles back. "Well, it was on a night just like this one, only it happened a long time ago...so long ago that even grand-mére forgot the date..."

Chapter XIV
"…there's only one guest at a pity party."

Jimmy

It's early morning, just after sunrise and Jimmy is sitting on the back porch swing, untouched coffee cup in his hand, completely still. It's been four days since the accident, Duplantier's funeral is tomorrow and it's a struggle to put pants on in the morning. He finally got Johnny to agree that they should make Mama's bread pudding for the repast after the funeral. Jimmy found the recipe tucked away in Roger's recipe box. He's going to make the pudding and Johnny will make the bourbon sauce.

They've barely spoken ten sentences since they left the hospital and Jimmy's beginning to worry about his brother. All Johnny does is sit in the living room, arm in a sling, listening to Harry Connick Jr. over and over with particular emphasis on the song *Careless Love*. "I'm going to buy myself a shotgun and shoot you four or five times and stand over you and watch you finish dying." Jimmy avoids the living room.

He takes a sip of coffee and immediately spits it back into the cup…cold and no sugar. He dumps the coffee in the zinnia bush. That just about sums up his day so far.

He goes into the kitchen and starts a new pot. While water is boiling, he checks the pantry for brown sugar, raisins, and French bread. The spice rack for cinnamon, nutmeg and vanilla extract, and the refrigerator for eggs, butter, half and half and heavy cream. He'll have to remember to check the liquor cabinet for a good Kentucky Bourbon…Johnny will need that too.

By this time, the water is boiling, and he finishes making the coffee. Staring at the coffee pot, Jimmy realizes he has no more excuses…time to actually make the bread pudding. He whisks the eggs, sugar, and spices together.

He came to Lake Charles to bury his brother...then to find his brother's killer and somehow it became most important to find a treasure. A treasure that he always thought Pop had made up, and now someone else is dead. He buried Roger, the killer is caught. Time to forget treasure and go home.

Jimmy finds himself staring at the mixing bowl...he's forgotten something...bourbon. He steps into the living room, careful not to disturb Johnny. He finds the bottle behind the Couvoisier.

He turns to head back into the kitchen when Johnny opens one eye. "Find the bourbon?"

Jimmy turns back. "Yup."

Johnny narrows his brows. "Jim Beam?"

Jimmy shows him the bottle. "Yup."

Johnny nods in approval. "Don't forget Mom's secret ingredient."

Jimmy frowns. trying to remember. "Love?"

Johnny smiles. "Rum...a tablespoon."

Jimmy nods remembering, turns back to the liquor cabinet and picks a bottle of Zacapa XO.

In the kitchen, he adds a quarter cup of bourbon and tablespoon of the Guatemalan rum. Jimmy tastes it and memories of Mama come flooding back. He whisks it all together and when it's smooth, he adds the half and half, raisins, and pours it over the cubed bread. He sets this aside to sit for two hours, pours himself a cup of coffee...remembering to add sugar this time, and leans against the counter trying to decide whether three or four more batches are needed.

Johnny pokes his head in. "My turn yet?"

Jimmy shakes his head. "Not yet...pour yourself a cup and join me...I'm trying to decide whether to make three or four more batches."

Johnny thinks for a moment. "Four more, you know how much people like it...and there's apt to be a crowd."

The brothers lean against the counter sipping coffee in silence. Finally, Jimmy looks over at John. "We sure made a mess out of this."

Johnny stares into the dark recesses of his coffee cup and nods. "We sure did."

Jimmy finishes his coffee, washes out the cup and returns it to the cupboard. "I think it's time to finish up here and go home."

Johnny cleans his cup and turns to Jimmy. "Amen, to that, brother."

Daz and Diz

Lagniappe House is almost glowing in the late morning sun. Rain is expected for the afternoon, but for now everything is bright and peaceful. A clarinet softly plays the sweet refrain from the old Shaker hymn, "Simple Gifts."

We find Diz standing on the balcony, eyes closed, playing the old song. It is wistful and somber at the same time. Daz, saxophone hanging around his neck, pokes his head out from the balcony door. "Whatcha doin?"

Diz glances back at Daz. "Nothin'…noodling."

Daz shakes his head. "You ain't noodling. Your noodling gives me a headache."

Daz shrugs. "Just playing, then."

Diz cocks his head. "You want to play that at Howard's funeral, don't you?"

Daz smiles briefly. "I do."

Diz considers this. "Me too."

They play a few bars, before Diz stops and motions Daz to sit and they begin to swing. Finally, Diz looks at Daz. "Seen Margot?"

"No…she hasn't been out of her sanctuary since the hospital."

The swing stops as Diz stares off. "Yeah, that's what I thought. Haven't heard a peep from the Chretiens either."

They start swinging again and Daz says what they are both thinking. "Howard's death must be weighing on them."

"Anything we can do about it?"

Daz considers this for a minute. "Maybe."

Diz' eyes narrow. "What you got goin' on in that brain of yours?"

"I'm thinking we need to make a couple of phone calls…one to the Chretiens and the other to Margot."

"Okay, but I think we should go down and pay Margot a visit…we are far more lovable in person."

Daz smiles and agrees. "I can't argue with that…but I think we should be careful. We have to do this just right."

They begin to play a very melodious but melancholy version of Simple Gifts. It's solemn yet hopeful...subdued yet optimistic. When they finish, the final note lingers, floating on the breeze until it fades completely. Diz and Daz are still for just a moment letting the love permeate Lagniappe House. Daz grins around his mouthpiece. "That was awesome."

Diz outright laughs. "No, my man, we were awesome."

Robert

Robert is in the back of Louragan and Son washing and waxing the hearse. Nothing is too good for Officer Duplantier and his family. Robert stops for a minute, trying to understand it all. He was the driver after all, and he feels responsible. But what he doesn't understand is why Howard...why did he have to die? Robert knows what he has to do. He just has to keep waxing.

Robert doesn't notice his father standing in the doorway, until Phillip clears his throat. "Careful, Robert, you'll rub the paint right off." Robert stops, trying to let go of all the stress, guilt, and anxiety he feels about the accident and tomorrow's funeral.

"How do you do it, Pop? How do remain so calm in the face of so much tragedy."

Phillip raises an eyebrow. "Only on the outside."

Robert looks doubtfully at his father. "Really?"

Phillip thinks for a bit and shrugs. "Sometimes...not always. You are always going to feel...something because of what we do. The trick is not let it get to you...personally."

Robert briefly goes back to buffing the limo but stops abruptly. "What if it is, Pop? What if it's very personal?"

Phillip rubs his face. "Then, I'm afraid, you just have to feel what you feel."

Robert closes his eyes. Phillip puts a hand on his shoulder. "Have you spoken to her...have you called Jenny?"

Robert looks away before tossing the rag onto the roof of the limo. "Not since the hospital." He looks to his father. "I don't know what to say...I'm not even sure she wants me to call."

His father shrugs. "Do you want to call her?"

Robert thinks about this before going on. "Why? It's all a jumble." He gives his father a long look before deciding to go on. "It's so many things. The accident...Officer Duplantier's death and something else that I learned at Chretien Point Plantation."

Phillip looks off...he always knew this was inevitable. "What did you learn, Robert?"

172

Robert runs his hand through his hair. "I learned that we are descendant of one of Lafitte's pirates." He studies his father. "And that you knew about the treasure and even passed a clue about it on to me."

Phillip exhales a lungful of air. "Yes, I knew about the treasure...and Chanceaux Louragan. The chant is passed down father to son. I was going to tell you when the time was right... I guess this is the time."

Robert doesn't understand. "But why didn't you tell me before?"

Phillip shrugs. "No good reason, really...I was building a business. Everybody knows that nearly every black man today has people in his past that came from a plantation...that were slaves...but a pirate? I always planned to tell you when you got older...I guess you're old enough now."

Robert can't help but chuckle. "Yes, pop...yes, I am."

Margot

Everything in the room is in shadows. Margot, still in her pajamas and robe, is curled up and dead to the world with the remnants of breakfast before her. She woke up this morning almost back to her normal self. Her first mistake was making an elaborate breakfast of pain perdu, eggs over medium, bacon, sausage, and French press coffee. Her second was turning on the year-round holiday movie channel. The combination of the two was like taking an Ambien with a shot of bourbon.

She manages to focus on the television for just a moment. "Is that still Candace Cameron? It can't be...I've been asleep for..." She checks her watch. "Almost four hours...how many of these movies did she make?"

She is saved from going down that rabbit hole by a soft rapping on the front door and a voice she almost recognizes calling her name. She stubs her toe on the coffee table and hobbles to the front door. She opens it a crack, shielding her eyes from the bright light streaming in, and trying to focus on the two shapes on the other side.

A concerned Daz and Diz stand on the porch looking at a clearly disturbed woman. After an exchange of looks, Diz puts his arm around Margot and leads her back to the couch. Daz picks up the remote and shuts Candace off.

Diz sits beside her and takes her hand. "Okay, Margot, what's going on?"

She is about to say "nothing" but then collapses in Diz's arms. "Oh, Diz, how did it go so completely wrong?"

Diz holds on to Margot letting her cry it out. She finally wipes her eyes and leans back on the couch. "It's all a mess…Howard is dead, and we accomplished nothing."

Daz shares a look with Diz. "Have you spoken to Jenny?"

Margot wipes her nose and shakes her head. "I haven't spoken to anybody…what am I going to say? It's all my fault. If I hadn't shown Roger that brooch none of this would have happened…Roger and Howard would still be alive."

Daz sits on the other side of Margot and takes her hand. "Margot, Roger and Howard are dead because some lunatic murdered them…end of story."

Margot leans back and closes her eyes. "I want to believe that, but right now I can't."

Diz has had enough. "Okay, pity party is officially over. You've got responsibilities. Howard's funeral is tomorrow so you've got less than twenty-four hours to pull yourself together."

Margot looks at him doubtfully, but he's having none of that. "It's the Louisiana way…the Lake Charles way. You've got to pull yourself together and make a Goddamned casserole."

Daz stands up in support, "First, take a shower, get dressed and get into the kitchen. That casserole isn't going to make itself."

Jenny

Jenny can't stand the thought of staying in this house another minute, but, looking out the window …at the bright and shinning day outside makes her hesitate. She, finally, picks up a pair of sunglasses from the table beside the door, and while she has no idea who the glasses belong to, they are dark enough.

She walks outside turns left at the sidewalk and wanders down Engleside Street. She goes only a few blocks when she happens upon Drew Park. She strolls down a path until she comes to bench under a spreading magnolia tree and sits there for…she doesn't really know how long.

A few days ago, she was in the midst of a great adventure a long side the man she was falling in love with. Jenny can only marvel at how quickly everything went to hell. She hasn't heard from Robert in days...she's beginning to loath Louisiana in general and Lake Charles in particular...she hates all the people in the park and can't stand the smell of magnolias.

On the other hand, the thought of going back to Los Angeles and law school doesn't appeal to her at all. She tries to imagine a future that includes torts, briefs, summary judgements and 'Chretien and Chretien: Attorneys at Law' on the door of some swanky L.A. high rise. She's can only shake her head .

A squirrel scampers down the tree and stops at her feet, expecting to be fed. Jenny searches in her pockets and can only find one stale Altoid gathering lint on the bottom. She tosses it to the squirrel, who sniffs it, glares at her and chatters something that Jenny can only imagine is extremely rude. She glances up at the gathering clouds and hears the rumbling of thunder. It's time to head back.

Maybe she should become a nun...a cloistered nun devoting herself to self-flagellation, self-sacrifice, and humiliation. She shakes her head...that's too much like being a lawyer. She looks up to find she's standing outside Uncles Roger's house.

The rain begin to fall as Jenny opens the front door and walks in hoping to find her dad. She hears the squeaking of the back porch swing and heads there, stopping for a cup of coffee before joining her father on the swing.

They sit in silence, swaying back and forth, listening to the soft rain before Jenny turns to her dad. "I'm trying to decide my future."

Johnny looks at her skeptically checking his watch. "What, now? At 2:37 in the afternoon."

Jenny ignores her father. "I'm trying to decide whether I should be a lawyer or a nun."

He stares at his daughter, considering. "Both good choices." Johnny gets serious. "Have you spoken to Robert?"

Jenny shakes her head, and he raises an eyebrow. "Perhaps you should give him a call."

"Perhaps he should give me a call."

"You've become a very stubborn young lady."

Jenny glares at her father. "I don't know where I got that."

Johnny

Leaving Jenny on the back porch, Johnny goes into the kitchen. The smell of Mama's bread pudding fills the room. Jimmy has done his part and now is the time to make Mama's famous bourbon sauce. This is what separates Mama's pudding from every other bread pudding in the State. He checks to make sure that James left enough ingredients for him...Jim Beam...Steens...heavy cream,...and butter.

He finds a large saucepan, melts the butter, and whisks in some sugar. Then comes the heavy cream...he lets that thicken a bit and then comes Mr. Beam, and the Steen's syrup. Johnny leans against the stove and lets the concoction simmer.

Jimmy appears at the kitchen door following his nose. "Smells like Mama's in the house."

Johnny smiles at his brother. "Well, let's see how it turns out before we bring Mama into this."

Jimmy slaps Johnny on the back. "No, son, Mama's right here." Johnny beams and punches Jimmy on the arm. This is male bonding, Louisiana style...food and family.

Jimmy takes a step back and appraises his brother, "So, what happened to you...you seem to be feeling better."

Johnny shrugs. "Well, as Mama would say...there's only one guest at a pity party."

Jimmy nods, remembering. "That she did."

Johnny looks out toward the back porch. "Jenny's struggling though, and I've got to find a way to help."

Jimmy's gaze follows Johnny's. "She called Robert yet?"

"No...she says he should call her."

Jimmy chuckles. "She's definitely your daughter."

Jenny appears at the door as if cosmically called. She smiles at the bread pudding in the oven and bourbon sauce on the stove. "That is a glorious smell."

Johnny cocks his head and wistful smile spreads across his lips. "I wish Roger was here, he loved that smell."

Jimmy's eyes mist. "And Howard...that boy loved to eat."

Johnny puts his arms around his brother and daughter. "I'm sure Mom and Pop are making Roger and Howard a meal they'll never forget."

Jimmy closes his eyes. "Amen to that, brother."

After a moment Johnny breaks the spell and moves to the stove, stirring the pan before turning off the burner and putting on the lid. "Now we let it cool...all those wonderful flavors coming together. Tomorrow it will be perfect."

As they stand together thinking about tomorrow, Jenny's phone begins to play Alicia Key's *Girl on Fire.* Jenny mouths "It's Daz" and goes back to the porch to take the call. Johnny cocks his head. "Maybe he can help."

Jenny comes in from the back porch, frowning. Johnny looks over at her. "What'd Daz want?"

Jenny considers this for a moment. "He was trying to find out if I've spoken to Robert...I wish everyone would mind their own business."

Jimmy is about to speak when his phone pings...then Johnny's...then Jenny's. They all check their phone. Jimmy is the first to speak. "A text from Sergeant Durel."

Jenny, concern spreading across her face. "He wants to see us at the station...now."

Antoine

A light rain with thunder in the distance falls as Jenny pulls her Fusion into LCPD parking lot. Johnny notices Phillip Louragan's Mercedes parked two spots over. He thinks it unlikely that Jenny didn't see. They sprint for the main door and Johnny ushers James and Jenny in out of the rain. Officer Thibodeau, at the main desk, barely looking up, points to a hallway off to the right and announces: "Conference Room."

They dutifully follow the hallway until they arrive at a door clearly marked 'Conference Room.' They take off hats, remove coats and smooth hair before opening the door. Jenny sees Robert sitting beside his father. Johnny guides her to a chair directly opposite from Robert's. He and James sit on either side. As Johnny sits, he meets Phillip's eyes, who smiles briefly and nods toward Robert. Johnny returns the smile and nods toward Jenny shaking his head. They both get the message. "Kids."

Margot enters flanked by Diz and Daz. She surveys the room. Margot, ever the picture of a perfect southern lady, goes first to Jenny, kisses her cheek, takes her by the hand and leads her to the chair beside Robert's and dares her to sit down. Margot walks back around the table and sits between James and John. Her message is clear…there are no sides in this room. Following her lead, Daz takes a seat beside Jenny, while Diz sits next to James.

Jenny and Robert remain stoically staring forward. The silence is broken when Antoine enters the room with a curt, "Good Afternoon."

He takes his place at the head of the table and looks from one side to other. He will never…not in a thousand years…understand these people.

He, finally, clears his throat and forges ahead. "First, there is a massive storm that just passed over the Yucatan Peninsula and is in the Gulf gathering strength before making landfall as a category 5 or 6." He consults the notes in his hand. "Its current trajectory puts Lake Charles right in the middle of its path."

A confused group of people share looks. James speaks for them all. "Why the weather report…why did you have to drag us down here for that?"

Antoine glares back. "Because I don't want any of you getting any fool notions to go out treasure hunting in the middle of a hurricane."

James speaks for all the Chretiens. "You don't have to worry about us, Sergeant, we're leaving just as soon as we can after Officer Duplantier's funeral."

Antoine nods. "It may be while…if the forecast holds, the hurricane will hit by late afternoon tomorrow."

Johnny looks toward Antoine. "Is that all, Sergeant?"

Antoine stares him down. "No, actually, it isn't…I've just come from the hospital."

The room gets quiet. Antoine has their attention now. James is the first to speak. "Is it Drago? Did he finally wake up?"

Antoine shakes his head. "No, Mr. Chretien." He stares at each person in the room. "Vincent Drago is missing."

Chretien Home
20 years ago

Roger Chretien opens the front door and enters followed by Jimmy and Johnny. Their mood is somber as befits a meeting going over Pop's final wishes. They stand in the living room sharing unspoken memories of their father. Pop had left this house to all three of the boys, but Roger is the only one who wants to stay. James can't wait to get the hell out of Dodge and Johnny has a family waiting for him.

Roger looks first to James, then to John. "So, what are your plans...when do you plan to leave?"

Johnny shrugs. "I'm here as long as you need me...you know that Roger...but it should be soon."

Jimmy lays a hand on his brother's shoulder. "You know I love you, but I have to go...tomorrow if I can get a flight,"

Roger understands, but there is something else...something that Roger wants to share but isn't sure if he should. After a moment Roger gestures for his brothers to follow him. He leads them into Pop's study, sits at his desk and turns on the computer, before looking up at them.

"After Pop died and before y'all got here, I began going through Pop's stuff to gather things we might need for probate...and I came across this."

Now curious, Jimmy and Johnny gather around the computer screen and look over Roger's shoulder. Staring at the screen, Roger goes on. "Well, it seems Pop subscribed to one of those family tree sites."

This isn't at all what James and John were expecting.

Roger goes on. "If you follow Pop's tree...not on his dad's side but on his mother's, you find that his...our great, great, great, great grandmother was Marie Lafitte...sister of Jean Lafitte."

Jimmy considers this and shrugs. "I admit it is interesting...but so what?"

Roger turns around so he's facing his brothers. "Well, just suppose those stories Pop would tell about Jean Lafitte and his treasure were not just legend or things Pop made up, but actual family stories?

James shares a look with John. "You're saying that there really is a treasure somewhere around Contraband Bayou?"

Roger nods. "That's what I'm thinking."

John rubs his face. "So, you want us to go off on a treasure hunt?"

179

Roger squints up at his brothers. "No...I'm saying I do what I do best and research this."

James shrugs. "Well, of course, if you want to...but I can't help thinking this is a complete waste of time."

John agrees. "I wouldn't spend a lot of time on this."

Roger thought they'd be as intrigued about this as he is. But he has always known that his brothers have never shared his sense of adventure or interest in the unique culture and history of Louisiana. Roger smiles to himself. He is a history professor after all and he'll do what he does and when he finds the proof, his brothers will get on board.

Chapter XV
"The world will be a little less without him."

James

James sits in the backseat of Margot's Prius looking at the long stream of cars ahead of them. How did it come to this? He tries to remember the way he felt when he first arrived in Lake Charles. Roger's death was really nothing more than an inconvenience. He had wanted to deal with Roger and be on his way. Now he sits watching Lake Charles pass by trying to remember how it used to be. Why he hates it so much. He believed he had outgrown it…that he was somehow superior but now it's almost like he stood still, and Lake Charles grew up without him.

James shakes his head…in death Roger changed his life. Just for moment James had felt alive…that he was a part of something. For the first time in years, he had felt connected…connected to John…to Jenny and Roger. Something at long last was more important than the end of the fiscal year.

James stares at his own reflection in the window, and he doesn't like what he sees. He's become a self-pitying and bitter old man. He sneaks a look at John…what does he feel? He looks at Margot and Jenny in the front seat…what do they feel? If nothing else Roger's death has to mean something. Officer Duplantier…Howard's death has to mean something.

Antoine

Antoine stands beside his squad car as an almost unending motorcade turns left from Common Street, enters the cemetery and winds toward the grave site. Police from all over Louisiana…even some as far away as California and New York…have come to pay respects to their fallen comrade. Antoine wishes he could focus all his attention on the funeral, Officer Duplantier, deserves that, but with Vincent Drago on the loose, he has no idea what to expect next.

As the motorcade comes to stop, Antoine hears the first strains of "When the Saints go Marching In" and knows that Diz and Daz are in the house. He doesn't know how they manage it, but the song is both solemn and hopeful. He reflects, for just a moment, on the lyrics: "Lord, I want to be in that number." Antoine smiles briefly, thinking of Duplantier marching...probably starting on the wrong foot...with all the Saints. Tears well up in his eyes, as his smile fades. His eyes linger on the hearse as it rolls to a stop. "You keep the streets of heaven safe now, you hear?"

He wipes a tear from his eye, all the while scanning the perimeter for some danger...something out of place. Diz and Daz begin *Simple Gifts* as Antoine watches as Robert and Phillip exit the hearse. Phillip moves to the right side of the limousine behind them, opening the door for the grieving family while Robert opens the rear door of the hearse as the pallbearers, in their full-dress uniforms stand ready to escort their fallen brother to his final resting place.

Antoine is vaguely aware that Diz and Daz have stopped playing and a lone piper begins playing "Amazing Grace." He is intently watching as Margot, far back in the line of cars, exits her Prius followed by James, John and finally Jenny.

He wishes they had stayed away, but he knows they need to pay their respects to the man who died protecting them. It will be a huge relief when they go back to California, but for now, it's his job to protect them.

Officers stand at attention as the pallbearers process through the honor guard. Antoine checks in with his team, placed strategically throughout the cemetery and gets an "all clear."

He is acutely aware of the ceremonial, Last Call, remembering the actual moment when he realized that Officer Duplantier would never respond to his call again. He winces with every shot of the Twenty-One Gun salute. Though his eyes never stop moving, he hears the minister give the final blessing. As he makes the sign of the cross, Antoine can't help but remember the Catholic Requiem Mass and the Latin words, *"Dona eis requiem, dona eis requiem, dona eis requiem, sempiternum.* Grant him rest, grant him rest, grant him eternal rest."

Antoine makes his way to the podium, pausing at the foot of the casket to give Officer Duplantier one final salute. Once he arrives at the podium and gazes out at the people before him…the family…the Brothers in Blue…the many mourners, Antoine realizes that no words will ever be enough. No words will ever relieve the pain. All he can do is speak from the heart.

"It is with almost unbearable pain but also great pride that I stand before you to pay my respects to a fellow officer, who died tragically doing his duty. It's a strange relationship that develops between a training officer and his rookie. A bond develops based on loyalty and trust. It is a sacred bond that only occurs between people that risk their lives, day in and day out, to protect each other. Even though Officer Duplantier died miles away from me…I feel the weight of his death. I feel responsible because he was one of us…one of mine…and I wasn't there to protect him. He was a good officer…a good man and a good…friend. The world will be a little less without him."

A tear runs down Antoine's cheek and he hurries from the podium before anyone notices. He wishes that Vincent Drago were here right now so he could kill him with his bare hands.

Daz and Diz

Diz is only half listening as Antoine begins to speak. His mind is too busy It would help if he had some idea what Vincent Drago looks like. He doesn't even know who Drago is targeting. It could be any of them. He has to keep reminding himself that they are dealing with a mad man and logic does not apply.

Daz is busy scanning the perimeter trying to outthink Drago. He looks for any telltale signs, like sun glistening off of the scope or birds suddenly startled but sees nothing. He looks over at Diz and sees that he is just as frustrated. This is the most likely place for Drago to make his move, but they have no idea what that move will be.

Antoine finishes speaking and moves away from the podium. Two officers remove the Flag draped over the casket and with precise movements fold it into a perfect triangle, placing it in the arms of Duplantier's mother. They begin "Nearer my God to Thee" as Duplantier is lowered into the ground.

As their last note lingers, people begin to get up and pay their respects to the family. Diz notices Adrienne hug both Margot and

183

Jenny, before coming to the front to offer her condolences to the family.

Officer Duplantier's mother approaches. "Thank you so much for the music...I didn't know you knew Howard."

Diz takes her hand. "It is our pleasure. Howard was a dear friend."

Diz and Daz pack up their instruments as Margot makes her way through the crowd followed by the Chretiens. Margot embraces them. "That was just beautiful, guys." Diz nods his thanks as Daz waves to John and James. Jenny, as if unsure of her place, hesitantly approaches. She is embraced warmly first by Diz and then by Daz.

John approaches. "I didn't know whether we should come or not."

James moves to his brother's side. "But we couldn't stay away."

Daz understands. "It's a strange time for us all."

There is an awkward silence. James clears his throat. "Well, we have food for the repast, so we need to drop that off, but..." He lowers his voice. "We should really talk."

Before Daz can respond, Margot cuts in. "Are you guys coming?"

Daz looks to Diz, who shrugs. "I think we'll stop by for a bit."

Jenny hangs back, giving them a small wave. "You sounded great."

Diz nods and watches Jenny as she walks away, searching the crowd for someone.

Daz cocks his eye as he turns to Diz. "You think she's looking for Robert?"

Diz watches her. "I'd bet on it."

Daz shrugs. "Well, you know what they say, 'God looks after fools and lovers,' and they need all the help they can get."

Daz smiles in agreement.

Robert

Robert is silent as he maneuvers the hearse behind the long procession of motorcycles focusing all his attention on the task at hand. He doesn't have to think about Howard...about the accident...about the pain...about Jenny. He knows that she is somewhere behind him, and he tries to convince himself that he isn't looking for her.

Phillip watches Robert out of the corner of his eye. He has no idea how to help his son. Every time he begins a conversation, Robert finds a way to escape...not to talk about how he feels. Phillip knows that if Robert can't begin to talk about his feelings he will never be able to get past the pain.

With a side glance at his son, Phillip takes a deep breath. "Robert."

Robert shifts his eyes from the mirror to a brief glance at his father, before returning to road before him. "Not now, Pop...I have to concentrate on what I'm doing."

Phillip shakes his head. "Yes, Robert, now."

Robert looks forward. "I'm a grown man and you need to respect that."

"With all due respect, Son, you may be a grown man on the outside, but inside you are a boy trying to make sense of a world that has gone sideways."

Still nothing from Robert, but Phillip is determined. "There is a time when we outgrow our parents. When our pain can't simply be fixed by a word or kiss from mommy and daddy. When we need something more...someone more." For the first time Phillip sees Robert consider what he's saying. "I am no longer the person who kisses your booboo and makes it all better...Jenny is."

Robert shakes his head. "But what if she doesn't feel the same way...there is no way to know for certain."

Phillip smiles and puts his hand on Robert's shoulder. "Son, I know this doesn't help, but I know for certain. Her father knows for certain...everybody knows for certain...but you and Jenny. You need to make a leap of faith."

Robert's shoulder's slump. "But Pop...I'm scared."

"Of course, you're scared. That why they call it a leap of faith and not a skip."

Margot

They all rise as the procession begins. Margot cannot look at the casket...it's hard to believe that Howard is really dead. She thinks back to the last time she saw him...back at Chretien Point, standing on a chair, reaching into a hole in the wall...expecting to be bitten at any moment, before bringing out that cedar box. The box that they hoped would provide the last clue they needed to solve the mystery of Lafitte's treasure. How wrong they were.

She struggles to focus on the ceremony and hears Sergeant Durel "He was a good officer…a good man and a good…friend. The world will be a little less without him."

Those words echo through Margot's mind. Her eyes begin to fill as she realizes how much those words apply to Roger. So much has happened, there hasn't been time to mourn him. Good people are dead…and for what…a treasure that probably doesn't even exist.

As the funeral ends, Margot remains seated unaware of what is happening around her until her hands are enveloped within the warm folds of another pair. She looks up into the emerald green eyes of Adrienne Gray.

Adrienne smiles. "I'm sorry I didn't know Roger…he must have been a wonderful man."

With those words she rises and follows the others to pay her respects. Margot watches her go and sits back realizing she no longer feels hopeless and helpless, because, no matter what lies ahead, she is prepared.

Johnny

Johnny, following James to the car, turns and waits for Jenny and Margot. He shakes his head when he sees them, heads together speaking intensely to one another. Those two have become so close, it's easy to forget there's a forty-year difference in age.

He watches as Jenny breaks apart from Margot and hurries toward him. Johnny reaches out his hand and smiles when she grabs a hold of it…just like when she was a little girl. "We'd better head on over to the repast."

Jenny smiles and shakes her head. "You go on ahead, I'm going to find Robert. I need to tell him we've been idiots."

Johnny laughs. "I'm sure he'll be relieved to know."

Jenny runs off in search of Robert and Margot arrives embracing him briefly and kissing him on the cheek. "We should go."

They find Jimmy leaning against the Prius, checking emails and…whistling. Johnny can't remember the last time James whistled. Jimmy stops and puts down his phone. "Johnny, come on. We need to get my bread pudding over there."

Johnny shakes his head, laughing. "Relax, Jimbo. You're bread pudding ain't nothing without my sauce."

Margot opens the car door. "And don't forget my casserole."

186

Jenny

Jenny begins looking for Robert. At last, she spots him wending his way toward her. Her first instinct is to run to him…to leap into his arms, but suddenly she becomes shy and uncertain. What if Robert doesn't feel what she feels…what if it's over between them.

One look at Robert's face when he sees her standing there, changes everything. They hurry toward each other, careful not to disturb the graves around them, and tenderly embrace in front of the living and the dead. For the moment, they are the most important people in the world.

They slowly break apart and for a long moment simply gaze into each other's eyes. They are overwhelmed with emotion and don't know where to begin. There is so much to say…so many feelings…that it's hard to contain. Hard to contain such love.

They walk hand in hand back to the hearse lost in their own special world. When they arrive, Jenny looks up…conscious of her surroundings. "I suppose we should go and pay our respects."

Robert murmurs. "I suppose." Neither of them move.

"I told my dad we'd meet him there."

"Then, that's what we should do."

Still no movement. "Should we wait for your dad?"

"No need, he left in the limo."

"Then there's no reason for us to stay here."

"No reason at all."

Still, they remain exactly where they are. Oblivious to anything but each other. Oblivious to the darkening clouds. Oblivious to the light breeze changing to a steady wind. Oblivious to the thunder approaching. Oblivious to the soft pattering of rain as it becomes more insistent. Oblivious to the shadow as it approaches slowly, silently…relentlessly. Oblivious until it's too late.

The sudden torrential rain…flashes of lightening and the explosion of thunder all obscure the real danger. Jenny doesn't realize that anything is wrong until Robert is lying in a heap at her feet…blood from his wound mixing with the puddles of water on the ground. Until something is placed over her head, and she is manhandled into the trunk of car. Until, with a roar of the engine, the car speeds off into the darkening gloom of the storm. Until there is no one left…no one but Robert…bloody unconscious, Robert.

187

Laguna Beach, California
Three Weeks Ago

Laguna Beach is a magical place...ten square miles of absolute heaven. Sandy beaches...with surfers and tidepools...caves and caverns. Ten square miles of gourmet restaurants...of luxury yachts...of beautiful people...and one James Chretien who finds himself stuck in a conference room listening to a quarterly report.

When he was asked to sit on the board of this prestigious art festival he was told to jump at the chance. After all it would open doors, he was told...and it did. Doors to parties he didn't want to attend...doors to art openings he wasn't interested in...doors to other festival boards he didn't even know existed.

So here he sits listening to some guy, drone on about revenues...blah-blah-blah...and deficits...blah-blah-blah...and bottom lines...blah-blah-blah.

His phone vibrates and James takes a quick look at the caller...Roger...and sends it directly to voicemail. He doesn't have time for Roger...not today.

Again, the phone vibrates...again it's Roger...and again off to voicemail. Roger will have to wait.

With the meeting finally over, James races to his Tesla S in Midnight Silver Metallic with cream interior and 21-inch Arachnid Wheels. His plan is simple...quick stop at his place...throw a few things into a duffle, a quick drive to the marina and his boat. Then off to Ensenada, where he plans on spending the weekend not talking to...listening to...or interacting in any way, shape, or form...with other people.

As he pulls out of the parking lot with Good Vibrations from his Feelin' Cool playlist blasting, Roger calls again. He hates the way the music just stops, and this disembodied voice announces, "Roger." Not now...not when he's pickin' up good vibrations. What can Roger possibly want? He pushes the connect button. "What." Silence on the other end...Finally, a timid, unsure voice comes on the line. "Mr. Chretien...are you James Chretien?"

James rolls his eyes. "Of course, I'm James Chretien...you called me...remember? Who is this? You're not Roger."

188

"Mr. Chretien, this is Margot Sallier...I'm a...friend of your brother's." He stares at his dashboard trying to see this Margot Sallier on the other end. "Okay, Ms. Sallier...why are you calling from my brother's phone?"

There's another uncomfortable silence on the other end and James is just about to hang up when the voice returns. "Mr. Chretien...Roger...your brother is dead."

Roger is dead? Roger can't be dead. He just talked to Roger not more than...six months...maybe seven months ago. This simply can't be. "How did...what happened?"

Again, an awkward pause. "He apparently drowned."

This makes no sense to James. "Drowned? That's imposs...what do you mean apparently drowned?"

He hears a sharp intake of breath on the other end. "At the moment things are unclear. You really need to be here."

No, no, not today...he needs to sail to Ensenada today...he needs peace and quiet today. "I'm sorry...Ms. Sallier, but I can't possibly think about this today. There's so much to process...I need time...next week. I can come next week. Tuesday...I'll be there Tuesday."

Before Margot can respond, James disconnects. He can't deal with this today. He'll deal with it Monday...after Ensenada.

Chapter XVI
"What am I missing?"

Jenny

Locked in the trunk of a car with a blanket over her head and hands bound behind her back, Jenny is terrified...confused. Robert lying at her feet with his blood swirling in a pool of water is all she can see. She was so happy a moment ago. So happy to be with Robert again...to feel love again...to feel safe.

She has to believe he will be okay, but she needs to concentrate on what's happening right now...to her. Where is she? Have they left the cemetery yet? Did they make a right or left turn onto whatever the name of that street is? Why didn't she pay more attention when Margot was driving?

Jenny forces herself to stay still...to take deep breaths...to reach out with her senses. What can she tell about where she is right now? Jenny waits, trying to think. Okay...she's in a trunk. It's still raining. There must be a leak in one of the seals because she can feel a trickle of water on her right ankle. What else? She's jammed against something. Something soft, but not too soft. Now...what direction are they going in? Jenny shuts her eyes...she doesn't know why she needs to shut her eyes, but she does. She shuts her eyes and tries to feel it. North...she doesn't know how she knows...but they are heading north.

Wait, she needs to stop. She's beginning to feel claustrophobic and nauseous. Jenny recognizes the signs...she's beginning to panic. Jenny takes a deep breath, letting it out...slowly. Okay...let's go back...she is heading north. Can she tell anything about the road? Jenny considers this. It's paved. Maybe they are on highway. Any traffic? Not much...that she can hear anyway.

Alone in the dark trunk, Jenny considers. Her dad knows she was going to find Robert. He won't be expecting her immediately. Will he be concerned if she doesn't show up at the repast at all? Probably not, he'll figure she's spending time with Robert.

So, they may not be missed until tomorrow. This is not good. She tries to sit up and hits her head, sharply on the trunk roof. Through the bright flashes of lights before her eyes, she tries to think. Robert is unconscious…bleeding. Someone needs to help Robert.

Jenny panics for just a minute…until she remembers…Diz and Daz. God bless Diz and Daz. They were still there. They'll notice the hearse. They'll notice Robert. They'll get him the help he needs, and he'll tell them about me. She has to believe that Diz and Daz are still there, and Robert is alive.

Jenny closes her eyes and concentrates on breathing. She needs to gain control. She begins to feel her body relax. Okay, let's start at the beginning…She is in the crowded trunk of a car, heading north on a highway with little or no traffic…

Diz and Daz

Diz and Daz are still schmoozing when the first raindrops begin fall. It's amazing how quickly people scatter when Mather Nature makes an appearance. As they run to the Corvette, Daz points to the hearse about seventy-five yards away.

In the car Diz peers through the rain. "I guess Robert is still here."

They continue to look, but Daz frowns. "I don't see him." He wipes the now fogged windshield. "Do you see him?"

Diz shakes his head, squinting through the rain. Diz and Daz exchange looks. Diz' eyes wander back to the hearse. "Maybe he's having engine trouble."

A silent agreement is made…Daz nods. "Let's check it out."

The Corvette roars to life and slowly moves the seventy-five yards until it is nose to nose with the hearse. Diz looks into the darkened cab but can't make anything out. "Well, I don't see him."

Daz shakes his head. "I don't either."

They both try to look through the slanting rain as the wind begins to pick up. For the tenth time Daz wipes his fogged window. "This is very weird."

They sit back in their seats and try to think. Suddenly, Diz sits forward. "Wasn't Jenny going to look for him?"

Daz nods in agreement. "Right…they must be together."

Diz nods and they begin searching for two people now. After a few minutes, Daz sits back in total frustration. "This is ridiculous, I still don't see anything."

Diz leans his head against the cool window. "Great, now, we've lost two people."

Daz continues to search when out of the blue something catches his attention. He grabs Diz' arm and points. "Diz, do you see?"

He turns to Diz, but only gets a blank stare in return. He points more emphatically. "There…just where the ground begins to rise."

Nothing from Diz. "On the ground…"

Daz can't wait any longer. He throws the door open, sprinting between gravestones and calling over his shoulder. "Bring a blanket."

Diz watches him run off, still not seeing what he sees. He feels around in the space behind the front seats and grabs a blanket that is miraculously there and runs after Daz.

He finds him crouched beside Robert's crumpled body feeling for a pulse. Diz holds his breath until Daz looks up and utters one word. "Alive."

Relief surges through his body as he spreads the blanket over Robert's sodden body and is already dialing when Daz looks up and says, "Call 911." As they stand in the pouring rain Diz scans the area. "No sign of Jenny."

Daz thinks for a minute. "Maybe she left before this happened." They stare at each other, while sirens get ever closer.

Diz and Daz turn in unison as the ambulance arrives, followed by three police cruisers. They move silently back as the paramedics surround Robert and watch as Sergeant Durel walks toward them.

Antoine squats next to the paramedics. "Alive?" The paramedics all nod as one and Antoine exhales and slowly stands turning to Diz and Daz. "You found him?" A statement more than a question.

Diz looks at Daz and nods. "Yeah, we saw the hearse and wanted to make sure he was okay."

Durel nods, but Daz reaches out. "Jenny…we think Jenny Chretien may have been here."

Antoine looks off into the pelting rain and shakes his head in disgust, "Shit." And trudges back to his squad car.

Daz watches him sit silently behind the wheel and turns to Diz "We should call, someone."

Diz looks up. "Who?"

Daz is suddenly aware of rain trickling down his neck and hunches his shoulder. "I don't know, they're all together...call Margot, she'll know what to say." Diz nods and hits speed dial.

Margot

Margot, dry and warm, patiently waits in line for her turn at the bread pudding. She ladles a scoop into a bowl and pours a healthy dallop of bourbon sauce over the creamy goodness. She takes one bite and instantly feels the glow. A sense of wellbeing transports her back to her childhood.

She looks for James and John and sees them holding court with Philip Louragan. She makes a beeline for them, not caring whether she is interrupting or not. "This is the best bread pudding I have ever had."

James beams with pride, but John waves the compliment aside. "Don't tell him that. It's not the pudding...it's the sauce. You could put my sauce over an old tire, and it'd taste great."

Margot laughs and is about to reply when her phone vibrates. She holds up one finger and turns to answer. All the color drains from her face as she turns to Phillip. "They found Robert unconscious at the cemetery."

John's laughter is cut short as a horrific thought assaults his mind. He turns and meets Margot's terrified eyes. "What about Jenny?" Margot shakes her head. "She isn't there...and they have no idea where she is."

John and Phillip move to each other, both trying to draw strength from the other. Instinctively James drapes his arms protectively around the shoulders of the fathers. When will this nightmare end?

Margot finishes the call and joins the huddle. "Robert is awake and they're taking him to St. Pat's."

John gives Phillip's shoulder one final squeeze as they break apart. John looks lost as he watches Phillip rush from the room. Margot tries to be of some comfort. "Diz and Daz said they will meet us at your place." John nods absently.

James picks up his cue. "Let's go. We can't do anything here."

Margot watches as James gently guides John out of the room.

On her way out she looks heavenward. "Roger, get with Howard. We need help." At the door she pauses and looks back. "Now!"

James sits shotgun as Margot weaves her way through the building storm. He pulls down the vanity mirror in the visor and watches John in the backseat. He can't tell if John has completely zoned out or if he's plotting some diabolical revenge. The hurricane is still a day out and with any luck will go around them. Of course, they don't seem to have much luck. Good luck anyway. Luck...that's a funny word.

James leans his head back on the headrest and closes his eyes. His brain has turned to mush. He has got to focus. Johnny needs him...Jenny needs him. Margot pulls up in front of the house and without a word John throws open the rear door and walks out into the rain heading for the front door. James is steps behind, opening the door and John, without a word, stomps into the house, through the living room, dining room and through the kitchen door.

James watches him through the swinging door march through the kitchen and out onto the back porch. He hears the unmistakable squeak of the swing as John settles in. Margot joins James at the door and peers into the house. She looks up at James and frowns. He shrugs. "He's thinking. He does his best thinking swinging on the back porch." James walks in the house and toward the kitchen.

Margot follows and finds James leaning against the sink with an empty coffeepot in his hand. He stares at the pot for a moment before looking to Margot. "You know, I can't just stand here making coffee while one brother is dead and my other brother is out on the porch, hurting. While my niece is missing...while her boyfriend is in the hospital...while some guy named Vincent Drago ruins our lives."

The kitchen door swings open, and Diz and Daz walk in. Diz looks back over his shoulder. "Did you know the front door is standing wide open?"

Jimmy nods toward the back porch. "Johnny's out there. Y'all go out."

James watches them. He needs time to think. He keeps going over it and it doesn't add up. Vincent Drago escapes from the hospital, right under Durel's nose? Then he attacks Robert and takes Jenny...again on Durel's watch. It doesn't add up. Unless...unless Durel is as much in the dark as we are.

James goes out onto the porch and sits beside Johnny swinging slowly. He looks at Diz and Daz. "You found Robert? What did

Durel say when he arrived? What did he do when he found out Jenny was missing?"

Daz looks at Diz before answering. "Honestly, he didn't do anything. He sat in his car while the paramedics took Robert away."

The swinging stops and James leans forward. "I'm thinking that Detective Sergeant Antoine Francois Durel could use help."

Robert

Robert sits upright on the examination table waiting to be discharged. He's been poked, prodded, stitched, and given a tetanus shot. He would have left an hour ago if his dad weren't sitting across from him glaring every time he even thought of leaving. "Dad, let's just go...I'm fine."

Phillip just shakes his head. "I know, Robby...just hang tight. We'll be out of here in a minute."

It's not very often that Robert gets exasperated with his father, but his dad doesn't get it...he doesn't understand. How can he make him understand?

"Robby, I know you've got to do something to help Jenny. But let's just wait and hear what the doctor says."

Phillip is interrupted when the cubicle curtain is drawn back and the doctor walks in. He shines a light in Robert's eyes...checks his pulse and glares at him, pulling up a rolling stool. "Okay, Robert, what gives? You were just in here. You've suffered another concussion... not as bad as the last one, but bad enough."

He looks to Phillip. "I don't know what your son is doing, but it's got to stop." He turns his attention back to Robert. "I'm tempted to keep you in here."

Robert begins to object but the doctor simply raises his hand. "But I won't as long as you promise to get some rest and stop doing...whatever it is you're doing." He glares at both father and son. "Now get out of here before I change my mind."

Robert jumps from the table to get dressed but sits down abruptly to stop the room from spinning. Phillip just sits with his arms folded. "What did the doctor just say, Robert?"

Robert frowns at his father and stands much more slowly this time. "He said I could leave and that's what I'm doing."

Phillip looks heavenward. "And then what Robert. What are you going to do then?"

Robert, pulling up his pants, doesn't hesitate. "I'm going to find Jenny."

Antoine

Antoine sits at his desk, glowering and absently takes a sip of coffee. He feels like he's just spinning his wheels. What did they miss? What did he miss? He has no illusions. This is his mess. He made this mess. He looks deeply into his grandma's cup. "Mamére, what am I not seeing...what am I missing?"

He sits back rubbing his eyes. Okay what does he know? Almost everyone had left, and the storm had just hit. Everyone was running for cover, but Drago was there. "I was still there, for Christ's sake. It happened right under my nose." He doesn't have time for more recrimination because his phone buzzes. He picks it up, fumbles the receiver for a moment and finally, "Whatcha got?" He doesn't wait for a complete answer. "Be right there."

He jumps from behind his desk and runs out of his office and down the hall. He throws open a door into a darkened room and commandeers a seat in front of a bank of computers and without looking up, repeats, "Whatcha got?"

A technician looks up from the screen. "Cameras...we got cameras."

Antoine doesn't take his eyes off the screen. "Show me."

The technician nods. "Okay, the service was over about 11:45 and the crowd started to disperse about fifteen minutes later. By 12:30 most of the people had left. Now watch."

He presses play and the image on the screen shows an empty cross street just as a deluge begins. Antoine frowns. "What am I looking at?"

The technician hits stop. "This is where Cemetery Road meets Common Street. Watch."

He presses play. Then, through the pouring rain, Antoine watches as a dark sedan comes into frame and turns right. Antoine looks up. "That all?"

The technician grins. "Nope." He turns to a different screen and brings up a new image. "Here we have the same street where it meets Highway 10."

Antoine leans forward and watches the same sedan as it merges onto the highway heading west. Antoine sits back. "Where does it go after that?"

The technician turns to a third computer and hits the play button, and we see the same sedan, exit the highway and head north on the road to Westlake. "Now we don't have any more footage of the sedan, but if I'd have to guess. I'd say he's headed to…"

He's interrupted by Antoine. "Sam Houston Jones State Park." He's out the door shouting over his shoulder. "I want choppers in the air…now. Tell SWAT to move. I want to be at the park in twenty minutes and I want an exact location by then."

He runs into his office, takes a final gulp of coffee, and sends up a silent prayer to his grandmére. He checks his sidearm, grabs his vest and is out the door.

Eighteen minutes later Antoine is standing in a clearing at Sam Houston Jones State Park surround by the SWAT team. He points to a map. "We have eyes on a dark sedan parked here about 50 clicks in." He looks up. "No sign of activity, but let's be careful. This guy has killed before and I don't want him to get another chance." He looks around. "Let's move."

Antoine moves just behind the SWAT team and when they stop, he waits for the team leader to report. "We're here." Antoine checks his sidearm one more time. "Okay…secure the vehicle. Let's go."

The team fans out, surrounding the car. The team leader looks up…it's empty. Antoine looks at the closed trunk and barely nods his head for someone to pop it open. He hears the trunk latch give and the lid swings up. The world stops for only a minute as they all see a shape covered in a blanket. Antoine slips on a pair of gloves as he walks to the trunk and pulls back the blanket.

Vincent Drago. Antoine sits on the rear bumper. "Now what?"

Johnny

In the midst of the discussion on the back porch, Johnny gets up and goes into the kitchen. He knows they are only trying to help, but they have no idea what's going on in his mind. He'd gladly change places with Jenny…to spare her whatever pain she's going through, but of course that's absurd. Jenny is much more capable of getting herself out of this situation than he ever would be. The thought that she's making this Vincent Drago guy's life a living hell makes him smile…just a bit.

Johnny hears a commotion coming from the living room. Phillip calls out. "Hey is anybody here?"

A very determined Robert comes into the kitchen and stops before Johnny. "I'm here to save Jenny."

Phillip follows Robert and pauses just a moment looking from Robert to Johnny, settling on Johnny. "Do you know, your front door is open?"

Robert looks for just a moment at his father before focusing intently on Johnny. "Do you have a plan…we need a plan."

Phillip puts his arm around his son. "Is there a place to sit? Robert insisted on coming here right from the hospital, but I'm afraid he's a bit wobbly."

Robert picks up a kitchen chair and goes out onto the back porch.

Diz scoots his chair over. "We wondered when you'd show up."

Daz smiles. "Avengers, assemble."

Robert puts the chair down and almost collapses into it.

Johnny stands in the doorway. "He came to save Jenny…and he wants to know if we have a plan."

Johnny looks from James to Daz and Diz. "Do we have a plan?" James shares a glance at Diz and Daz. "Well, maybe the beginning of one."

Jimmy begins. "What does Vincent Drago want? The treasure. So why did Drago take Jenny."

Johnny thinks for just a second. "He thinks Jenny knows where it is."

Margot nods. "That makes sense, but she doesn't…does she?"

They sit in silence until Robert speaks up…softly. "She might."

All eyes shift to Robert. "She kept the box, remember. She was going to try and figure it out."

All eyes turn to Johnny and Jimmy asks the obvious. "Did she?"

Johnny shrugs. "I don't know. She could have…she had the box…it must be somewhere in her room."

They all run into kitchen and are stopped by a loud boom coming from the living room. Johnny opens the swinging door and peeks out. Antoine is standing, alone, in the entry, bellowing. "Why is the Goddam front door just standing wide open?"

Johnny hurries out followed by the rest. "Have you found Jenny? Is she okay?"

Antoine shakes his head. "No, Mr. Chretien. That's what I came to tell you." He looks at them all. His glance lingers on Robert. "We found the car, but no sign of Jenny."

Johnny is deflated and sits abruptly on the couch but looks defiantly at Sergeant Durel. "If you can't find my daughter, we will." He looks at the others before continuing. "We know what Vincent Drago wants and why he took Jenny."

Antoine looks at them all before sitting next to Johnny. "That's the other thing I came to tell you. We found Vincent Drago…stuffed in the trunk…dead."

Los Angeles, California
Downtown
Three Weeks Ago

Johnny is standing in just about his favorite place in the world...in front of a jury giving closing arguments. He's spent a large part of his adult life in various courthouses, but this one, the Stanley Mosk Courthouse in downtown Los Angeles, is his favorite.

Johnny's leading them step by step through the evidence. It's the only time during a trial that he can let his passion for justice shine through.

Just as he finishes, Jenny walks into the courtroom. This is not unusual...Jenny likes to come hear his closing arguments, but today she has something to tell her daddy that he's not going to like.

Johnny has to wait for the judge to be done with jury instructions and the jurors to leave to deliberate. He throws his things into his briefcase and motions for Jenny to meet him in the hall. She follows him through the big double doors and finds her father sitting on a bench outside the courtroom. She gives him a peck on the cheek and sits beside him. He's looking at her curiously and Jenny decides just to come out with it. "Daddy, Uncle Roger is dead."

Jenny clears her throat. "I got a call from Margot Sallier. She said she's been calling you." Johnny holds up his phone. "I was in court...who's Margot Sallier?"

Jenny shrugs, "I'm not sure...a friend of Uncle Roger's?"

Johnny thinks about this. "I don't know any Margot Sallier. I know Salliers, but no Margot? What did she say? How did Roger die?"

She looks up at her father. "She said he drowned."

"Drowned?"

Jenny looks away for a second. "Actually, she said that Uncle Roger apparently drowned."

Johnny leans back against the wall. "Apparently? How does someone apparently drown?" Johnny gets up and starts to walk to the elevator. "Get me a flight...Monday red eye. I need you to go today."

Jenny nods as the elevator door slides open, and they get on. Johnny turns to his daughter. "Apparently drowned?" The door slides shut.

Chapter XVII

"They're heading somewhere...that's for certain."

Margot

Vincent Drago is dead...but then where is Jenny? Margot's watching Johnny out of the corner of her eye. What he must be feeling right now, she can only imagine. Less than an hour ago they had a plan...they were on a mission...and now?

Margot turns to the others, realizing. "Vincent Drago was murdered. Whoever killed him doesn't need him anymore. He thinks Jenny knows where the treasure is."

Understanding begins to spread throughout the room but Robert shakes his head. "But who is he?"

Margot puts a hand on his shoulder. "I don't know...but first things first...does Jenny know where the treasure is?"

All eyes turn to Johnny. "I don't know." He shrugs. "We didn't talk about it since...you know the accident."

Margot has another thought. "God we're stupid...before Durel we were on our way to Jenny's room to look for the box."

Everyone stares at each other for just a second before running up the stairs, coming to an abrupt stop outside Jenny's room. Johnny suddenly finds himself frozen...he can't bring himself to open the door. This room holds such meaning. He looks at James and their eyes meet. This was their room when they were kids...their room with Roger. Now Roger is dead, and Jenny is missing. Johnny reaches out and slowly opens the door. The room is impeccably neat...it's so Jenny. It doesn't look anything like it did when they were kids.

For Robert it brings everything back. The last time he was in this room he kissed Jenny. They were sitting on that very bed...that neat no wrinkle bed...and now she's gone. He doesn't know if he'll ever kiss her again.

Margot looks around the room taking inventory…bed, desk, nightstands, chest, closet. She turns to Johnny. "Do you have any idea where she might have the box?"

Johnny thinks. "She'd put it somewhere safe. Ever since she was little, Jenny didn't like to leave things just lying around…and this was important."

Margot moves to the desk and Daz and Diz come to help her. They search on the desk, in the drawers, in every cubby…but nothing.

Suddenly Johnny has a vision…he can see it clearly…Jenny lying in bed in the middle of the night trying to figure something out…schoolwork…boys. He turns to Margot. "The nightstands…look in the nightstands."

Margot moves to one side of the bed, while Diz moves to the other. Margot finds it in the first drawer she opens and holds it up. "Got it." She opens the lid of the box and takes a folded piece of paper out, unfolds it and smooths it out on the bed. "Out of the Water." And on the second line "Desapparitions Fantomatique Apparaissant."

Margot looks up at the others. "But what does it mean?"

Silence, until Phillip speaks softly. "Something about spirits or ghosts appearing. I grew up speaking French." Margot nods. "Okay, so now we have 'out of the water and ghosts appear." She looks around room. "Any thoughts?"

This is met with silence. Frustrated, Johnny runs his fingers through his hair. "This is getting us absolutely nowhere."

Margot agrees. "We can't think any more."

Phillip puts an arm around Robert. "Robert has to rest."

Robert is about to protest, but Margot cuts him off. "Your Dad is right. We all need rest…let's call it a night. We'll sleep a couple hours and come back first thing tomorrow morning."

They all reluctantly agree…even Johnny has to agree. He needs rest as well.

Jimmy

Jimmy can't sleep and is on the back porch swinging. Ever since he was a kid, Jimmy has enjoyed rain. He remembers summers on this porch with Pop…swinging and listening…talking about things only fathers and sons talk about. This was something they shared…this love of weather. Fragrant Spring rains...Summer cloudbursts...Fall soakers, and Winter's cold, driving rains.

Jimmy closes his eyes and stops swinging...his senses heightened. Something has changed. Something has changed within him. He doesn't feel helpless any more...or alone. He had cut himself off from people. Cut himself off from people who mattered...from family. Johnny and Jenny were only tolerated at times. Thanksgiving and Christmas and then he was done for the year. Roger not even that...a couple of phone calls was all it took.

Now, however, it's different. It took death to bring him closer to Roger. It took death to bring him closer to Johnny and Jenny. Now there is Margot and Diz and Daz and somehow Robert and his father...and he can't forget Howard. He's got his family back...he even has extended family. He has people who care about him and who he cares about. He won't let anything happen to them. He starts swinging...and thinking.

A hurricane is coming, and Jimmy can't stop it. He hates to think of Jenny, alone and frightened, out in this weather. Time is crucial and the hurricane will only hold them up. He tries to think logically. What do they know? Whoever has Jenny must be after the treasure and they think Jenny knows where it is, but does she? What will they do if she doesn't? Jimmy doesn't want to think about that. There must be a way to find her.

A blinding flash of lightening and accompanying clap of thunder jolts Jimmy back to the here and now. He looks up to see Johnny standing in the doorway, staring at him. "Where did you go Jimbo?" Johnny looks around and shivers. "I hope it was somewhere warm and dry."

Jimmy smiles and shakes his head. "I was just thinking about... stuff."

Johnny sits beside his brother. "I know...I keep going over and over it in my mind." He looks over at Jimmy with pleading eyes. "I can't bear the thought of Jenny being out there and I can't help her."

Jimmy nods and looks out into the storm. "What was last clue say?"

Johnny thinks. "Something about ghosts appearing out of the water."

Jimmy nods absently...somethings almost clicking into place. "Do you remember...I think we were on this porch...You, me, and Roger, listening to Pop tell one of stories? It was about Contraband

203

Bayou...far out where some small island would appear and disappear depending on the tide."

Johnny smiles at the memory. "Ghost Island...I always thought Pop made that up."

Jimmy smiles in agreement. "Me too, but supposing he didn't."

Jimmy and Johnny swing back and forth until Jimmy stops and looks at his brother. "It fits...the clue fits with what we know about Lafitte...about Contraband Bayou...about the legend of the treasure."

At last, something tangible to investigate. Is there really a Ghost Island and where, exactly, is it?

This feeling of accomplishment is short lived when a horrible thought crosses Johnny's mind. He looks at Jimmy. "This may be important, but it doesn't help Jenny, even if she's figured out the clue it won't help her. She doesn't know anything about a Ghost Island."

Jimmy gets it. "And if she can't tell them where the treasure is, she's useless to them and..."

Johnny fills in the thought. "She's expendable."

Jimmy nods. "Still, it's something to go on."

He looks at his brother and Johnny agrees. "Who do we know that can tell us whether Ghost Island exists or not?"

They look at each other and nod. "Diz and Daz."

Antoine

After spending three hours wrestling with the couch in his office, Antoine gets up. Every bone in his body aches. He hasn't gotten more than four hours of sleep a night since this whole Chretien thing started and he won't be getting any more until Jenny Chretien is found.

He remembers Jenny Chretien kneeling on the ground next to her wounded father...Robert Louragan on the ground after being struck from behind...Roger Chretien draped in a pirate flag. Nothing in this Goddamned case ever gets solved.

Shaking his head, Antoine knows he can't make another move without coffee. Without looking up, he bellows, "Duplantier, I need coffee." He raises his head listening to that reverberate down the hall. Slowly he gets to his feet, shuffles to the break room, and brews a new pot of coffee. Sitting at a table, drinking from his favorite China cup he gazes out the window at the windblown, driving rain.

Antoine returns to his office and sits at his desk putting pieces together. Drago was found stuffed in a trunk at Sam Houston Jones Park. So, he either had a partner or there is a new player. The treasure must be the goal and Jenny Chretien is the key.

The park must have been a diversion…Contraband Bayou fits much better according to the legend, but where? That area is completely different than it was two hundred years ago. There are hotels and a golf course…even a university there for Christ's sake.

As he sits at his desk, it hits him…he needs a map…there must be a map showing what Contraband Bayou was like two hundred years ago. There must be.

An idea emerges…he has people. What is the name of the rookie at the front desk? Thibodeau. He punches in a number and waits. As soon as it's picked up, the words tumble out of his mouth. "Thibodeau, this is Durel, I need a map."

A very calm Officer Thibodeau responds, "Certainly, sir…a map of what."

Antoine thinks for just a minute. "I need a map showing Contraband Bayou about 200 years ago…do we have that?"

A brief silence. "We might, sir. I'll check the archives."

Antoine leans back. It's great to have people…and archives.

Diz and Daz

Daz is annoyed. It's still dark outside and he's awake. The magnolia tree outside his window is beating on the glass in a very unmusical way and the water pouring off the roof sounds like the Sunset Limited, barreling through Lagniappe House at one hundred miles per hour.

Daz hates hurricanes. This one isn't even here yet and he's already having flashbacks to Audrey, when he was a kid. Taking cover in the courthouse basement with his mom and dad, Holding onto his sister for dear life as the entire building shook in the 125 mile per hour wind. When it had passed, he remembers going home and seeing half the roof gone…taken apart shingle by shingle.

He imagines Jenny out in this storm somewhere. They've got to do something. Maybe Diz has an idea. He takes a look at his watch wondering if it's too early to wake him up. He looks up as a flash of lightning reveals Diz standing in his doorway. "Got a call from Johnny Chretien."

Daz gets out of bed and puts on a robe. "Now, in the middle of night?"

Diz motions to the scene outside. "If you had a daughter out in this, I don't expect you'd be getting much sleep."

"Yeah, I was thinking the same thing. What did he want?"

Diz gives him a look. "What do you think…he wants his daughter back."

Daz glares back. "I know that…I mean specifically what does he want."

Diz sits in a chair next to the window. "He did ask something odd. He asked if we knew anything about a Ghost Island on Contraband Bayou?"

Daz takes the seat opposite and stares out the window. "Why does that sound familiar?"

Diz leans forward. "Because it is. Do you remember a few years ago…maybe five or six now, during the Pirate Festival…after our set? That old Cajun going around calling everyone le crétin because they didn't know anything about real pirates."

Daz nods. "Couldn't understand much of what he said but I do remember him saying something about Contraband Bayou…about how it was ruined here but still the same further north."

Diz scratches his chin. "Yeah, that didn't make much sense, and I tuned him out, but I do remember him babbling something about Ile Fantôme."

Diz and Daz look intently at each other…wondering. Finally, Daz gives voice to their musing. "What if the old guy was right…what if Contraband Bayou continues farther north."

Diz considers this. "And remember the clue…something about spirits rising from the water."

Daz nods. "It's beginning to make sense. Do you have any idea who this Cajun guy is?"

The wheels turn in Diz's mind until he smiles and turns to Daz. "You know, I think I just might know a guy."

Robert

Robert quietly opens the back door onto the carport. He hasn't sneaked out of the house like this in ten years, but he can't stay here…he has to bring Jenny back home. He looks out into chaos. The wind must be gusting at over 70 mph and the rain coming in at a 45-degree angle in small tight pellets that sting when they hit. Even in the car port he needs help standing upright and making his way to his Passion Red Nissan Z. The only way he can tell that it's morning is that the sky has turned from black to dark grey.

Robert tosses his hurricane go bag behind the front seat and slides behind the wheel. The Z roars to life as he throws it into gear and turns left out of the driveway. Trying to see well enough to maneuver, he turns the wipers off since they're useless and turns on the defogger. Almost every block he has to get out of his car and drag branches out of the road. Finally, he pulls up outside the Chretien home behind Margot's Prius.

Robert grabs his bag and sprints for the front door fighting his way through the howling wind and driving rain. It's no better on the porch as he bangs on the door and rings the doorbell, hoping someone will hear him over the din of the storm.

Finally, the porch light come on and the door is flung open by the wind. Margot is there with a towel in hand and together they wrangle the door shut. Robert stands dripping water all over the entry floor trying to dry himself off with an already wet towel.

Margot watches, amusement twitching around the corners of her mouth. "There's coffee in the kitchen." Robert mumbles a thank you through the towel and heads in that direction, pushing open the kitchen door.

James is standing, coffee cup in hand, just inside the door as Robert stumbles in. He looks up to see John standing next to the sink and walks to him like he's reporting for duty. "We can't leave her out there. We have to find her before…"

John puts his hand on Robert's shoulder. "I know…and we will." He looks at James. "We've got a plan. Sort of."

James meets them at the sink. "Diz and Daz are finding out a few things for us.

Johnny shrugs. "They know a guy."

Margot comes in looking at the bedraggled Robert. "You got other clothes?" He nods. "In the bag." She sits at the kitchen table and rests her chin in her hand. "Good, I don't know what we're going to do or how we're going to do it…but at least we should be dressed properly." She looks up to see a bemused James staring back and smiles briefly. "It's what I do."

Jimmy can't help but laugh and turns to Robert explaining. "She said the same thing to us as soon as she arrived." He sneaks a look at Margot. "Luckily, we found Roger's rain gear." Margot manages a smile. "Like I said…it's what I do."

A low rumble is felt more than heard. It builds until dishes begin to rattle and the good crystal begins to tinkle. They look at each other. An earthquake on top of a hurricane? They rush from the kitchen and peer through the window out into storm…not understanding, at first, what they are seeing.

A mammoth sized beast lies in wait growling outside the house. A throbbing GMC Yukon Denali, twelve feet high and with massive sixty-six inch off road tires sits at the ready. It's only when the engine is turned off that they realize the truck completely drowned out the sound of the raging storm.

A drenched Daz and Diz arrive on the front porch, flinging the front door open. and again, a struggle to shut the door against the raging wind. Diz takes off his hat, leaving puddles on the hardwood floor. Diz looks to Jimmy and Johnny. "You were right."

Daz takes out a folded map. "Contraband Bayou continues about a mile north of the city." He unfolds an old map and spreads it out on the dining room table.

Diz tries to fill in the blanks. "We tracked down this old Cajun…Boudé…who not only had this map but claimed to have seen…Ghost Island."

Jimmy squints at the map. "Do you believe him?"

Diz and Daz exchange looks and Diz shrugs. "Don't know…he was drunk at the time…but to be honest I think he's drunk most of the time."

They all stare at the map, following Contraband Bayou as it winds, north of Lake Charles, deeper into the swamp.

Robert looks up confused. "This doesn't look right to me."

Daz shrugs. "Well, you have to remember, this map is over 100 years old."

Robert rubs his forehead. "Is this any help at all?"

Diz glances away. "Well, yes and no."

Johnny shakes his head. "I'd like to hear the yes part, please."

Daz begins to explain. "Boudé says there's an old firebreak that runs beside where the bayou used to be. If we follow that we'll find the rest of Contraband Bayou."

James shakes his head. "Sound like a big if to me."

Robert heads back to the front door and grabs his bag. "Sounds like the only if we got."

Margot follows him. "Robert's right."

Johnny looks at his brother and agrees. "Let's go get Jenny."

Diz watches them as Daz folds up the map. He holds up the keys. "You need to wait for us...I've got the keys."

Daz swoops by and snatches the keys. "I'm driving...you practically killed us on the way over." Robert is waiting by the front door. "I don't care who drives...let's go get Jenny.

As they pile into the Denali, a dark squad car parked about halfway down the street goes unnoticed. Officer Thibodeau watches through the downpour. She keys the microphone. "You were right Sarge. They all got into the biggest vehicle I've ever seen. They're heading somewhere...that's for certain."

There's a burst of static and muffled, "Shit" on the other end. After a brief pause, Antoine comes back on the line. "You'd better follow them, officer...but please be careful."

Johnny

Johnny is sitting in the third row of the Yukon, beside Jimmy and behind Margot and Robert, who are behind Diz and Daz. He can't see much, but he supposes there isn't much to see. The pandemonium around them reminds him of when he was a kid, watching the Wizard of Oz on the television for the first time...when Dorothy was inside the tornado. He half expects to see a pig fly by.

Lake Charles is unrecognizable outside the window. He has no idea where he is...every block or so Robert and Diz have to jump out to move something out of the way...but he can hardly contain himself. He finds himself leaning forward, pushing on the seat in front of him, trying to get them to go faster...cursing to himself whenever they slow down. Suddenly they come to a complete stop...the SUV throbbing all around them. Daz looks back over his shoulder.

"A tree is down...the road is completely blocked...any suggestion?"

James stares out the window and sees the university. "Bayou Contraband goes right through the university. Can't you just follow it...I mean physically drive in the bayou?"

Daz tries to see through the madness of driving rain and flying trees. "Maybe."

He puts the Yukon into gear and bumps over the curb, onto the grass, churning through the soaked ground and between two buildings. He follows the terrain as it slopes down toward the bayou. Two days ago, this was a lazy little stream, but today it's a raging torrent. He slides into the bayou bed, shifts to all wheel drive, and slowly heads upstream while the current batters them. For the first time, they are all afraid this beast may not be big enough.

Johnny, eyes closed, feels every gush of the raging current and every one hundred mile per hour blast of wind as they buffet them in ten different directions at the same time. His eyes pop open when Daz comes to skidding stop. "The bayou ends here. It disappears into a grove of cypress trees."

Diz peers through the windshield trying, vainly, to see more clearly. "If Boudé is right we should find a firebreak somewhere along here. I guess we'll have to get out and look...any volunteers?"

Robert slides the back door open. "I'll go."

Johnny looks at the sling holding his left arm. He doesn't care if he needs it or not...it's in the way. Making a decision, he rips it off, throws it on the floor and climbs around the middle row. "Me too."

Jimmy follows. "Wait for me."

As soon as Johnny slips into the waist deep pool of water, he realizes he can't stand up and grabs a hold of a huge cypress root. Using this he pulls himself out of the water onto more firm ground. He turns back to see how the others are making out and finds they are following him.

At first, they find it impossible to fight against the wind and rain, but as they move farther into the cypress grove it becomes easier. The canopy of branches offers some protection and they spread out in search of some pathway or clearing through the tight foliage.

After about an hour...Johnny checks his watch...okay 12 minutes, Johnny's got nothing. He just too old for this...although he doubts there is a right age for running around in a category four hurricane.

Over the bellowing wind and pouring rain, Johnny hears a shout and looks up to see Robert waving his arms. They all struggle toward Robert and find him looking down a narrow path that disappears into the dense vegetation before them. Robert shouts into the wind. "Is it wide enough?"

Johnny looks from Robert to the path disappearing into the gloom and shrugs...shouting back. "It'll have to be."

They help each other back to SUV and climb inside momentarily letting the outside chaos into the cabin. Margot watches silently for a moment but can't contain herself. "I thought y'all had drowned…did you find anything?"

Robert, wipes rain from his eyes. "Oh yeah…we're good to go." He points toward the path and Daz puts the Yukon into low as the beast climbs out of the water.

As Johnny watches the vegetation scrape by outside, Daz pushes the vehicle beyond its limits trying to force their way down this path. Finally, they come to a stop and Johnny stares through the window seeing the path open up revealing the bayou, the current raging, flowing beside them.

Jenny

Jenny wakes up…or comes to, still crammed in the trunk of some car. The stifling heat, incessant pounding of the rain and howling wind rocking the car all make it impossible to focus. She remembers talking to Robert and then being thrown into a trunk. She finds herself caught between hoping Robert will come save her…and hoping he's still alive.

She remembers the car stopping and being dragged out and thrown into another trunk. This one is bigger and not as damp and smelly. They had driven for, what seemed like, hours and then just stopped. With the storm raging around her, she had drifted off, but now…she wakes to a different sound…human sounds.

She knows she has a chance here. When the trunk opens…she has to make a run for it. Even with a bag over her head and hands bound behind her back she has to be ready. She waits for Vincent Drago, trying to hear above the storm. She curls her legs ready to thrust them out, catching him by surprise and giving her time to run. Straining to hear that pop of the trunk latch, she coils her legs tighter. Jenny hears the release of the trunk…feels the rain and wind attack her savagely as it opens. Trying to ignore the mayhem around her, she focuses all her strength and uncoiling her legs like a spring she lashes out at…nothing.

Confused and exhausted, she lays half in and half out of the trunk until she feels two pair of hands grab her and drop her callously on the rain-soaked ground. Hands grab her collar and drag her up wooden stairs and dump her unceremoniously in the middle of some room tearing off the bag covering he head.

From where she lies, she can see one large room and two feet...she cranes her body until she is facing up, trying get a good look at Vincent Drago, the man who killed Uncle Roger and Officer Duplantier, but instead locks eyes with Etienne Bastineau.

She is unprepared for the savage kick that sends her sliding across the floor into the legs of an old woman. It takes a moment to click...the old woman from before...Lafitte's niece, Zora.

Jenny is at first unaware of the conversation going on around her...unaware until she is kicked once again. Etienne crouches down beside her and grabs a handful of hair, twisting her head until she sees his face.

"I asked you a question. I ask...you answer. Got it?"

Jenny doesn't answer in time and Etienne cruelly twists her head again and repeats. "Got it?"

Jenny manages a "Yeah," before Etienne lets go of her hair allowing her head to slam into the hard wood floor. He grabs a wooden chair and pulls it up next to Jenny. "Good, now we understand each other."

Etienne sits, staring down at Jenny. "So, where's the treasure...I know you've got both clues...so where is it?"

Jenny maneuvers herself into a sitting position. "Are you kidding me...that's what this is about...the stupid treasure?"

A kick reminds her there is someone else in the room. Zora crouches down beside her. "I assure you, mon enfant, that we are not kidding you." Her mind racing, Jenny tries to come with an answer. "Yes, we have both clues, but it doesn't make any sense to me."

Zora stares deep into her soul. "It might not mean anything to you, chère, but it might mean something to us."

Jenny can only tell them what she knows and hope it's enough. "Okay...the first one..." She looks up at Etienne. "Led us to Chretien Point."

Etienne looks at her impatiently. "We know that...get to the second clue."

Jenny shakes her head in frustration. "It just says something about spirits or ghosts rising out of the water." She readies herself, expecting another kick, but sees a satisfied smile spread across Zora's face as looks up at Etienne.

212

"See, I told you, Vincent Drago was a fool. It's all there in my uncle's journal."

Etienne rolls his eyes. "Pardon me for being skeptical of something some lunatic wrote down two hundred years ago."

Zora's eyes narrow as she takes out a 12-inch Bowie knife. "Oncle Jean has been right so far has he not? I can go on alone…if I must."

Etienne backs off. Old Oncle Jean is not the only lunatic here.

"Okay…what'll we do with her?" Jenny is real interested in this part. Zora stares down at her.

"She's no longer of use, just like the other one. We'll dump her in the bayou…no one will ever find her there."

Etienne stares at Jenny a moment. "Now?"

Zora shakes her head as she puts the knife away. "Non, we'll take her further into the swamp. Now we need to look for Oncle Jean's Ghost Island."

Only sort of relieved, Jenny watches as they leave the cabin, locking the door behind them.

Straining to hear over the maelstrom outside, Jenny waits until she hears the car start up and drive away before she tries to get loose. She slowly tugs on the cloth strip that binds her hands. One way the strip tightens, and other way gives, just a little. She patiently works her hands back and forth until there's just enough room for her to slide her hands out.

Now, next step. The door…of course it's locked. She thinks about Nancy Drew…she was always locked in some room…how did she get out? Jenny shakes her head. Nancy always had pins…hair pins…bobby pins…hat pins and here she sits…pinless.

She examines the door again. It's locked but not too sturdy. She looks around…nothing about this cabin says sturdy. She can probably wait for a gust of wind to blow it all down. Then she remembers the trunk. She lies down on the floor next to the door and brings her legs into tight coil. Taking in a gulp of air she kicks out her legs…hearing the splintering of wood as it begins to give way. Two more kicks and the door swings open, hanging by one hinge.

She stands facing the raging storm. She doesn't know where she is. All she knows is she can't stay there. Remembering her Girl Scout training, she understands she must follow the water.

Lake Charles, Louisiana
Contraband Bayou
Three weeks ago

Roger sits in his silver Buick LaCrosse in the Golden Nugget parking lot, near where Contraband Bayou empties into Prien Lake. He wants to get a sense of what it would have been like for Lafitte, being chased by the British or Spanish, to disappear into the shallower bayou. No hotels...or golf courses then...but still, seeing Margot's brooch has somehow made it more real. If all the stories about Lafitte and the Salliers are true, it makes him wonder if all the stories Pop told about Lafitte...about the treasure...about Contraband Bayou...about Ghost Island might also be true.

Then Jimmy and Johnny will have to pay attention...will have to come home. He doesn't know exactly when they started to grow apart, sometime during college. Ever since Pop died, he has felt the need for family...for his brothers and this may be the answer. What he needs is proof. He needs tangible evidence that this isn't just one more of Pop's stories.

As Roger sits thinking about family, another set of eyes are watching him. Vincent Drago sits two rows away from Roger in his black SUV, waiting and watching. He first noticed Roger Chretien because he was always with the Sallier woman. It seemed that wherever Drago went to find information about Laffite and the treasure, he would find Roger Chretien...one step ahead. Drago thinks that maybe it was time to have a conversation with this Roger Chretien.

Roger climbs out of the LaCrosse and walks through the parking lot to a dirt path that winds its way down toward the water. The path isn't too steep, but Roger needs to pay attention...this may be part of civilization now, but it's still home to alligators.

Arriving at water's edge he can see across to Coon Island and the spot where Prien Lake, the Calcasieu River and Bayou Contraband all come together. He imagines Jean Laffite maneuvering the Pride up the Calcasieu River into the dark recesses of the bayou...completely disappearing.

Drago silently follows him and stops, unseen, five yards behind Roger. He too sees the confluence of the waterways and imagines Lafitte running, one step ahead, into the depths of the bayou. He must have made some noise, because Chretien turns, and their eyes meet.

214

At first is seems casual, almost natural, but Chretien realizing that something isn't right suddenly turns and tries to run. His feet can't find purchase in the loose dirt, and he loses his balance and falls, sliding down toward the water. Drago follows and towering above Roger places a foot on his throat, slowly pushing him into the water.

"I can't have you getting in the way any longer. I'm afraid you'll just have to go. I can get all the help I need from your girlfriend." Drago continues to push until Roger's head is completely under water...his body thrashing, searching, in vain, for air.

At first, all Roger can think about is the need to breathe, but as water begins to seep into his lungs he becomes acutely aware of choices. Choices he made and choices he didn't make. He regrets the loss of a life with Margot...the pain this will cause her and just before he loses consciousness, he regrets all time missed...with Jimmy and Johnny...and not telling them that he loved them.

Drago waits, holding Chretien's head under water...until he stops thrashing. Drago stares at the lifeless body before him feeling an almost sense of regret. If only Chretien hadn't forced his hand, but Roger Chretien hadn't given him a choice. Now Vincent is forced to clean up this mess Chretien caused. He needs a diversion...something that will cause confusion. A smile spreads across Vincent's face. Chretien was looking for pirate treasure...he deserves a pirate funeral.

It isn't until later...much later...that Vincent Drago discovers he lost his coin. Somewhere along the water...somewhere next to where Roger Chretien died...he lost his lucky coin.

Chapter XVIII

"...a look of surprise still on his face"

Officer Thibodeau

Officer Thibodeau can barely see them ahead. Squinting she tries to see the road before her when the radio crackles. "Officer Thibodeau...Durel, what's your twenty?

She looks around to reorient herself. "I just turned from Lake onto West McNeese heading East. I can't see them ahead, but my guess is that they are heading for the university, Sergeant."

There's a pause but finally. "Okay, but I think they're following Bayou Contraband...it goes right past the university. You follow that, you'll be okay."

Thibodeau nods to herself. "Got it, Sarge, 10-4."

She tries to stay calm...she'll be fine until she reaches the university. That's where the bayou curves briefly to the North before heading East again. She isn't sure what road to follow then, but she'll deal with that when she gets there. Now she needs to concentrate. The road seems to be clearer, but there's still no sight of them. This may be the perfect time to catch up.

She increase her speed, hoping she can react in time to any obstacle she encounters, when out of the gray blur ahead of her, a huge dark mass appears. She slams on the brakes, skidding to a stop inches from a huge, fallen magnolia tree blocking the road.

She spends a moment waiting for her heart to slow to something resembling a normal rhythm. She reaches for the microphone. "Thibodeau, here."

It's answered at once. "Durel."

"Sarge, there's a downed tree blocking the road and no sign of the Chretiens."

There's a long pause before, "Okay...any indication of where they might have gone?"

Thibodeau looks out at chaos around her. "I'll get out and check."

She leaves the squad car for the utter mayhem of the outside. At first glance there's nothing, but on closer examination, she sees the curb has been broken and deep ruts running into the university, itself. She climbs back into the SUV and keys the mike. "Thibodeau here…it looks like they headed into the university."

There's a moment. "Okay…we think they left the road to follow the bayou. I mean actually getting into the water itself…Is that doable?"

Officer Thibodeau tries to imagine it. "I'm not sure, Sarge. Let me check it out."

She backs up and turns into the university, jumping the curb. Just as the Yukon before, she follows the slope down to the bayou and heads east against the raging current. She comes to a stop where the bayou turn north, before contacting Durel. "It's going okay, Sarge, but still no sight of them."

"That's okay…keep going…That map you found is ça c'est bon."

Thibodeau smiles at the radio before Durel goes on. "The bayou ends a few miles in…but there's an old fire break that should be on your right. You follow that…the best you can, until you see the bayou again on you left."

She smiles. "Got it."

Durel comes back. "We found a way to follow the bayou from the east…so, hopefully, we catch them between us."

Thibodeau nods and replies, "Okay…10-4," before clicking off. She turns north and keeps following the bayou.

Etienne

Etienne fights his way to his prized Mercedes S 550. He had bought this new almost twenty years ago and had taken exquisite care of it…until now. Now this vielle folle is going to ruin it. He can't wait to get rid of her. He turns to look back to see Zora fighting against the storm. Etienne shakes his head…he hopes she blows away.

Reaching the car, he slips in behind the wheel. Enjoying, for the moment, the feeling of the supple leather. He looks up to watch Zora struggling against the storm and has to admit that while she may crazy, she's as tough as the come. He also has to admit that she's been right so far. This fishing camp was exactly where she said it would be. They took the long way around, but it was here.

Etienne reaches across the front seat and opens the door for her and watches as she uses both hands to battle the door against the raging wind until it's shut. He sits waiting for her to give him some indication about their next move.

Zora looks over at him with a sneer spreading across her face. "Hurry on."

Sometimes it's so difficult speaking to this woman. Etienne puts on his most ingratiating smile. "And where do you suggest I go?"

The sneer gets bigger as she waves vaguely forward. "Ahead... follow the bayou...is it so difficult? Do I have to do everything?" Zora shakes her head and mumbles under her breath. "Roi des cons."

Etienne looks heavenward for strength, thinking. "Well, at least now, I'm King of the Idiots...I've come up in the world."

Etienne turns on the defogger. It's hard to tell with the rain and flying debris, but he thinks he can see a narrow road running parallel to the rushing water. It won't be good for the car's finish, but he supposes that with the treasure he'll be able to afford a new paint job. He smiles to himself...he'll be able to afford a lot more than that. He puts the car in gear and gently gives it gas. The wheels spin briefly before they catch hold, and they lurch forward.

The drive is excruciating. He barely has control, and it seems as if every few feet the car slips beneath him threatening to slide into the bayou itself. This may not be worth it. This treasure may not be worth risking his life for. This makes Etienne stop and think. It's not worth risking his life for...at least, not for half a treasure. He takes a side glance at Zora...but how? He doesn't have a clue where they are going. He'll just have to wait...accidents happen.

A blinding flash of lightening completely disorients him. There's a loud crash and Etienne slams on the brakes causing the Mercedes to fishtail into a downed cypress tree. With his heart racing it takes a moment for him gain control...for his hands to stop trembling. He looks to his right, making sure that his companion is okay, only to find her glaring at him in contempt. "We don't have all the time in the world. What are you waiting for?"

"We can't go anywhere. Can't you see? There's a tree right there."

Zora's glare intensifies. "Get into the water...follows the bayou."

Etienne's eyes move from Zora...to the downed tree...to the steep slope leading down to the wild, raging water. This is enough. "Are you crazy?"

Zora looks calmly back at him...reaching into the recesses of her voluminous skirt ...calmly pulling out her twelve-inch blade and pressing it against his throat...calmly. Etienne looks into her crazed eyes. If he wants to live beyond the next few seconds, he better do what she says. He puts the car into gear and begins to follow the steep slope down to the bayou.

He doesn't go far when the earth beneath them seems to turn to liquid and they begin to slide...faster and faster...toward the tumultuous water. Horrified, Etienne can only watch as they slip toward the water and then...after a moment's hesitation...into the water itself. They are swept up by the current, turning uncontrollably until coming to a stop...wedged against a fallen tree.

Unable to think...unable to move, Etienne watches Zora reach up and open the sunroof. Pulling herself up, she glances back. "Hurry up...it's not far now."

He watches her climb down the car and into the water...using whatever she can find to pull herself against the current. He looks around at the water, rapidly filling the car, and decides he has no choice but to follow.

Jimmy

As Jimmy sits in this mammoth vehicle surveying Bayou Contraband. He's scared. Scared he's going to die...there are so many ways a hurricane can kill you. He looks at the raging torrent...at the fierce wind and diving rain...at the destruction all around him. And he's afraid for Jenny. He looks at Margot...at Diz and Daz...they are here for no other reason than their devotion to Jenny. They are risking their lives for someone they've known less than a month.

He looks at Robert and tries to imagine his feelings. James has watched his relationship with Jenny blossom and grow only to fade then rise from the ashes like a phoenix. He knows how desperate Robert must be.

And lastly at John...Johnny is frantic to find Jenny. James is afraid that his brother is going to crack under this strain. He sits back and realizes his biggest fear. He's afraid he's going to lose everyone. He's finally found a family again and he realizes that whether they live, or die is completely beyond his control. He reaches over and

219

takes Johnny's hand…something he hasn't done since they were kids. Johnny looks back with pain and fear etched on his face.

James is slammed back in his seat as Daz puts the Yukon in gear and lurches ahead fighting their way through the storm. At least they are moving forward…at least they have hope.

He sits forward in his seat and puts his hands gently on Margot's shoulders. "How are doing, up there?"

Margot puts her hand on his and shakes her head. "I'm wishing this was over and we were sitting on back porch, drinking coffee."

James manages a smile, when a huge gust of wind sends them flying to the ends of their seat belts and they feel the SUV straining against the wind.

James sees the strain of Daz's face. "We're not making much headway against this wind. I'm afraid the engine is going to blow."

Diz pipes up in his best Scotty voice. "I dinno how much more she can take, Captain. She's giving everything she's got. I'm afraid she's going to blow."

There is absolute silence in the cab, until Johnny begins to laugh. "Fire photon torpedoes." James watches John carefully.

Johnny returns Jimmy stare and manages a smile. "I thought Diz was right. We need as much Star Trek as we can get right about now."

Daz skids to a stop and points ahead. "Is it my imagination or is there something over there?"

They all strain to look and Robert finally nods. "It looks like a cabin."

Diz nudges Daz. "Let's check it out."

Daz fights for every foot they gain until he comes to a stop next to a cabin.

James is first to speak. "Look at the door. It's hanging by one hinge."

Before anyone can speak, Robert opens the rear door and scrambles out…battling his way to the door.

The others follow, bending to avoid the broken door, they enter to find Robert crouching next to a pile. "It's a blanket."

Johnny kneels next to him. "And it's still damp."

James sees relief spread across Johnny's face. "If I had to guess, I'd say Jenny was here." He points to the splintered door. "And did that to escape."

Johnny stares out at the violent storm. "Now, she's out in that."

James puts his arm around him. "But now we have evidence she's still alive."

Margot joins them. "And since we didn't pass her, we know what direction she went in."

Robert nods. "All we have to do is follow her."

Daz holds up the keys. "And that's just what we'll do."

Now they have hope. Now they stand ready to fight any storm…any adversary to bring Jenny home. Just before stepping out into the madness around them, Diz stops. "Wait…maybe we should split up…we don't want to miss her."

It takes a moment for that to sink in. Finally, Johnny nods. "He's right. We should split up.

Daz and Diz

Fighting the raging turbulence, Diz helps Margot into the Denali, while Daz climbs behind the wheel. They watch as Jimmy, Johnny and Robert struggle against the elements finally disappearing into the wind whipped rain. Taking a deep breath, Daz puts the beast into gear and drives slowly into the bayou…travelling parallel to the others.

They drive on in silence, praying to stay safe…praying that they will find Jenny…alive. Daz drives slowly forward trying to see through the raging storm for any signs of Jenny or for any possible hazards until, unexpectantly, the bottom of the bayou drops off beneath them. Plunging nearly two feet. they find themselves resting at a forty-five-degree angle.

After a moment of stunned silence, Diz wonders. "Can we move at all?"

Daz looks around before confessing. "I don't know. I'm afraid to try." He takes a deep breath and lightly presses down on the accelerator. Hearing the wheels spin he stops immediately. "Now, I'll try reverse." He shifts the gear and again presses lightly on the pedal. This time they feel the tires grab, but only move inches.

Margot pipes up. "Do you have it in four-wheel drive?"

Daz is about respond sarcastically when he looks at the display and reaches over with his left hand and turns the dial from 'two-wheel drive' to 'off road.' "It is now."

Margot grabs Diz's hand as Daz gently presses down on the accelerator. This time they can feel both the front and rear wheels dig into the mud beneath them and slowly…ever so slowly…the SUV begins to back up…teetering for a moment before dropping into position. Horizontal, once again, Daz continues in reverse until they are safely away from the hole. Breathing a sigh of relief, he looks at the others. "Let's head for higher ground."

Even with four wheel drive the way is difficult. Reaching the top, Daz closes his eyes. "I think we should rethink this."

Diz nods. "First of all, stay out of the bayou...bayou bad."

Robert

Robert is fighting to keep up. He stops briefly holding on to a gnarled cypress tree, listening as Bayou Contraband surges inches away. His eyes clamped tight against the driving wind and rain; Robert recognizes the futility of it all. He is supposed to be searching for Jenny, but she could be anywhere. Right now, she could be three feet away, and he wouldn't know. He wouldn't see her...he'd pass right by.

He opens his eyes and sees Johnny and Jimmy, about fifty yards ahead, waiting for him. He doesn't know how they do it...they are at least twice his age, and they keep trudging forward. He squints ahead and using the cypress trees pulls himself forward against the wind until he reaches Jimmy and Johnny. The brothers watch him carefully. Johnny puts his hand on Robert's shoulder. "You sure you're, okay?"

Robert nods. "Yeah, I've just need to rest for a minute and catch my breath. Jenny is out here somewhere, and I have to find her...I'll be okay." He slogs ahead and following his lead Jimmy and Johnny trudge after.

After what seem like an eternity Robert has to stop. "Nothing...I haven't come across any sign of her."

Jimmy looks around trying to take stock. "Unless we're completely wrong, she must be following this same path."

Robert looks around helplessly. "Unless we missed her somehow."

Johnny shakes his head. "No, we haven't missed her...she's still ahead." He looks intently at the other two. "I feel it."

Robert nods...takes a deep breath, grabs a cypress root, and pulls himself forward. He doesn't hear the ominous crack as a huge cypress tree breaks free at the roots and crashes just feet from where he's standing. Robert hardly bats an eye, near death experiences are becoming the new normal.

He looks back at Jimmy and Johnny. "Have to find a way around."

The three of them hunker down and rest against the tree. For a brief moment they are protected from the worst of the wind. Johnny looks back over his shoulder and sees the Mercedes in the middle of the bayou wedged against a fallen cypress tree. He points to it, but all he can manage is. "Look."

Jimmy, fighting the wind and rain, drags himself to bayou's edge to get a good look at it. "There's nobody inside, but the sunroof is open." He looks back at the others. "I'm thinking that whoever was in the car pulled themselves out and continued on foot."

Just then a low growl cuts through the wailing of the hurricane. They peer through the wind ripped rain and see a dark mass slowly approaching. They have to cover their eyes when rooftop lights of the Yukon momentarily blind them.

As soon as they stop, Daz and Diz jump from the truck and run to help. Diz is the first to arrive. "No offense but you three look like drowned rats."

Margot

Margot watches as Jimmy and Johnny climb into the rear seat and Diz and Daz help a struggling Robert into the seat next to her. For a moment no one in the truck speaks...all lost in their own thoughts.

Finally, Margot looks up and sees the half-submerged Mercedes in the middle of the bayou. "What gives with the Mercedes."

Johnny shrugs and smiles briefly. "Don't know...it was here when we arrived. The real question is where is Jenny? Assuming we're correct in our original assumptions, whoever was in the Mercedes left Jenny in the cabin to find the treasure."

After a brief shake his head, Diz says, "Which brings us back to the question...where is Jenny?"

Johnny stares ahead for a moment. "Well, knowing Jenny I think she got here, saw the Mercedes in the bayou and decided to turn the tables on them...I think she's stalking them."

Margot rubs her brow. "But what's our next move?"

Johnny exchanges looks with Jimmy and Robert. "It's obvious...we follow her." With a flourish, Daz gestures forward. "Once more unto the breach, dear friends."

Margot holds up her hand. "Stop right there, Shakespeare. Do you really think that any of you are ready to go back out.

Robert sits up straight. "Yes, we are."

With that, Margot shakes her head, but finally opens the rear door...gets out and begins to walk away. She looks over her shoulder. "You guys coming or what."

Jenny

When Jenny escapes from the cabin the first decision she has to make was what direction to go. She was taught to follow the water and that would clearly take her to the left, but a vehicle had recently taken the road...if you could call it a road...to the right and must be headed to civilization of some sort...only a fool would drive further into the bayou. She knows it's risky, but if she follows the car, it would either lead her out of the bayou or take her to wherever Etienne and Zora are going...and she's curious.

After an agonizing time of grab...pull...and slog, her hands are raw and legs ready to give out. Seemingly, out of nowhere, a downed cypress tree appears completely blocking the road. She takes a moment, using the tree to block some of the wind and rain, to get her bearings and sees the Mercedes wedged against a tree in the middle of the bayou. She takes in a huge breath and slowly lets it out. On one hand she was clearly right about the direction Etienne and Zora were going; on the other they had escaped from the car and could be anywhere.

Jenny looks at the tree and realizes she could climb through it. Slowly, she begins to move through the tree. Pulling the last branches apart, she surveys the road before her. No sign of either Zora or Etienne. She half runs and half crawls, landing face first in the mud next to an ancient cypress tree.

Wiping mud from her eyes, she peers through the branches and can clearly see Etienne huddled against a rock up ahead. As she rises into a crouch, she feels a knife point just below her ear. Standing slowly, she looks over her shoulder and sees Zora, a menacing smile on her lips. Jenny feels the knife point break the skin and an ooze of warm blood trickle down her back. "Thank you for joining us, my dear, it saves me the trouble of going back to the cabin to kill you." Impervious to the wind and rain, Zora pushes her forward.

Standing in the open, Jenny suddenly feels the wind and rain fall off and sunlight bathes them in a warm glow. Jenny looks up, she's in the eye of the hurricane. All the wonder of the moment is destroyed when Zora, roughly, pushes her to the ground in front of Etienne. He looks down at her, a snarl on his lips. "I blame you for all of this...I wouldn't have lost my car...I wouldn't be out here wandering in a swamp, looking for a goddamned treasure if it weren't for you.

Zora steps over Jenny and stands glaring into Etienne's eyes. "I am sick of your whining and since I don't need you anymore..." In one fluid movement Zora brings up her right arm and slices Etienne's neck with her knife...neatly severing his jugular. Jenny watches Etienne, a look of surprise still on his face, slide to the ground in a pool of blood.

Zora grabs Jenny by the collar and pushes her forward. "Not far now."

The sun disappears and the wind, coming from the opposite direction, and rain descends on them.

Johnny

Johnny, sitting in the truck, sees Margot standing in the middle of a hurricane daring them to follow her, but he can't move. He feels defeated...hopeless. Until he notices the air around him change. The wind and rain drop off and a bright sun shines overhead. He looks up into the eye.

Feeling rejuvenated, they all pile out of the truck and join Margot, who's staring into the fallen tree. She points into the tangle of branches. "There seems to be a couple of fallen trees here, but I think we can get through. We should go now. Take advantage of the break in the weather."

Johnny looks up at the patch of blue sky above them. The calm and quiet are almost overpowering, but he knows Margot is right. They need to follow her now. Taking a deep breath, he follows her into the labyrinth of branches.

Robert pushes his way through and stands, gaining strength from the sun. "There's nothing here. We've got to go...Jenny could be right ahead."

Johnny puts a restraining hand on Robert's shoulder. "Let's not rush into anything...we don't know what's up there."

225

Diz points to a fallen tree in front of them. "Let's keep to the tree line and meet there."

One by one, keeping low to the ground, they run from cover to cover until they arrive at the cypress tree, pulling branches apart. Johnny moves his hand to get a better grip and feels something wet and sticky. A smear of blood. He jerks his hand away and finds droplets of blood on the branch. Is this Jenny's blood? He nudges his brother showing him the blood on his hand and where it came from.

John holds up his hand to the others. "I found blood on the branch."

There are a jumble of questions each tumbling over the other.

"What does this mean?"

"Whose blood is it?"

"Could it be Jenny's blood?"

"There's not very much so that's a good sign, right?"

Robert doesn't say anything. He feels more than ever that Jenny is near...alive or dead he doesn't know. All he's aware of is a primal force, deep within him that's driving him forward.

He forces his way through the branches until he is standing on the other side, face covered with scratches. Johnny follows, staring at Robert, whose eyes are focused beyond the clearing. As the others join them, Robert points. They follow his gaze and see a body lying crumpled on the ground.

Johnny tries to hold him back, but Robert scrambles forward until he stands over the mangled body. Johnny joins him and gazes down at the man before him. "Bastineau...Etienne Bastineau...what is he doing here?"

James looks at John. "Who did this?"

They all stare at Etienne...throat slit...blood mixing with water swirling around the body.

The sun disappears, the wind and rain return with even more ferocity and suddenly they realize that they have no idea what's going on.

Zora

Pushing Jenny before her, Zora struggles to move forward. She doesn't want to admit how much she relied upon Etienne to help her. Zora wonders, perhaps she acted hastily...she hadn't planned on killing him until she had the treasure, but his constant complaining, and grumbling had become too much. The older she gets, the less patience she has for nonsense. She gives Jenny a shove, scowling at her. Now she must rely on this girl...she has to keep reminding herself. Don't kill her until you have the treasure.

Through sheer will, she pushes down the agonizing pain jolting through her body. She tries to concentrate on the treasure. All her life she has been waiting...convinced the treasure was real...that her uncle's journals would lead her to the fortune that was rightfully hers, but he held something back...just like all men...the key...the most important piece of information...he hid from her. But this girl provided the clue without realizing what it meant. Now the gibberish in the journals make sense...everything she thought were the ravings of a madman would lead her to what is rightfully hers. She feels the weight of the journal deep within the folds for her cloak waiting for the right time...waiting for it to reveal the final answer.

A faint sound, coming from behind, puts her on high alert. Pulling Jenny close and clamping a hand over her mouth...Zora waits and listens. The sound...there it is again. Silently, she reaches into the deep recesses of her voluminous skirt and draws out an ancient revolver. She waits silently until she hears the sound once more. Then she turns and fires. The shot rings out...a sound different from the sounds regularly heard during the height of a hurricane. Zora smiles when she hears a cry of pain. That should buy her some time.

She grabs Jenny by the neck and drags her forward through the muck and the mud. She doesn't mind the raging wind or torrential rain...she's almost there. She stops and reaching under her cloak she pulls out one of Lafitte's aging journals and flips through pages until...there it is...the map, ink beginning to smear in the rain. It's all there. It all makes sense now...all the wasted days behind her.

She drags Jenny out into the raging bayou toward a small thicket of cypress trees being battered by the powerful storm. She lets go of Jenny who tumbles with the current until she's able to grab hold of a protruding root. She turns back to look at Zora, struggling against the current, trying to get to the trees.

Robert is the first to arrive on the bank of Bayou Contraband. He looks between Zora and Jenny and wades into the rushing water to get to Jenny.

James and John arrive and watch silently as Robert fights his way to Jenny. Then a gurgling sound begins...getting louder and louder. The current seems to stop for a moment and then begin to swirl.

James turns to watch as Zora stands in the midst of the spiraling water, watching as a small island, beneath the cypress trees seems to rise out of the bayou itself. Zora pulls herself forward until she can stand, triumphant on Ghost Island and Jean Lafitte's fabled treasure.

Antoine

Antoine sits in a BATT-X tactical vehicle, hoping against hope that people are still alive. He kooks out a very narrow window and shakes his head. While hurricanes have been getting worse and worse, this may be the fiercest storm to ever hit Lake Charles.

Antoine is becoming more and more frustrated. They are headed down the middle of the bayou, knocking all obstacles out of the way, but he hasn't seen anybody, and he hasn't been able to reach Thibodeau. Still, he has to hope that everyone… the heroes and the villains, victims, and assailants…Chretiens and…everyone else will survive.

Antoine sits, looking out his little window trying to put all the pieces together, but no matter which way he looks at it, there is a piece…a big piece that's still missing. He sits up when he hears a crackle from the speaker and a faraway voice says something he cannot understand. Antoine keys the microphone. "Thibodeau…please repeat I can barely hear you."

A pause before she answers. "Sarge, the road is blocked here. The SUV is here…but it's empty."

This is not good. "Do you see anybody?

"No, Sarge, but in the bayou…right beside the downed tree is an abandoned Mercedes…I ran the plates, and it belongs to an Etienne Bastineau."

Antoine scowls. "Who the hell is Etienne Bastineau?" This remains unanswered when Thibodeau comes back on the line. "I have to leave my vehicle and proceed on foot."

Antoine stares off. "You need to be careful out there. I can't afford to lose another officer."

Thibodeau comes right back. "Yes, sir. I'll be careful."

Antoine rides in silence…the storm raging around him. He sends up a silent prayer, hoping he reaches them before it's too late. His reverie ends abruptly when Thibodeau comes back on the line. "Sarge, I think I found him…I think I found Etienne Bastineau."

Antoine sits up and Thibodeau continues "Dead...he's dead, Sarge...throat cut."

Antoine rubs his forehead...when will something make sense. He has no idea who Bastineau is and now he's dead...why? Antoine leans forward...an idea forming in his brain. "Is Etienne Bastineau the one who took Jenny Chretien...and in an attempt to get away did she cut his throat open?"

Try has he might, Antoine cannot quite picture Jenny doing that. Suddenly an excited Thibodeau reports. "A gunshot...I heard a gunshot just ahead."

The line goes silent, and Antoine is left staring at a deathly quiet speaker. Thoughts of Duplantier come flooding back. One thought keeps going through his brain...not another one...please not another one.

Finally, the speaker crackles and Thibodeau is back. "I found them."

Thibodeau is offline for a minute...and Antoine is going crazy "Officer Thibodeau...where the hell have you gone...is everybody there?"

A long pause before "Well, yes sir...I think so."

Antoine glares at the speaker. "What do you mean, 'you think so'?"

Dead air...finally. "Well, it's confusing, Sarge. Miss Chretien is in the middle of the bayou...maybe unconscious and Robert Louragan is going out to get her...someone is injured...either Mr. Dampiere or Mr. Brousard, I don't which is which, but the rest are here and seem to be okay."

Antoine's whole body relaxes. "That's great news...I'm almost to you."

Suddenly the line goes silent. Antoine, eyes shut...waits an excruciating thirty seconds, before: "Sarge, there's something else...there's a women trying to stand in the middle of the bayou, brandishing a knife."

Antoine comes around a small bend and sees what Officer Thibodeau just described. Before he can make any sense out it, the entire bayou seems to change. The water stops flowing and begins to spin and swirl. He feels the earth beneath him start to give way...and then...like nothing he's ever seen before...an island rises out of the depths of the bayou. The woman climbs onto land and in the midst of the storm begins to shout.

Then, a sudden stillness descends on them...Antoine is filled with dread as the storm begins to build toward a new fury. The rain cuts through the air like knives and the wind gets stronger and stronger sending trees crashing down all around them. Then the lightning starts...bolt after bolt, striking all around them. The smell of ozone is almost overpowering, the pounding of thunder deafening. Though he can barely see right in front of him, a shape begins to form through the blinding rain.

Antoine squints through never ending streaks of lightning and sees a two masted schooner careening toward the island with a lone figure standing at the helm. At the moment of collision, the storm intensifies. The deafening sound of thunder...the raging fury of the hurricane and the blinding flashes of lightning all converge on this small island. Antoine realizes he has his eyes shut tight and when he opens them, the island...the ship...the woman...all gone...vanished.

The air is amazingly calm...it's as if in a final frenzy, the storm has blown itself out. Antoine steps out into the swift current of Bayou Contraband. After gaining his balance, he wades toward a visibly shaken Thibodeau meeting her where the island was just moments ago. She looks up at him. "What the hell, Sarge?" There is long pause before Antoine finds his voice. "What the hell, indeed?"

They silently slosh their way to shore, where Jimmy Chretien is waiting. Their eyes meet and Antoine can only repeat. "What the hell."

He looks past Jimmy and speaks in a low voice. "How are y'all?"

Jimmy turns and looks at the others...at Johnny watching Robert hold on to Jenny, afraid to let her go...at Margot and Diz tending to Daz. He turns back to Antoine and shrugs "Some better than others...We just want to go home."

Antoine stares off into space and nods. "Me too, Mr. Chretien, me too."

As Jimmy turns to go, Antoine clears his throat. "Mr. Chretien...James... tell me...there at the end...what did you see?"

Jimmy looks off. "I saw a question answered and a problem solved." Jimmy starts to walk away, but Antoine calls out. "I have no idea what that means...and that woman. Who the hell was that old woman."

Jimmy waves over his shoulder. "Not now."

A very perplexed Sergeant Durel can only stare at Jimmy. "What do you mean, 'not now'?"

Jimmy stares off at the now empty bayou. "Let it go, Sergeant Durel...for right now, just let it go."

Epilogue
Chretien Home
One week later

It's been a week, and everything is back to normal...almost. Jenny still has nightmares...Robert suffers from vertigo...Diz, his whole left side bandaged, has trouble standing...Margot and Daz still recovering from total exhaustion...and Jimmy and Johnny, content to sit on the back porch swing, coffee in hand, laughing and crying, telling stories about Mom and Pop...and Roger...always Roger.

Plans are being made...Jenny is staying in Louisiana and planning to attend LSU's Paul Herbert Law Center. Jimmy and Johnny are planning to slow down and head toward retirement...maybe in Lake Charles. Robert will be taking on more responsibility at Louragan et Fils and for Margot and Diz and Daz life will go on much as before, but with more...many more new friends.

On this day, they have gathered to celebrate...celebrate life... in the only way permissible in Louisiana, over a meal. At the table, Johnny and Jimmy sit at the ends Margot, Diz, and Daz on one side and Phillip on the other. At the moment Jenny and Robert are in the kitchen, giggling, before stepping into the dining room. Robert looks to Jenny, and she steps forward still giggling. "We have asked you here today to celebrate life...our lives here and lives that are gone."

She looks at Robert who puts his arm around her. "In that spirit we have prepared a meal that is a combination of both Chretien and Louragan." Jenny, in her best head waiter voice. "We shall begin with an appetizer from the house of Louragan...Fried green tomatoes served on a bed of mixed greens, topped with crab remoulade." Robert steps forward. "And from the recipes of James Henry Chretien...Shrimp Etouffee, with roasted asparagus in a Hollandaise Sauce."

With all the pomp and circumstance such a feast requires, Robert and Jenny serve the meal. Jimmy pauses, raises his fork, and looks around the table. Johnny smiles and raises his fork and soon everyone has their forks in the air, Jimmy looks to Robert and Jenny. "To the chefs."

Jenny waits, watching as her father and uncle cut the tomato covered in remoulade and take the first bite. She grins at Robert as the smiles spread across their faces. Johnny looks at Jimmy. "Why have we never tried this before?"

Jimmy cuts another slice. "Because, dear brother, we hadn't met Robert and his father before now."

The meal progresses...each bite better than the last...until finally, the last forkful is taken, leaving them stuffed...but still wanting more...in other words, a perfect meal.

A sense of calm and serenity descends upon the table...but not for long. They hear the sound of the door being thrown open and slammed shut ...a voice bellowing. "Why doesn't anybody ever lock the goddamned door."

Antoine storms into the room glaring at everyone. Johnny looks at him and smiles. "We were just about to have coffee. Care to join us?"

Antoine's glare sweeps the table one last time, before he smiles and draws up another chair. "Thank you...don't mind if I do."

Contented, they all sit back enjoying coffee...when suddenly Jimmy turns to Antoine. "Sergeant, you know that you're welcome here any time, but I'm not sure of the reason for this visit."

Antoine takes a sip. "Well first, I wanted to thank you about the information on Etienne Bastineau and Zora Lafitte. That helped answer many questions." He eyes the others at the table. "And I don't know how quite to put this, but..." His eyes land on Margot. "I'm sorry that the treasure was lost...I know it must seem like Dr. Chretien died in vain, and so..." He fumbles his breast pocket and brings out the gold coin, laying it on the table. "I thought you should have this."

For a moment they just stare at the coin. Finally, Margot looks up, her eyes glistening. "Thank you so much...Antoine."

Still staring at the coin, Johnny smiles. "It was never about the treasure, Sergeant. It was about stories told a warm summer night...it was about family and legacy."

Antoine looks back, puzzled. Margot smiles. "For Roger the fact that the treasure actually existed was the treasure. The truth is the treasure."

Johnny nods and looks back at Antoine. "Anything else?"

Antoine stares into his cup, afraid to make a mess. "I know we've been over this...but I can't get what I saw in the bayou, out of my mind." He gets no response from those around the table. "I've been doing some research and I found something interesting."

Johnny looks across the table. "Really...what?"

Antoine scoots closer to the table. "I found a legend...about John Lafitte...it said that sometimes at the height of a hurricane...when innocent lives are at stake...Jean Lafitte appears, at the helm of his two masted schooner coming to their aide."

Jimmy puts down his cup. "That is interesting...tell me sergeant, is that what you saw?"

Antoine looks at the two brothers who are smiling enigmatically and shrugs. "Perhaps."

The two brothers raise their cups in a toast. Johnny takes a sip. "Then...perhaps, sergeant...that's exactly what you did see."

The End

About the Author

Thomas Leveque grew up and spent his life in Southern California but has deep roots in South Louisiana. He has been a motion picture and television studio executive, elementary school teacher and principal and a college professor and dean. Writing has always been a large part of his life, either his own screenplays and teleplays, or working with writers, producers, and directors to shape their projects. Education is another passion in his life. He holds a Doctorate in Education from UCLA and believes that literacy and knowledge are vital for our survival. He loves to read, travel, cook and of course eat. Currently Dr. Leveque lives in Lancaster California with his wife, Lisa, and son Grayson.

Printed in the USA
CPSIA information can be obtained
at www.ICGtesting.com
LVHW041209140923
757946LV00002B/272